SAFE
WORD
LOBO

By L. Concepcion

Copyright ©2025 L. Concepcion.

All rights reserved.

This is a work of fiction. Names, characters, places, and incidents are products of the author's imagination or are used fictitiously and are not to be construed as real. Any resemblance to actual events, locales, organizations, or persons, living or dead, is not intended or should not be inferred.

No part of this book may be used or reproduced in any manner whatsoever without written permission except in the case of brief quotations embodied in the critical articles and reviews; nor may any part of this book be produced, stored in a retrieval system, or transmitted in any form or by any means, electronic, mechanical, photocopying, recording, or other, without written permission from the publisher/Author.

ISBN: 979-8-9907520-2-3

This is for those that thought they couldn't be loved.
Those that have that inner Dom.
Those that command others to their knees
Slips on leather glove

Before You Read

Italics- Words written in italics are meant for either inner thoughts or when the wolf and their human host converse with one another.
Bold- Words written in bold are for telepathic communication between wolves or humans.

Characters and Their Wolves

Kristofer – Zeus (wolf)
Iris – Nora (wolf)
Atlas – Leo (wolf)
Cassius – Wolfie (wolf)
John – Keokuk (wolf)
Alex – Peyton (wolf)
Mavis – Ivar (wolf)
Demetrius –Alcide (wolf)
Hugo – Czar (wolf)
Scott – Elu (wolf)
Riley – Paxton (wolf)

*For trigger warnings please see last page.

1

Alex

"How did I end up here?"

I huff at my tired reflection in the mirror, fogging it slightly with my breath as I lean into it with my forehead.

I thought we were happy, and my mate would never treat me like he did. Yet, here we are. Demetrius isn't speaking to me. He barely looks my way the few times we are in the same room. I thought our love was inseparable. But with the way he turns on the cold shoulder tells me otherwise. What's worse is the fact that he looks more hurt than angry. For the life of me I just can't fathom why. He says he needs space, and I am giving it to him. But what does he need space for when he can just talk to me?

Even with all of this, my heart holds hope that Demetrius will come back to me when he is ready. But the look in his eyes the last time he looked my way did something to my soul. I'm shattered inside. I have no idea how to mend the pieces he left. I hit my forehead against the mirror in frustration. There is nothing going on for it to provoke such Demetrius to pull away from me like he did.

The silent treatment hits too close to home. Similar to the feeling I got when my father did the same to me. The memories rush through me like a flood of childhood sadness. It rattles me in a way I didn't expect. I'm exhausted by the constant roller-coaster of emotions. The way they are weighing me down, draining everything from within me, has me spent. It's too much and I don't like the feeling.

Demetrius blew up on me a week ago, on Christmas day. He refuses to tell me anything and says I should know what I did wrong. But I don't. We welcomed the new year separately because of it. While everyone else counted down, drinking and singing songs with one another, I cried. I brought in the new year sobbing like I used to do so many times before. Curled up in my blanket, in my closet, and tucked into a corner.

I walk out of my ensuite bathroom and drop down onto my bed to lay down, tired, lonely, and most of all, hurt. I finally got used to having my mate's warmth constantly around me. Now, it's gone. I am finally blessed to feel something as great as someone's undivided affection. Goddess only knows I never had that from anyone, only to have it ripped away from me.

Then again, I consider myself lucky to have experienced warmth at all, precisely because of the life I lived. My life has never been easy. For as long as I can remember, living was always something I had to work at doing because if I didn't, I'd want to give up. I never had happiness, love, or a family. It all started when my mother left. For the longest time, I thought I had to accept things as they were because I was no one to question my father.

My ceiling fan wobbles with a slight creak to it, pulling me from my mental monologue. The blades spin quickly, and I can't help but find how it resembles my thoughts. Spinning nonstop. I grab one of my decorative pillows from behind me and chuck it across the room to join my other pillows previously tossed in frustration. The pillow instead hits the dresser I have against the wall with my television and cologne assortments. The colognes rattle a bit, but all is safe in the sea of eau de parfum. I grab my blanket and cover myself into a cocoon.

It pisses me off that I have to find out the hard way the truth about my mother. More than anything, I'm baffled it never occurred to me to question my father until recently.

Even though my father told me my mother died, it hit me hard in the gut to later find out that she is alive. She is happily living somewhere else without me. She simply didn't want my father and I. Well, okay, it's not entirely true. My mother did want me at one point at least. My father just blames me because she rejected him, but I was a few months old according to him when it happened. I still don't understand how I was to blame or why she didn't take me with her. At least it's the story he tells me whenever he is drunk and starts to ramble about my mother.

From what he told me, after Mom left us, Dad couldn't handle being near anyone in my mother's family and packed up our things to get away from Mom. We left our country, Wilderness Den shortly after. We ended up here in Lunar River roaming around for a month before former Alpha Jude found us and took us in. I don't know how life would have been for me had we never found this pack after bouncing from home to home. Having Alpha Jude and then Alpha Kristofer made growing up alone less lonely.

I am surprised my father made the long journey with me being so little considering his short temper and how he treats me now. I doubt he treated me any better when I was just a pup. That's not even considering the dangers of travelling alone. We could have been attacked by rogues or starved to death. But the determination to get away from anything which reminded him of my mother must have been what kept him going.

No one takes kind to rogues roaming around with nowhere to go. And as far as anyone is concerned, that's what we were at the time. As advanced as we are with our species, rogues are still a threat to a pack. Guilty until proven innocent is the way of the wolves. Rogues almost always have ill intentions. It could put a pack at great risk because they are either seeking revenge for being kicked out of their pack or they become crazed from being a lone wolf. So being lucky enough to meet former Alpha Jude was the key to our survival. I will always firmly believe that.

I honestly don't remember any of the travels then. I was too young. So, for me, my life started here. My father and I have our small cottage close to the pack house. Although my memories only go back to when I was five years old, like fragments, there is one feeling that has been with me since. I was three and holding on to one feeling—I hated being alone with my father.

The only time some sort of happiness graced me was when Cassius was found and brought into the pack. I was either six or seven and we quickly became friends. We spent so much time playing together just to avoid my father's random mood swings in the cottage. Eventually, I developed a major crush on Cassius. It confirmed for me I was indeed gay. I ran to my room so quickly after that because I knew what it meant if my father ever knew. I first had the thought I was gay when I was in school. We had to change in the locker room for gym class. I felt funny looking at the boy change and one time I had to fake a stomachache because I had my first erection. I cried all day and then told myself I was tired, and it wouldn't happen again. I was so wrong.

And so, like I predicted, it was another thing Dad learned to hate me for.

Unfortunately, because of Dad, I lost all my trust in male figures with authority. Between his abuse and neglect, I vowed to never rely on anyone but me. At least until Kristofer showed me how to trust again and so did my wonderful Beta, Demetrius. They never went back on their word and always made sure to include me in everything. I was family no matter what and growing up with them allowed me to reduce my hatred of male figures to just my father.

Stupid Demetrius.

I forgot I was thinking about that jerk. That stupid, annoying, gorgeous, delicious jerk. I miss him.

I toss in my bed in a silent scream, hating the cold that the lonely sheets provide. I miss his body next to me with his big arms wrapped around my waist. I need my mate and his touch to settle the storm in my heart. Being depressed and covered in self-hate is all too much of a comfortable state to live in. It is a state of mind that I made friends with long ago and I don't want to revisit it again.

Being alone in my thoughts, means being trapped within the walls I carefully build around me. These walls were once meant to protect me. Eventually it became my prison under my father's scrutiny. Nothing in this world makes me feel worse than the dread and hopelessness that knots in my throat from the thought of my mate not wanting me anymore.

As I open the cocoon so I can breathe, I stare at the ceiling. The fan assists my tears to cascade down my temples and pool within my ears like wells keeping my sadness hidden from the world. These familiarities of having lived in fear my whole life creep back in like licked wounds that reopen. I hadn't even told Demetrius I loved him yet. My plans were to do so during the holidays until everything went to shit, and I was left alone.

A sob escapes my lips as the image of him turning his back on me pops into my mind.

I squeeze my eyes tightly trying to hold back the unshed salted droplets lingering there. The only other thing besides my mate that can calm this raging storm right now is showering and allowing the water to soak its magic on my body.

With leaded feet, I drag myself back out of bed and trudge into the bathroom again to fill up my tub with hot water. My eyes skim over my body in the mirror when I step back. From my waist up to my face, my reflection mocks the slender arms removing my clothes.

How does Demetrius even find someone like me attractive?

I look starved.

Even though I have gained a good amount of weight in the last several months, I am still too skinny for my liking. I want to be more like Demetrius with muscles and bulk. Not the gangly looking mutt I am right now. My ribs aren't as prominent anymore, but they are still noticeable if you looked closely. My face is filling out nicely and I admit it's my favorite part of my body. I love my green eyes but the rest of me has a bit more to go.

My heart skips a pained beat—a warning that the bond between Demetrius and me is deteriorating. A tear manages to break free. Whatever my mate is doing is slowly severing the bond.

Does he hate me that much already?

Then again, it could simply be because we have been apart and stewing in whatever this is. Bonds can break if both parties are at odds with each other without resolution, but I'm sure my self-hatred is also playing its part in all this. The damage might already be done. Maybe it is time I accept it. I cry as quietly as possible into the mirror with my shoulders slumped. This is a different hurt. I don't want to accept that it may be over.

My chest clenches unbelievably tight. No matter what is going on. I still want him. I need him in my life. The bond is breaking. I can feel it slowly coming undone. I can't. I won't accept it.

DEMI, TE QUIERO. PLEASE, COME BACK TO ME.

I scream in my mind as my heart shatters. Yet, those broken fragments pound harder than I ever thought possible. They are embedded within me like shrapnel.

No, something is wrong.

My breathing quickens, making it hard to fill my lungs. Gasping desperately, I claw at my chest looking for a way to breathe. I haven't felt like this in a long time. Like my world is imploding and all I can do is be a bystander as it happens. I can barely fill my lungs. They are on fire as air struggles to inflate them and fail with each attempt. A bang from my bedroom door faintly makes its way to my ears right before my vision tunnels and I hit the side of the tub and black out.

***

I open my eyes, wincing as a throbbing pain pulsates through my skull. If I were ever hit by a bolder, I am positive this is how it would feel. I'm not saying I ever would get hit by one, but for some reason it's my first thought. My damn anxiety is getting the best of me. It has been years since I last had a panic attack to this extent. Sniffling and soft whimpers fill the room around me, and I can't tell if it's from me or someone else.

Pain radiates again and I groan in my attempt to move. The

slightest movement makes the pounding worse. It sends a wave of nausea to catch right at the base of my throat. I swallow the bile as my heart pours down my cheeks in salted streaks. Only now I realize I am in my bed.

"Chiquito!" The deep, beautiful voice I love so much is calling out to me. He must have moved me.

It's him sniffling. As much as I want to look his way, I'm scared to see him. I'm scared he is going to check if I'm okay and disappear again. I can't bear to watch him leave twice.

A finger wipes the moisture from my eyes before the bed sinks in with what I assume is his weight. His strong body spoons into me and his arms wrap around me in a comfort so sweet I cry harder.

I never deserved a man like him. After having a taste, how can I let him go? I grew up thinking I am meant to be alone. *Am I not allowed to be happy?* I turn into Demitrius's arms and sob uncontrollably. His heat radiates off him and seeps into me in a welcomed embrace. I miss his warmth against me so much that the chills ripple through my skin as he hugs me tighter, bringing me the relief I crave.

Yet, even as his presence is bringing me the comfort I need, I can't help but think as to why we argued in the first place. He never gave me a proper answer and now, so many scenarios are racing through my mind. They all shout at me and scold me. Each one tells me a possible story of his anger and they are all filled with pain. Demetrius giving me the cold shoulder during Christmas replays in my mind, swirling in circles as I cry.

Why? Why? My mind shouts, projecting everything I am feeling. My heart goes off in another round of panicked rhythm. The irregular beating of my cruel thoughts thumping starts another attack.

"Chiquito, please breathe. Calm down for me." Demetrius strokes my wet hair.

The thing about anxiety is that once it starts, it's hard to refocus. I never just have one attack.

Demetrius continues to try to sooth me and strokes my head while holding me tight. I only now realize I have dry clothes on. He must have changed my shirtless body. But why is my hair wet?

"Shh, I'm here now," my mate continues to soothe me, intensifying his scent so I can find comfort in it.

My mind continues to attack me. Words I've heard since childhood—mutt, weak, bastard—continue on repeat, like a chant. My own thoughts betray me, just like everyone else. Over and over, I was reminded how useless I was. My father made sure I knew I was never wanted and could never be loved.

After all this time, I am starting to believe him.

My Goddess, his scent is everything.

Musk and Rosewood hug every inch of my soul.

After long agonizing minutes of ragged breathing, I manage to finally calm down enough to think.

PLEASE STOP HATING ME. DON'T REJECT ME. I'M SO STUPID. I KNEW I'D NEVER BE LOVED.

"Whoa, Alex. What is going on in that pretty little head of yours?" Demetrius pulls away a bit to look at my snot-ridden face. I squeeze my eyes tighter knowing if I look at him, I'd break yet again.

"I I-Demetrius. Please tell me what I did wrong."

I know I sound like a mess. How could I not? Demetrius is the only man I have ever fallen this deeply in love with.

He's my mate, my other half. The sole reason why I'd fly to the moon and back. The only reason I can stand tall. He is my strength.

"Chiquito, breathe. Please don't scare me." Demetrius hugs me, bringing me back into his chest. "Your thoughts are screaming at me. And I don't like what I'm hearing. Alex, you obviously did nothing wrong. I can see that now. I'm so sorry. I was so angry thinking I was being played for a fool, I never sat down to talk to you about it. I just assumed everything was true. I didn't mean for you to hurt like this."

I push him away confused, this time looking him straight in the eye.

"What do you mean? I don't understand." I can barely see him through my watery blurry vision. Demetrius wipes my nose with his shirt with a half-broken smile and sighs.

"What I mean is, listening to your thoughts, it's obvious you don't want to break our bond and leave me. You weren't planning on running away either." Demetrius is tearing up now.

Is this what he thought?

"When did I ever say that's what I wanted!?" My voice cracks like a prepubescent teen.

"Hugo came to me on Christmas and gave me an envelope with a bunch of documents. I asked him what they were, but he simply said for me to decide and left." Demetrius pauses to wipe his tears. "When I opened it, there were papers with you opening new bank accounts and a lease to a new apartment. Your passport and other things were in there too. It all pointed to you leaving. But why did you have those things if you weren't?"

Demetrius closes his eyes as if to fight more tears from coming out. He was hurt.

"Wait, my father gave you that?" Demetrius nods, still with his eyes closed, unable to speak as his lip quivers. "Son a bitch. Yes, what you found there is right, but not for the reasons you think. I also decided to stay a long time ago and canceled the lease because I fell for you. All those plans to leave were before I wanted you to be mine."

I sigh and dig my face back into his chest, inhaling his scent allowing his pheromones to calm me down so I could think straight. Hints of relief invade my senses, but the pain still lingered.

"I'm not ready to tell you my story, but before I realized you were my mate, I had every intention of leaving after the new year." I nuzzle further into his chest, making sure our bodies touch from head to toe.

"But, not anymore, right?" My mate asks with a sadness dripping in his voice. He is hurting as much as me.

"No Demi, not anymore," I whisper back.

"Did you mean what you said earlier?" Demetrius whispers with his face buried in my hair.

"What did I say?"

"That you still liked me. When I heard you and felt your emotions through what was left of the bond, I ran as fast as I could. I was happy but scared because I thought something happened. I thought I lost you for good and when I got closer to your room, I felt this wave of nausea and heard you hit your head." Demetrius squeezes me a bit, making my tension fade.

"Yes, te quiero mucho." I look up and kiss his trembling chin.

"Me too, Chiquito," his shaky voice replies. He is ready to cry again but does everything possible not to do so. I'm tired of the waterfall that has been draining from my face. I snuggle my face into his neck to take in his scent. All my adrenaline fades as quickly as it came and sleep kicks in. Relaxed in Demetrius' arms, I let go of my pain.

Sleep overcomes me and I dream of our future together.

2
Alex

I wake up to something hard on my stomach and the weight makes it difficult to breathe. As I yawn, my eyes struggle to open with the way they are crusted shut from my salted tears. After a gentle rub, the crust crumbles off, allowing me to open my eyes. With how they feel, they must certainly look like puffy pink balls of cotton candy. Looking down through my lashes at the massive hard-on my mate is sporting through his pants, I sigh in relief at the welcomed feeling of his nearness. His heavy arm on my stomach is not appreciated since I have a full bladder waiting to be emptied.

"Good morning, Chiquito," Demetrius pulls me in and shifts himself, causing his wood to rub against me.

I groan because the movement makes it harder to hold in the pee. Demetrius smiles and rubs himself against me on purpose, now making me roll my eyes. It amazes me every day that I can take in his size. Makes me almost proud even. *Or am I loose? ...Nah... never.*

"Good morning, Demi," I reply, still fatigued from crying all night.

I try to pry out of his hold to go to the bathroom, but his arm doesn't budge.

"Babe, I gotta pee," I groan.

Demetrius shifts again and lifts me up to carry me to the bathroom.

"What are you doing?" I ask while cradled in his arms like a newlywed wife.

"I am going to make up for the week we weren't together. You are not leaving my side or lifting a finger."

He sets me down and pulls down my pants. Had it been any other person I'd throw a fit. Hearing him say it was only a week makes my emotions feel so small, but it felt like a lifetime in the moment. Everything we went through simply because of miscommunication caused by my father.

"Are you trying to say my dick is a finger?" I try not to laugh because I know what he means, but I love teasing him.

"BABE. Never. I love your size!" Demetrius blushes but positions me in front of the toilet. "You're almost as big as me." Demetrius grabs my dick and aims. He isn't wrong. I may be ridiculously skinny but I'm packing well.

"Demi, that's enough. I can pee on my own now. Besides, I'm mad at you." I give him the best stern voice I can muster.

"Okay, okay. Fine. I'll be in bed."

He lets me go and closes the door behind him. Beyond the wood that separates us is the sound of the bed springs squeaking under his weight.

I turn around and slump onto the toilet, rubbing my swollen face as I relieve myself. The thought of standing to pee is exhausting and I've always hated standing up unless I am in a public bathroom. I flush my business and take a good look in the mirror while I wash my hands in my favorite floral soap.

I look like a hot fucking mess.

My face is puffy and sunken in with dark circles. All the luster my skin had is gone from the crying I put myself through.

Hopeful that my skincare routine is enough to rectify the situation, I put it to work before I brush my teeth to start the day. Thankfully some of the inflammation seems to already be going down, but it is still noticeable. The green color of my eyes is barely visible with how dull and tired they seem.

When I open the bathroom door, Demetrius looks up at me as he lays naked in all his glory. A bit sleepy-eyed with messy hair on his face, he poses most suggestively with one leg bent up to his chest against the bed while lying on his stomach. A devilish smile pulls at the corners of his lips, and he bounces his butt as if humping the bed. I'm suddenly very jealous of my stupid mattress. It is currently getting more action than I have had in the last week. His gorgeous plump ass jiggles in the process, like perfectly made Jell-O. I want nothing more than a bite of his bubble butt.

"Stop, I can't get distracted," I plead.

But man, what I wouldn't give for the distraction in front of me. He is as tempting as it gets. A chuckle leaves my lips and it's something I haven't heard in what feels like ages. Even though it was only seven days of sorrow I suffered, seven is long enough. Demetrius continues to hump the bed, and I swear I will be done for if he makes those juicy cheeks clap.

"Why not get distracted then?"

He perks his ass up a bit more and there it is. The. Fucking. Clap. I look away, but the sound makes the struggle against giving in nearly impossible to withstand.

"I'm going to confront my father. Besides, didn't I tell you earlier I'm still mad at you?" I quickly blurt out and look away.

Demetrius stops in defeat and drops his ass back down on the bed. He is the world's biggest tease between his fat clappers and the rod-like weapon between his legs, but my heart aches still with the knowledge of what my father did. This time, no amount of sexiness can overshadow the hurt my father inflicted with the lie he let my mate believe.

"Why are you mad at me? I apologized," he pouts.

"I fell asleep, so I wasn't able to scold you properly, but I am upset because you chose to believe my father and never gave me a chance to explain. You let me hurt for a week and allowed our bond to suffer because of it."

This time, the stern look isn't hard to muster, and I almost feel a bubble of emotion forming in my chest.

"I'm sorry, mi amor," Demetrius whispers.

"We can talk about it later." My voice isn't angry, but I put out a hand to stop him from talking.

While I'm glad we are talking again and cleared it all up, he can stew a bit more on his own.

I am wounded and I was ready to give up on it all just to stop the pain I felt. My father almost destroyed my relationship and for what? His amusement? To prove that I continue to be worthless in his eyes. Nothing in this world will amount to the hatred in my heart for my father. If he could just leave. There's nothing keeping him here because I sure as hell won't live under his roof again. He is almost right up there with Rick.

I quickly change into a pair of baggy cargo pants and a loose band tee. Demetrius stares at me the entire time almost with a ravenous look which almost makes me second guess my resolve to speak to my father.

"Before you go bat shit crazy, whatever you hear me say, because I know you will try to listen, trust me. Don't do anything and wait for me." I wink at my mate who now looks puzzled. He nods in agreement and out the door I go to find Alpha Kristofer.

A shudder races down my spine, but with a determined mind, I link with my father as I walk asking if we can talk in Kristofers office. It is a talk I don't want to have, but I drag my feet out of my room and down the hallway to end this.

Alpha Kristofer is in the kitchen eating an apple as he leans against the counter. He drops his smile at the sight of the gloom on my face and the obvious swelling from all the crying. Not that I blame him for his immediate concern. It definitely isn't my finest hour, but here I am, about to face my fear.

"Hey, I called Hugo over. Can we all talk in your office when he gets here? I'ma need you there for backup." I try to sound strong, but I think Kristofer can see right through me. He agrees and leads me to his office so we can wait for my father. The sweat builds in my hands as quickly as I can wipe them against my clothes.

I wish I didn't have to confront him or have anything to do with my father. Messing with me is one thing but to use my mate to hurt me even more is going too far.

We wait a few minutes in tension filled silence as my palm grows damp. I know Kristofer is itching to ask what is going on. He keeps looking between me and the door. His actions only make me more nervous because the moment my father arrives; I see it in Kristofers face.

My father walks in just as I am about to say something, and his presence sucks all the air out of the room. Hugo freezes on the spot when he spots our Alpha leaning forward on his desk with hands laced into one another and pressed against his mouth. If it were me walking into the room with Kristofer sitting like that and staring at me, I'd probably shit myself. Hugo turns on his heel to leave like the coward he is when Kristofer speaks, finally understanding why he is present for the conversation.

"Hugo, in here, now!" Kristofer's Alpha tone makes me shrink in my seat despite it not being directed towards me. It's so strong when he uses his Alpha command. Even my wolf instinctively tucks his tail. A conditioned reflex. He is unparalleled as an Alpha. He is a leader like no other I've seen. I even find him to be a better leader than his father was before his death. His father was too lax, and it got the pack in trouble a lot with the locals.

My Beta, on the other hand, is still all-around better in my eyes, but I'd never say that to Kristofer nor Demetrius. I am sure it's my bias speaking since I'm blinded by all that my Demi is.

My father walks back into the office and closes the door with a sour face. When he sits next to me, he shoots a glare that would have killed me if it could. Luckily, he can't do that. I am safe. At least for now...

"Okay Alex, the floor is yours." Kristofer is stern but I can tell it's more because of my father's reaction. He is now weary of the situation. I nod my thanks and begin.

"So, I am sure everyone is aware that Demetrius and I are not together anymore. This past week has been hell because of it and this morning, our bond finally broke off." I mind-link Demetrius reminding him to go with whatever I say. It's the only way to prevent him from bursting into the office and ruining my plan. "However, it was brought to my attention as to what caused our downfall in the first place."

Kristofer glares at my father who is sporting a smug expression as he sits there cleaning his nails. I follow his gaze to the man I know as Father. He almost looks proud of what he thinks he did with the half grin lifting the corner of his lips.

"Hugo, why did you give the envelope to Demetrius on Christmas?" I asked my father.

"Hugo? It's father, you insolent brat!" Hugo spits as if that's what matters most. His constant need for validation on his authority is stifling. But my conceding to his title ends today.

"Not anymore, now answer the question old man," I spit right back.

Hugo keeps his composure, but barely as eyes lose focus, most likely because he is searching for an answer in the vault of lies he keeps in his head. I, however, keep my features in check with ease as I grow more confident in the room. Although the proximity to Hugo tempts me to beat him senseless and runaway all at once.

"Answer his question," Kristofer demands as the silence from Hugo is deafening.

"You are planning to leave, and Demetrius has the right to know."

Kristofer snaps his head over to me, but I hold out a finger to stop him from speaking which provokes a look of surprise.

"That is not something you would have known unless you secretly went into my room and looked through my things. Not only that, but you would also have had to remove my picture frame from the wall to find the envelope attached behind it with tape. So, what were you really looking for to come across my secret information instead?" I ask with courage.

Hugo shifts in his seat not expecting my blunt confrontation.

"That is not the issue here. The issue is you abandoning your mate. Guess the apple didn't fall far from the tree. Like mother, like son." Hugo smirks but I roll my eyes along with my head.

"I'd like to know why you went through his room as well," Kristofer adds. Hugo thinks he avoided the question, but he isn't leaving here without answering. I honestly wasn't expecting Hugo to dodge this much. Instead, I expected him to be the shit father he is. But he's lost his poker face now, and Kristofer and I see through it.

"Well...I... I knew something was up. I was simply trying to find out what. How else will I know unless I look in your room since you are never home now," Hugo stutters. The sweat beading on his forehead. His lies are weak.

"Well, for starters, how about you ask me instead of snooping? It's not like you can't link with me. I called here with the link, didn't I? Besides, I know you're lying. You see, several months ago, that was my original plan. I was tired of your shit, and I wanted my freedom. Then something amazing happened and I found my mate. My life changed from then on. I canceled everything that was in the envelope because I wanted to stay with my mate no matter what. Even if it meant having to put up with you.

"So again, I ask, what were you looking for? Because I have been nothing but happy, so I'm sure the so-called suspicion you had would have disappeared by now."

I cross my arms to see what lie he spews next.

The cold sweat beading on his forehead intensifies at this point. This man is looking for something that I might have but what?

What could be so important?

"I will not sit here and be interrogated. And by a child no less," Hugo yells, standing up to leave.

"SIT DOWN!" Kristofer's voice booms through the room.

I shrink under the pressure in the air. My alpha is angry on my behalf, and I am grateful for it. Hugo sits down, whimpering before his Alpha, and it is a beautiful sight. My father submitting is never something you see.

Kristofer looks at me and eases the pressure of his Alpha tone when he notices how uncomfortable I am.

"Fine," Hugo starts. "I was looking to see where he hid the necklace he stole from his mother's belongings."

I narrow my eyes on him. That crazy bastard. He knew I had the necklace, which means he might know I was planning to go find her.

If I had left, I was planning to live with her to start over, all because of what I found in the locket. This man, who calls himself my father, hid so much from me, including the truth about my mother.

I had been cleaning my cabin, or rather my father's cabin one day, gathering the last of my things before moving out. As I'd tidied the room, I picked up a book I found sticking out from beneath my father's dresser. When I opened it, there was a letter from my mother stating how much she missed me and that she didn't want to give me up. The letter was dated around the time Dad moved us here. It went on to talk about the necklace enclosed. It was a gift from her to me. Something to remember her by if I never saw her again.

I cried so much when I found the letter. Everything was a lie. If living with my father isn't bad enough, to find out it is also a lie from the very start about her leaving us, broke me. I held the necklace tightly to my chest wishing that somehow, I'd get whisked away.

I admired it for a while before realizing it was a locket. When I opened it, an even smaller note was folded inside. It had her address and her signature. However, her last name was different. I kept the note and put the necklace in my pocket. I returned the book and left.

I don't think he knows about the note inside the locket, but he must have known I would try to find her. I glare at my father.

Why does that worry him? All he has ever done is lie to me. Unless....

"You mean this necklace?" I reveal the locket hidden under my shirt.

Hugo's eyes grow wide.

"You fucking thief." He rips it off me. The chain scrapes against my neck. "This does not belong to you." He growls at every word.

I rub my neck where it stings. "Yes, it does according to the letter it was attached to. You know, the letter you hid from me. From my mother, who is very much alive. It still doesn't explain you wanting to sabotage my relationship with my mate."

Kristofer chokes on the air and eyes Hugo with disbelief.

"You should be happy I saved you from that disgusting gay shit. It was revolting watching you with the Be-"

"ENOUGH. Hugo, you are dismissed. Go await your punishment in your cabin." Kristofer eyes my so-called father, waiting for him to leave.

Then Kristofer turns to me.

"Punishment?!" Hugo barks.

Kristofer stands up with a raised brow releasing a wave of his pheromones, creating that immense pressure alphas are known for.

"Yes, Alpha." Hugo lowers his eyes and leaves.

I wait for Hugo to be out of earshot before I speak to my alpha.

"I think I know what he is afraid of me finding out. I know my mother's maiden name and it's not Santos." I whisper and Kristofer leans in. "My family name is Neverdeen."

Kristofer's eyes pop out of his head, and he quickly stands up to close his office door.

"As in the family that founded the council?" He gasps.

I nod in agreement.

"This is huge! Maybe she can help us," Kristofer suggests.

I honestly don't see how her family or pack could help us with finding Finn. He has been missing for so long already. My mother probably even forgot about me by now.

We sit there as the silence grabs hold. *Alex Santos Neverdeen.*

3

Demetrius

My beautiful mate walks into his room finding me still in his bed. His irresistible scent strengthens in the room, wrapping me in his happiness with a hint of lust. A hint of sadness hangs underneath it all. The remnants of the hurt from his father fades away with every step he takes toward me as it's veiled by the newfound hunger in his eyes.

I know what's coming. This is the other side of Alex. The one that is strong, commanding, and sexy as hell. The one he uses when he is in the mood to do something wild. But from what I know about my mate, it is also something he uses when he wants to hide.

Sometimes I feel like there is something else he isn't telling me, but I let it go and wait for the day that he tells me on his own. Pineapple and coconut seize my senses the closer he gets. I never thought I would like the smell of coconut this much. I was never one for fruity scents. I would always gag when a girl would pass by with fruity perfume. Here I am now, swimming in the delectable exotic drink that is my mate. Alex snaps me out of my daydream with his nearness. The heat from his body, reminding me of what he is wanting to do.

"Can you stop licking your lips at me? What are you even thinking about, to put that look on your face?" Alex chuckles. I love the sound of his laugh. So pure and sweet, opposite to the man he is in bed. Opposite to the man he is about to turn into. His smile though, no matter which version of himself he is, is the best on him. There is nothing I wouldn't do to make sure that smile never fades.

"You. You're all I ever think about," I answer and pull him to me with a smile.

His legs stop at the edge of the bed, and I bury my face in his crotch as I sit eye level with it. I want him in ways that should never be spoken of. The desires that stir within me whenever he is around, is akin to one of a lust crazed succubus. Luckily for him, that's not what I am because those things are nasty little bastards. Lucky for me, my man has kinks. Each time we are intimate, I seem to discover a new kink I like more.

"If you'd like. I could use a distraction. Kristofer is going over to Atlas' house with Iris to go over some leads on where Finn is after handing my father his punishment. Will you keep me preoccupied in the meantime?" Alex runs a hand through my hair and pushes my face harder into him.

I moan against his heat. But I am right. He is going to use sex to mask what he is feeling, and it leaves me torn between telling him no or caving to his needs. It is a bit odd for him to be acting this way, especially after meeting with his father. But I nod because I am afraid that he will close up on me.

"Okay. Good." Alex shoves my face to the side and walks away from me. The click from the lock on his door echoes before he steps into his closet. The things he has in there would make former Luna Cecile lose her shit if she knew her little Alex had them. She already freaked out when he bought a penis mug.

I wait in anticipation with my dick throbbing as it grows to full attention. The eagerness drips from my crown and soaks my tip, begging for someone to lick it off. But I know better. My Master will punish me if I were to touch myself without his permission. It is a huge turn on how he flips his switch so drastically from everyday Alex to Master Alex. And lately, the roleplay is more frequent.

My gorgeous and seductive mate is Dominant in bed even though he is a submissive in everyday life, while I play the complete opposite for him. My feisty mate is a power-bottom and it's the sexiest thing in the world to me. We don't always role play, but when we do, I obey his every command, and he makes really good use of it.

"Come here, Suga." Alex uses his nickname for me when we are in play and walks out of his closet dressed in leather shorts hugging his sexy ass, perks of his Latin genes. Even with his slim build he has the sexiest plump ass I've ever seen. Black leather heart pasties cover his nipples while his torso is adorned with black leather suspenders that crisscross his chest.

Master traces his leg with a whip. My cock twitches at the sight of the leather strips and what he plans to do with it.

The leather mask he is sporting is the icing on the cake to complete the look. His electrifying green eyes stand out in contrast to the black of his mask. The puffiness on his face must have gone down a bit more or at least enough for me to enjoy the way his eyes sparkle when he is in this mindset. His irises intensify as his stare bores into me with a hunger that is both deep and carnal.

He taps his leather boots waiting for me to obey and, of course, that's what I do. Following his command, I crawl on all fours over to his feet, slowly, like a wolf on a prowl. One thing I know for sure is that he enjoys watching my ass sway when I crawl. The smirk pulling on the corner of his lips only proves that I am right.

"Sit," he commands.

I do so without hesitation. Master runs his whip against my face and down my arm, pleased by my obedience. The cold leather leaves a shiver on my skin and draws a breath of excitement from my lungs.

He smiles down at me. "Good boy, now strip."

Master hits the whip on the floor at a speed I wasn't expecting, and it cracks with power. I jump at the sound and squeeze my muscles in hopes that I can keep myself from coming too soon. If I had known that we were going to initiate play, then I would have added a few more layers of clothes. Instead, I only put on my underwear and pants while I waited for him. With a few more layers than I could have extended the play a bit more.

I remove my two pieces of clothing before getting back in a seated position for my master. My dick is wet and dripping with excitement while standing at full attention despite my underwear soaking up a good amount of my precum. Throbbing and barely keeping my senses together, I take a deep breath. Master trails the whip along my hard shaft and sucks his teeth in disappointment like I knew he would at the sight of the mess I made on myself. He sees that I am dripping with pleasure all over the place and it displeases him that I did so without his permission.

"Why is my little Suga spilling his milk?"

I blush listening to how his heels click as he walks around me, leading his whip across my body.

"Speak when asked a question," my master commands.

His whip comes down onto my back with just enough force to feel both pain and pleasure. I accidentally moan. Quickly, I respond between my teeth trying to hide the pleasure.

Woof Woof I bark at my master and then whimper.

I'm so turned on I could die a happy man. This way of behaving in front of him behind closed doors is exhilarating and freeing. I would never do this in front of anyone else. Only he deserves to feel the power and control of having me at his feet.

"Good boy. Now come lay on my lap face down."

I crawl over to the bed and climb onto his lap. The palm of his hand softly circles my ass and then smacks my cheek with a resounding echo filling the room. I flinch in pleasure, moaning uncontrollably as the sting on my skin pricks under his hand as he rubs the spot once again. Another slap comes down to even out the tingling on the other cheek. I yelp from the sting as it sends unbelievable pleasure to pulsate straight to my dick.

"Speak," my loving master commands as he rubs the spots he struck.

Woof Woof! I bark.

"Louder!"

WOOF WOOF!

My Master spanks me again and I gasp as his hand lands much heavier this time. My aching member wags beneath me, proof of my ecstasy dripping steadily on the floor.

"Now *that* is what I like to see. Your beautiful ass is nice and red for your master." Master's voice is gravely and deep.

Woof I respond.

I want more. With his spanks alone I can climax at any moment and be completely satisfied. If I'm honest with myself, anything he does to me sends me over the edge. It is all a game of chance on whether I can hold it in or not.

"Get on all fours, on the bed," he commands without giving me the opportunity to move and standing up. I almost lose my balance, but I get in position as my master repositions on the bed and sits back by the headboard. His hard-on is evident by the perfect outline of his cock straining under his leather shorts.

Absolutely delicious.

I look up to him, only to be entrapped by his attention.

My body blushes with his penetrating gaze licking over every inch of me. The heat of his stare rolls over my body like a wave of lava scorching my skin. My body feels hot, leaving my heart to race in anticipation. My breath quickens as the seconds turn to minutes. The blush over my body turns to embarrassment with the fingertips of his most likely perverse thoughts touching me repeatedly. But unlike times before, he doesn't let me hear what he's thinking. It's torture.

His pheromones scour every part of my skin and setting it on fire. The way his eyes dance over my nakedness, living out his wildest fantasies with me just inches away from him has me jealous of the *me* in his mind.

The silence screams in my ears and to me it sounds like the moans he whispers when I fuck him just right. The him in my mind is writhing beneath me, but I am too scared to close my eyes and envision him better. If I break contact with him now, I could risk losing the feelings I am drowning in at the moment. His scent violates every part of this room as it strips me down to my most basic animalistic instincts. It makes me feel vulnerable to a new degree.

My master cracks his whip against the bed and I jump at the sound as it sends my heart into a frenzy. "Touch yourself. You may also speak in human tongue." My crown weeps. The sound of his voice and the whip breaking the tension between us is the best form of edging we have done so far.

"Yes, Master."

I grab my cock quickly, swiping my thumb over the dripping precum to mask my insolence and pump as my Master commands. Then again, if he sees that I am dripping again, he just might give me another spanking. Not that I'd mind.

The whimper that leaves my lips at the feel of his gaze on my dick as I pleasure myself under his command is whiney. This game he is playing is putting me in a constant state of trying to stop myself from coming and he has yet to touch me. I want to shove myself in him but the moment I do, I am sure that I will come just from the heat of him alone.

My Masters cock twitches and his scent releases in a more potent dose of sex. The pheromones pierce my body and over stimulate me in the best way possible, almost tantric.

Being humiliated like this, giving up full control to your partner, obeying his every command, everything, is a rush I would have never known had Alex not introduced me to it.

As his first sex partner, he never had put to practice his fetishes, and I am glad that is the case. Not sure I can handle the idea of someone else doing this with him. The idea alone infuriates something fierce in me. To my surprise, all that he knows, he learned from the extensive amount of BDSM porn he watches.

My impending release multiplies with the thought of him watching porn and how he looks jerking off.

"Look at how well you're touching yourself. Are you ready to come, Chulo?"

"Yes, Master. I'm ready," I reply in a raspy, strained whisper.

He nods at my response with a wicked grin. Master stands beside the bed. The whip splits the air as it crashes onto my ass. My shot sprays all over the bed with that alone. I moan so loud I'm sure the whole house hears me roar my pleasure as I empty myself onto the sheets. But I don't care. It feels euphoric. It is a full body release of pain and pleasure that rides through me in waves.

"Oh, what a bad Sub. You dirtied my sheets."

Master runs a finger along the length of my body from my hip up my ribs, and to my shoulders as I pant. A trail ignites on my side, everywhere he touches me, with my senses on an all-time high. I turn on all fours to face him and watch Master finally unzip his shorts to release the strain he has been keeping hidden from me. I whine knowing I get to taste him soon, but I have to wait until I have permission.

"Why are you whining?" He grabs me from under my chin, scrunching up my lips. "Stick your tongue out."

Obediently, I stick it out through my puckered lips. My master waves his cock in front of me and then brushes it against my face. I close my eyes enjoying the sensation of his flesh on mine. I want to taste it and he knows it. Master finally rubs his tip against my tongue, making me tremble at how delectable he tastes. His dick is just as wet as mine. My member comes back to life in response, stiff and strong.

"Is Suga hungry?" my sweet Master asks.

I growl, "Yes, Master. May I please have some cock?" I give the best puppy eyes I can muster.

"Wow, since when does my little pet know how to beg so well?"

Master shoves his hard-on in my mouth and fucks my face. The tip of his dick hits the back of my throat over and over. I choke and gag against his thick length, but he doesn't pull out. Instead, he holds it there and slaps the silhouette of his member on my cheek. Just as I gag a bit too hard, he pulls out with a chuckle. A string of spit stretches between my mouth and his crown as I gasp for breath. My face is a thousand degrees red, fading down to my neck. The embarrassment of being gagged this hard is new. He has never done that before and… I like it.

"Okay, Suga, you may prep me now."

Those are my favorite words and the ones I have been waiting to hear. I grab his member and make him drip with a wet sloppy blow job he will never forget even if he tries.

Master shoots his load in my mouth, and I gladly swallow it all. A gift from my merciful Master. He lays on the bed and down I go to work on his rosebud. I eagerly use my tongue to push through his hole and lick every part of him. I bite his cheeks, his thighs, and spit against his hole. A moan escapes his lips. All I can think of is how we went a week without sex. The absolute torture of those days apart is making this so much more intense.

"Master, I am going to use my fingers now."

Master exhales softly with a nod and hands me the lubricant he keeps in his nightstand for us. I drench my fingers and his rose before I slip in a finger. He gasps and up goes his beautiful erection again. I pump into him slowly, feeling his muscles become more relaxed around my finger before gripping me again tightly. His bud pulsates as it readies to receive another finger. A second finger, and he squeezes me tighter than before.

"Master, do you wish to break your pets' fingers?" I joke.

Master pops up his head and grins as he squeezes around me again. I bite my lip with a smirk. This man is destroying my ability to show self-control. I thrust my fingers into him up to my knuckles and he throws his head back in pleasure with a moan of approval. Another finger slips in, and I continue to work, making my master perfectly ready for my size.

"Suga, I am ready. Fuck me." His wish is my command.

Sitting up on my knees, I align myself at his entrance and rub my head against him before pushing myself in slowly, allowing his body to accept me. Three fingers are nothing compared to the weapon I carry. At least that's what Alex calls it. Once fully inside, I wait for his muscles to relax around me as much as possible before I start moving. Master opens his eyes and licks his lips

An enticing little thing.

"Despacio," he whispers to me.

"Yes, Master."

I pull out and push back in slowly like he asked. With long fluid strokes, every inch of me slides against his quivering walls. Each stroke that I pump, his body sucks me in with a death grip. If I didn't know any better than I'd say that he will tear my dick off. Focused on not coming too quickly, I continue at this agonizing pace. All I want to do is pound away and fill this room with the sounds of my hips slapping against his ass. My Master is cruel and merciful all at once. He gives me the pleasure to feed him all of me but doesn't allow me to do as I please.

I moan with need.

"You're such a good boy. Would you like to go faster?" His playful, coy voice was egging me on.

"Yes, Master. May I?" I beg with the need to give him more of me.

"Then bark. While you pound into me, stick out your tongue like the good Sub you are."

I rumble deep in my throat. He really knows how to drive me crazy.

WOOF WOOF I bark loud and clear for him and stick out my tongue like the good little thing I am for my Master.

I thrust my hips. I increase my pace and pound into the tight hole that has been torturing me all this time. He bucks under me, receiving me all too well. My mind goes numb with the waves of sensation that course through our bond. It feels like home.

My wolf inside howls wildly. He enjoys this kind of play. Alex's wolf, Peyton, is also the only Master my wolf will ever submit to. He stirs inside excitedly relishing in the euphoria of it all.

"Flip me over," my Master screams and so I do. I place him on all fours and reinsert myself in one motion. I slam against his pure white skin that is now red.

"You're free my lil pet," my Master moans into the pillow.

"Yes," I growl in response.

Our play is over, and I can enjoy the meal before me in full control. Alex screams with pleasure and grabs himself to jerk off, chasing the orgasm building in us both.

"F-Fuck, I'm almost there," I moan and lift Alex off the bed.

I hold his slender body in my arms and pound away mercilessly. Our skin slaps in rhythmic echoes which fills the thin walls of the room.

"Demi!" He moans out to me in a husky voice full of need.

"Dime, mi amor", I pound harder. He throws his head back onto my shoulder. He is about to orgasm and so am I. I slam a bit harder into his prostate, over and over where he likes it best.

"Asi Papi," Alex growls as he tightens his hole. His Spanish words unleash everything in me, and I bust inside him. How does he bring me to the edge of the world and back so easily? He releases as well and squeezes my member with his ass at the same time. His chest is covered in ribbons of his ecstasy, and I am more content in that moment than I have ever been before.

4

Demetrius

I stretch in the bed, releasing the sleep from my bones and joints. It is the best sleep I have had in a week. Evident from the fact that I don't even remember falling asleep after sex. Alex and I knocked out quickly from the exhaustion of our sexy playtime earlier. Now it's sometime in the late afternoon next day and I need coffee. A sigh slips from my lips with content. I'm still baffled at the fact that I managed to go a week without his body wrapping around mine. The addiction I have to Alex is one I never care to fix. I can't help the smile that forms on my lips when he switches to his Master persona. Alex, despite us still being rather new as a couple, could ask me to move a mountain and I'd simply ask, where to? I truly found myself a keeper, but with that thought comes the feeling that he's hiding something that consumes him. Even with his smiles and kisses, a sadness always lingers in his eyes. If he looks at me long enough, I can see pain rising to the surface. It's almost as if he is silently begging for help.

The thoughts I heard when he cried yesterday worries me and only confirm my suspicion of there being more than he lets on. The feeling of no longer wanting to exist lingers faintly in our bond and to think that it isn't the first time that he has felt that way.

If I had not come running when I did, what would have happened?

I shake my head and push aside those thoughts for now. I don't want to ruin the good mood our makeup sex has put me in. The evening is approaching, and I need to check in with my Alpha about

Finn's situation. Maybe then I can ask my mate what is on his mind.

Alex squirms in his sleep next to me, tugging on my groin. His mindless action makes me flinch under his firm grip. What is he dreaming about for him to hold onto my dick like this? I look under the covers at the clutch my mate has on me. Just looking at it has made my junior grow a little and the initial thought of getting out of bed is becoming harder to accomplish.

"Chiquito, wake up." I shake him without prevailing. "Chiquito, come on."

I shake him harder, but the movement causes his hand to jerk my member a little. A wave of pleasure shoots up through me. I close my eyes and moan softly at the feeling. My hardening dick isn't listening to me and Alex, who is now grinning like a fool, knows exactly what he is doing.

This little faker.

"You're awake, aren't you?!"

I grab my pillow and slap him with it.

"Pero, te gusto!" Alex giggles from under the pillow.

His Spanish does things to me. I thank the Goddess I paid attention in school, because I love understanding his sweet nothings.

"Shut up." I smirk at the sexy little wolf beside me.

"Babe, random question."

"Okay, what's up?" I smile at Alex trying to read the pondering look on his face.

"Would you ever be into exhibitionism?" Alex bites his lip in wait.

"I am not sure. In front of people we know or strangers?" I ask, wondering where this is coming from.

"Either." Alex shrugs with a smile.

"I'll think about it."

Alex lets go and I hop off the bed, opting for a session under an arctic shower. The cold water is the best cure for relieving boners. Rather, it has the ability to perform a vanishing act, making both boners and nut sacks disappear into the body itself. I stare at the cold running water already dreading stepping into it. The moment I do, icicles hit me like a barrage of bullets that nearly take me out. I stiffen from the attack of the shower head and step out of the spray to warm the water a bit. Sure enough, looking down, my nut sack is taking cover, and my dick is no longer up. Keeping the water cool, I soap and scrub the sex off my body.

By the time I finish, Alex is back asleep, still naked under the sheets. I kiss him on his head and throw on my clothes before heading out to the kitchen for some food and much-needed coffee. Goddess only knows I can't function without that liquid concoction.

The house seems oddly quiet considering it isn't late enough for everyone to be in bed, reminding me how well sound carries throughout the old home. It makes me blush at the thought of everyone hearing all the things Alex makes me say, but no use worrying now. If someone heard me bark, then they can stuff cotton in their ears for all I care, because there's more where that came from.

The kitchen is empty and the cool floor against my feet sends a slight shiver up my spine. Grabbing socks would have been smart, but again, I need coffee. The coffee machine hums in a weird whirring manner as it warms up the water to brew my fuel while I whistle to myself. The machine doesn't sound like it has much life left in it and it wouldn't surprise me if it stops working tomorrow.

Listening to the gurgles of the coffee maker, I pat the machine and pray that it doesn't actually break down. The aroma of the delicious Colombian roasted beans waft through the air. Coffee is my weakness. There will never be a day that I go without it. It doesn't matter the time of day... or night. It is practically integral to my survival. The creamer I grabbed from the fridge swirls into the coffee, creating a dark caramel color.

"Mmm." My body dances as the strong robust elixir fills my veins with the first blissful sip. It's heaven on my lips.

My feet absentmindedly transport me to the hallway toward the living room where I can suddenly hear soft voices whispering flirtatiously. The scent of Iris and Kristofer in the air is thick in the living room which can only mean one thing. I peek my head in as Iris giggles at a very handsy Kristofer. Thankfully, they are still dressed.

This must be the Goddess playing a trick on me—payback from when Kristofer walked in on Alex and me.

It is about time my damn Alpha lost his virginity. He was turning into a grandpa with a hymen thicker than his eyebrows. Not that men have a hymen, but at the rate he was going, he might as well have grown one. His dedication to only be intimate with his mate had him almost becoming a monk.

I walk into the living room as if I don't notice any of what they are doing with a smile.

"Hey, so what's the update on Finn?" I lower my bottom in one of the armchairs and sip my coffee, enjoying the warm feel of the liquid working through me once more.

"Do you need a minute alone with your mug?" Iris jokes and

Kristofer chuckles.

"Hardy har har. Let a man appreciate his coffee in peace," I snap with a playful grin.

Then plaster a loud kiss on my mug as if it were Alex. Iris laughs while Kristofer makes a face of horror. I liked Iris from the very start. she gets my humor and goes along with it at times. Meanwhile, Kristofer is most likely cringing over the fact that I kissed a mug. He can be a real germaphobe at times. Imagine if it was his mug I kissed.

Iris brings her feet up onto the couch to cross them before Kristofer answers my almost forgotten question.

"Well, he was last seen by Mystic Lake. After that, there's no sign of him." Kristofer explains, but his eyes are narrowing at the hallway for some reason. His face contorts in thought and then falls serious.

Follow my lead, he links with me.

Both Iris and I nod at the message.

"So, tomorrow morning I am going to go with a few of my men and scout the area. I think it's best to see what the potential threat might be down there." Kristofer speaks, but his eyes are still narrowed at the hall. He tugs his ear to signal someone is listening. "Okay, so I'll make sure to round up our strongest fighters just in case."

I respond to Kristofer with a silent "Who?" in American sign language.

We never studied sign language to its full extent but know enough to quickly communicate certain things. The rest of what we use is made up by us. As kids we thought it was cool, and it stuck.

"Okay, sounds good. I hope we can find him soon. I have a lot of questions for that idiot."

Kristofer then taps his head to sign 'I don't know.'

Iris watches us in fascination as we simultaneously have two conversations. Yeah, the link works just fine between us, but oddly enough, old habits die hard.

"Yea, same, but damn losing a finger must have been tough." I point to my nose shaking my head as if to say why couldn't we smell the person that's listening.

"Well, that's better than what I would have chopped off for touching Iris, " Kristofer replies.

Iris hits Kristofer and we laugh while he signs the word 'hide' by placing his closed fist to his lips and then moving it under his other hand. Whoever is hiding is also masking their scent.

I nod in agreement and sip more of my coffee.

"Alright, I'm going to head into town for a few things." Kristofer says. "Demetrius, come with me. And you, my dear, beautiful, and oh-so-sexy Luna, keep watch and link me if anything happens."

Kristofer kisses his mate, and I follow him out of the house with my mug after putting on my shoes.

"Who do you think it was?" I ask while we get into the truck. Kristofer clearly doesn't need to go anywhere, but he drives off anyway so we can talk.

"I'm not sure yet, but I think it's Hugo. If I am right, he is up to something. And why did you bring the mug?"

The pick-up passes our property gate leaving a trail of dust clouds. He turns toward the town to create distance between the sneaky wolf we left behind and our conversation.

"Well, not like I planned for a drive when I poured myself coffee. Anyways, I know he is an asshole, but what could he possibly do?" I snorted, but Kristofer didn't laugh.

"Yesterday morning when Alex spoke to him, I was there, and some things didn't add up." He pauses for a moment, pursing his lips in thought. "Did you know that Alex's mother is a Neverdeen?"

His grip on the wheel tightens, making a weird squeak against the leather that wraps it. It does nothing to calm the anxiety that's overcoming him. If his pheromones didn't tell me as much, I'd say he was fuming instead.

"As in the founding family?" I gape.

Alex never mentioned this to me. Kristofer shoots a glare over to me, determined to not utter the answer we both know. Speaking it out loud is like admitting that we have been hiding a fugitive of not just the founding family of the council, but a pure blood.

"Alex only recently found out. His father was hiding the fact that she is still alive. I don't believe Hugo knows that Alex is aware of her real name though." Kristofer lets out a little curse. "I think you should talk to Alex and see if his mother could help us find Finn and discover what else Hugo may be hiding."

I rest my head back on the seat and gaze out the window at the passing scenery. The bald trees make the land look dead with a few evergreens scattered here and there. The way winter strips everything down to the bones is depressing. Maybe that's why humans have such joyous holidays during this time of year. My breath fogs against the window as we pass homes in the distance of our pack family with smoking chimneys before crossing into Atlas' territory.

After a few more homes and then a vast expanse of trees, we end up by a field of nothing. It stands bare before me as small pieces of everything that went down with Cassius' father and then Iris' begins to piece it together. The battle that went down with both men left our land in disarray. It isn't just our people that need time to heal but our mother earth as well. Yet, with all that has happened, it doesn't feel like it's over. Something big is coming. Like if an apocalypse is ready to take place, but only if we play our cards incorrectly would we not survive.

What is the right move? What should we be doing right now?

Kristofer pulls up to a random park for us to kill time. The sky darkens quickly as daylight saving moves us back an hour. The animals respond to the fading light and scurry to sleep while others come out to play. Small insects in the shadows sing their nightly songs and owls hoot in the distance.

"I think we should contact the council." My voice sounds too uncertain, betraying the suggestion of my words the moment they leave my tongue.

"Maybe. They could offer protection or even know what might be going on. But with the way they acted after the incident with Cassius' father and their involvement in Iris' dreams, I don't know. I am finding it hard to trust them right now." Kristofer shrugs.

I agree with Kristofer. Even if not everyone from the council is involved, it is hard to know for sure which one of them we can turn to. We sit the car in silence with the hum of the running engine, consumed by thoughts of all that is unfolding and how clueless we are to it all.

"Okay, I think he has had enough time." Kristofer pulls out of the parking spot and turns in the direction to head home.

"What do you mean?" I ask.

"Well, if the eavesdropper was listening to relay information, he would have taken the opportunity that I left to report it. Now we wait and see what happens."

Kristofer grins and it's moments like these that I truly admire his leadership. He is quick on his feet. While I sit processing information, this man already figured out the next three moves.

When we arrive home, Alex is in the kitchen with Iris and Cecile chatting away. My Alex smiles at something that Cecile says and something in my stomach flutters as if seeing him again for the first time. I missed this. It was only a week, but it was enough time to live a year's worth of loneliness. His scent hits me, and my heart skips a beat. Inhaling deeply, I smile and catch his gaze briefly meeting mine. Maybe he isn't a wolf, but a sly fox in wolf's skin sent to toy with me.

Kristofer and I walk further into the kitchen, and I smile at everyone in greeting as I pass the table.

They are having what seems like girl talk, so I kiss my mate on the cheek and proceed to the pantry. I never had the chance to make something to eat since Kristofer took me on a detour. I rummage through the pantry items and grab what I need to prepare a few peanut butter and jam sandwiches with a tall glass of milk. It's not dinner but at least the protein will fill me up for now.

I hum a tune that has been an earworm since a few days ago when I heard a song playing on the radio in one of my errands into town. In my own world of a musical masterpiece and my not so angelic humming, I pull out six slices of honey whole wheat bread and stack them on a plastic plate. I honestly hate doing dishes and would rather use disposable plates.

I open the jar of smooth and creamy peanut butter, because the chunky kind are for serial killers, and stare at it for a second. I need a knife but as I open the drawer, it reveals all the knives are gone and only a few spoons and forks remain. I turn to the empty sink and realize that luckily, they must all be in the dishwasher. Grabbing a warm knife from the steamy clean load of dishes, I return to my sandwich construction. I spread a thick layer of peanut butter on one side and then an equally thick layer of jam on the other. Three sandwiches later, I am ready to chow down.

The strawberry jam is perfectly sweet as I down two of them in a matter of minutes before a hand sneaks around my waist. Alex's face pops over my shoulder, eyeing my food. I turn to him with a mouthful of sandwich and give him a kiss and moan into his lips because at that moment I realize how much sweeter his lips are to me than this jam. But just as quickly, Alex pulls away, skipping and giggling. I watch, amused to see a grown man like him prancing around. Shaking my head, I reach for my last sandwich only to find an empty plate. That little sneak bamboozled me. You would think that I would be used to his sneaky ways when it comes to food. But no, once again my mate uses my body to steal my food, and it works flawlessly every time.

"Ladron!" I yell in Spanish and chase after a now-running Alex.

We run around the house and in the midst of it all, Alex shoves the sandwich into his mouth while laughing and screaming as I catch up to him. With a face like a chipmunk, I catch him in the den and tackle him to the floor. He burst into another fit of laughter with jam all over his lips and crumbs on his shirt, leaving proof of his mischief. He swallows the last bit in his mouth and smiles. This man is both my reason to live and the reason I will die from starvation if he keeps stealing my food. Little does he know I will gladly give it up for him if he asks. Yet, knowing him, he finds this fun and will continue to steal from me. So, I guess I'll have to serve myself extra food from now on. He will think he won, and I won't go hungry.

Alex is lucky that he is the sexiest thing in the world because only he can get away with something like that. I straddle him and pin down his hands above his head. His laughter fades as he takes in my shifting eyes. I can hear the laughter of the other in the kitchen most likely from how I barreled out of the kitchen after Alex. But it's a faint echo in the background as my focus narrows on his heavy breathing.

The ache in my groin against his hardening one stirs me more. I lean forward and lick the jam off his lips, nipping him a little. The stiffness beneath me throbs against me, sending a growl from my throat, wanting to have my way with him on the floor.

All I ever want to do is be inside him. It's where I feel at home. My hands run down the length of his arms and down to his chest before they slip under his shirt. His back arches into my touch with a growl of his own that vibrates against my hands.

"No wolf cannibalism allowed." Kristofer chuckles leaning against the doorway. "How is it that the two of you can run around like five-year-olds over a sandwich and somehow end up seconds away from devouring each other instead?"

I got off my mate and helped him up from the floor. Both of us flushed and still very much aroused. Well at least I am.

"Buzzkill," Alex sticks out his tongue at Kristofer and walks out.

"Yeah, what he said," I add following closely behind my mate.

"Wow, look how well you listen to your 'Master'. Aren't you a good Sub?" Kristofer's words drip in sarcasm while he makes air quotes with the word master. I snarl at him, earning a slap on the arm from Alex when I turn into the hallway bumping into him. His face horrified over something I must have missed. A snort comes from the kitchen and it's clear they are listening to what's going on here.

"Hey, what was that for?" I rub my arm even though it doesn't truly hurt while Kristofer laughs hysterically in the den. I take a step back to peek through the doorway and Kristofer is laughing and making faces while mocking me saying 'ow' in a girl-like manner. Alex slaps my arm again and I turn to him in question.

"That was embarrassing," Alex whispers.

"What do you mean? I'm the one he's mocking!"

"Yeah, but your hardon wasn't the one he noticed." Alex blushes.

"So why did you hit me?" My voice raises a bit in the end.

Man, I sound whiny.

"Well, I can't hit him, now, can I?!" Alex snaps back looking like an inflated red balloon.

My little wolf is adorable when he is embarrassed. I really could just eat him up.

"Yes, you can! Go, I'll back you up. I'll hold him down for you."

Kristofer peeks his head into the hall, "What did you say?"

"Nothing!" Alex yelps and runs.

I chase after my mate who pauses for a second considering my words, but with another look at Kristofer he dashes to his room instead.

5

Alex

Thump

A loud sound booms through the quiet of the house waking me from my sleep. I listen but nothing stirs. The sound of my mate breathing threatens to lull me back to sleep.

Another thump, like a bowling ball dropping on the wooden floor, jolts my eyes open. I sit up panting to scan my room for the cause of the sounds. My eyes quickly adjust to the dark and recognize the silhouettes of the furniture in my room barely visible beneath the moonlight. Demetrius doesn't seem phased by the sounds and turns over in the bed lightly snoring most likely from me sitting up.

I strain my ears, but I hear only the sounds of the settled pack house. Now I'm questioning if it was in my dreams. It would explain Demetrius not waking up.

The silence is so loud around me that it vibrates in the stillness of the night, but the feeling that someone was there pricks in the back of my mind. My skin crawls at the uneasiness. Annoyed at being awake, I slip on my socks and leave the room for a glass of water, taking the opportunity to see if anyone else is awake. The best part about my room is the proximity to the kitchen, so the walk isn't far. Easy access to the kitchen from your bedroom should be illegal. If it wasn't for my wolf metabolism, I would be obese by now.

Walking in the dark, I rub the sleep from my eyes, I open the cabinet and grab my favorite mug. It has little phallic rainbows and a puking unicorn that's farting glitter. The day I brought the mug home,

I remember Cecile wanting me to return it. She'd said it was inappropriate for the pups in the house. The look of confusion at the farting unicorn is what got her though it was hilarious. It was Demetrius who coaxed her into letting me keep it by telling her how I showed I have something that expressed me as an individual and I would promise to not let others see it. The three pups at the time eventually left when they were adopted by others in the pack. Demetrius had winked at me with what I now realized is his devilish smirk. Cecile still reminds me of the mug every day now. She always suggests getting one with only rainbows, leaving the phallic aspect of it out. But I always smile and remind her that is the only reason I bought it to begin with.

Thinking back, Demetrius always defended me, and I never noticed because my mind was always elsewhere with worry of my father. Or I was blindly following Cassius around all lovestruck.

Filling the mug with tap water, I take a sip of the cool liquid while looking out of the window. The sensation of the cool liquid extinguishes the burning desire that is creeping into me at the thought of my mate. Now that I have unlimited access to him, I am horny all the time. That man does wonders for me and my libido.

Satisfied with my drink, I rinse the mug and grab the towel to dry it. The hairs prick on the back of my neck again. I feel a presence before my nose catches a whiff of my father's scent. It always has this underlying cigar smell. I remain with my back turned away from the door.

It doesn't surprise me that he wants to confront me when no one is around. If I could roll my eyes endlessly, I would. His very presence irritates the core of my soul. That hatred I developed towards him tipped the scale for me to finally move out of the cabin and into the main house. I need to be away from him and to be free of the terrifying wolf that he is. This man doesn't deserve to be called my father. He is controlling, abusive, and a man full of anger for no fault but his own. I don't bother turning around at first but my distrust in him has me turning slightly towards him.

"What are you doing here at-" With a speed much faster than my own, a hand reaches around me and covers my nose with a cloth. I try to fight Hugo off, but in comparison, I'm much too weak against his strength. He is taller than me by a few inches and has enough muscle to hold me down. My head grows fuzzy the more I struggle and down I go as I black out to a sweet scent.

***

My eyes flutter open, but nothing registers. It is dark to the point where shadows are indistinguishable. Tears sting my eyes as I try to move and realize that my hands and feet are bound by something, preventing me from moving freely to explore the space around me.

My father just upped his assholery to another level.

Why can't he let me be?

Taking a deep breath, I listen to my surroundings. Faint voices filter through the darkness, but what's being said eludes me. I bounce a bit, jostled by the movement of whatever I am in. Nausea grips my throat with a bitter taste greeting my tongue. I close my eyes as my head spins again. Whatever drug my father took me out with must have been a high dose to make me this disoriented. A laugh filters through again and I black out once more.

***

Something bumps my head, and my eyes flutter open for a second time as I struggle with the groggy feeling. Music is playing rather muffled and that's when I realize that I am in a car. Between the muffled sounds, the movement of whatever I am in, and the music now rattling the bass of the speakers, all tells me that I have to be in a car. Rather, I am in the trunk of a car. It has to be why it's so dark. With my hands and feet bound, the numbness must have taken hold already because tingling starts to spread on the tips of my fingers when I wiggle. The tingling turns to pins and needles, the more I try to move and I almost groan from the pain. Squinting and hoping my eyes adjust to the dark better, all I catch is a bit of light coming in from what I assume is a rusted hole on the side panel of the vehicle.

The jostle again as the car goes over something like a speed bump considering the uneven movement. Another item rolls hitting me again and I squint at the oddly shaped object. The vehicle turns quickly, causing my body to jerk to one side and I slammed into the side panel. I groan at the newfound pain in my head and shoulder.

Shit.

I feel something drip down the side of my face. Whatever hit me earlier must have been made of metal. The throbbing on my temple intensifies as time passes. I try to link to Demetrius, but the brain fog isn't allowing me to focus. Whatever I am drugged with is still heavy in my system and I am sure that the multiple head injuries don't help either.

Eventually, the car comes to a stop, forcing me to roll forward and bang my knees against what may be the trunk door. A sharp pain pierces my skin. I will come out of here looking a mess.

Well, let's see what his grand reason is this time.

Car doors slamming closed shakes the car, rocking me slightly. Multiple sets of footsteps walk around the vehicle and approach me. The trunk door pops open, bombarding my eyes with glaring sunlight. I jerk my body back deeper into the trunk to avoid the brightness. I must have been blacked out for a while because the sun blaring in my face is strong. Slowly, my eyes begin to adjust to the invading light.

The dumb fuck in front of me pulls me out of the trunk with ease. I stumble with my numb feet from the restraints. The pain in my legs is unbearable as they regain feeling back in what feels like electric currents racing through my body. There are two other wolves with the idiot who yanked me out of the car, but before my vision clears enough to get a good look, a bag is placed over my head. It's thick like a canvas bag that barely allows light to penetrate through it. The smell is horrid, as if rotten food molded in the bag before they dumped it and placed it over my head. I close my eyes and walk trying to take in the sounds and smells other than the bag around me.

My feet barely comprehend how to walk properly as the blood flow makes its way back into my toes. I trip over something and one of the men grips me tighter to keep me from falling.

Nausea makes its way back to my throat and the fog in my mind pushes through. It is a feeling I know all too well, but the thought of it being that very same possibility scares me. The only things that disorient a wolf's senses are hard drugs, an insane amount of alcohol, or a very low dose of wolfsbane slowly administered to sustain a high of sorts. At this point, I put nothing past my father. If I make it out alive, my father won't, because I'd see to it myself that he takes his last breath or at the very least pays for his sins.

My senses fight to distinguish my surroundings. The faint sounds of water hit my ears in the distance and the terrain beneath my sock clad feet shifts to gravel. The shuffling of the small painful rocks drowns out any other noise with all our feet shuffling at once. Each step hurts more than the last as the pointed edges of parts of the gravel dig into the souls of my feet. But the water I heard earlier gives me hope. We were possibly near the river.

I struggle against the wolf holding me, but no strength is left in my weak body. The tired sigh slips away from my lips while the men lead me to a set of stairs. Very quickly I realized we were descending somewhere when I lost my footing and one of the men yelled to go down the steps before me. When we stopped, keys jingle, and a loud creaky door gives way. The men push me through the door before I am shoved to my knees with rough, strong hands.

One of the men finally removes the bag off my head, effectively yanking my hair with it. A grotty, rusted cell comes into view on the far side of the wall of the large basement. My eyes don't take as long to adjust as before since the light here is dim. Rust-like stains cover everything from the walls to the floor and the bed off to the side. As if it were the paint of choice, very little is left untouched by the iron-based stains. The smell in the room confirms the fresh round of bile to my throat. It reminds me of the time I slummed it a while ago when I ran away from home to go on a binge.

This may very well be how I die. The lackey behind me removes the bindings from my feet and unlocks the door. He drags me deeper inside the cell, cuffing my hands to the wall in one fell swoop.

I hit my head against the wall causing a barrage of dancing lights to blind me for a moment. The circles that dance through my vision give a halo to everything in its presence. Even the bastards that kidnapped me now look like angels.

As the halos disappear, I truly take in the condition of everything around me. Aside from the reddish-brown stains on the walls, the paint is peeling and revealing the bricks underneath. Mold grows on the corner of the ceiling and a line of ants crawl from a crack on the wall up to the small window. It is the only window to adorn my cell, but it is small and too high to see anything or enjoy the little bit of fresh air it provides.

A nice breeze could do me some good at the moment considering the unfinished floor is covered in dirt with lord knows what buried underneath. At least I'm assuming something is buried somewhere under here since the dirt seems loose. One of the men walks over to the other side of the bed and grabs the bedpan from the floor as something sloshes inside. Someone must have been here not too long ago, perhaps even just before me.

The bars are rusted but look sturdy enough to contain a weakened wolf like me. The horrid stench clings to the back of my nose, teasing the bile that's there. I swallow it down. In the corner opposite of the window where the unstable-looking bed is leaning at an odd angle, another set of chains hangs from the wall.

"Let me go," I try to bark through gritted teeth, but it falls on deaf ears as my voice cracks.

I continue tugging on the chains to no avail. "LET ME OUT YOU BASTARD," I yell as best as I can.

My outburst earns me a hard, backhanded slap across the face from the wolf who so generously showed me to my cell.

"Shut up you piece of shit," one of my captors demands. He spits on my head. Then the brute walks back out laughing like a madman and slams the cell door.

***

A familiar feeling comes over me.

Oh my god, no.

My heart races erratically against my chest. This can't possibly be happening. Not Again. Not after everything I've done to get clean. Sweat beads into droplets of despair that drip down my temples. My world swirls and my vision dots before me. The way my body is reacting is almost the same as before, but this is more intense. One by one, the side effects I know so well are coming to life like a haunt that was never fully exorcised. I'm holding on by a thread, dangling over a raging river, waiting for my inevitable fall.

The crawl of my skin, seeking the next spot the needle will pierce, grips me. I want this to stop. At least mentally I do but my body remembers, and it yearns to taste the sweet escape it once had.

The sound of boots stomping down a set of stairs, then dragging across the ground draws near. They stop in front of the cell door. My mouth goes dry, and my shaking becomes nearly uncontrollable. My head remains slumped as I tweak against the wall. My arms and hands have a mind of their own as the twitches intensify. My heavy head lifts to meet the wolf through droopy eyes. My eyes don't notice the person, but rather the needle he holds in his hand.

"I see you need another fix." Hugo pulls off his hood and unlocks the cell. His disgusting smile makes my insides turn in on themselves.

"You asshole, let me out of here," I pant as another wave of nausea hits me, forcing me to spit the small amount of my stomach contents onto the floor.

Who am I fooling? We both know my words are empty. My eyes wander back to what he holds. If I am going to die, then I might as well do so in my own ignorant bliss of the horrors of this world.

"Look at that. You can't even keep your wits about you. How does it feel to use it again?" He laughs with pure delight inching closer to me and waving the needle. "Think I didn't notice the drugs you used or your so-called cross-country trip that was really a stint at rehab? You have been nothing but a disappointment from the day you were born. Tan indeseable." Hugo scoffs.

He prowls forward and injects the familiar drug into my neck.

A sweet rush courses through my veins. My body's tension melts in false relief, and I slump against the wall.

Don't give in, Alex.

My wolf Peyton calls out to me, but it is a far echo in my mind. I know I shouldn't like this. Hell, I fought tooth and nail to kick my addiction. But this feeling—this deliciously, intoxicating feeling is what helped my mind escape my father. This bliss is what I called home for so many years.

Alex, please fight harder. You and I could die this time, remember? Stay strong. We can't spiral.

My wolf is right. I must fight to stay as clear-headed as possible. With wolfsbane, there's no control during the high. I lose my sense and go numb to the point of having no ability to move. However, afterwards, as I come down, I can use what little control I have in those lucid moments—for myself and my wolf.

I can't los-

My eyes roll back as the peak of the high hits and silences my thoughts. Like a remote pressing mute on everything around me. Euphoria takes hold and a series of colors and imagery become the ride I stay. I can no longer discern reality from the drug. The pains and aches are gone, replaced by sweet relief. Nothing but bliss seeps in with the feeling of non-existence.

If I die, then I die in this world of make-believe and hope that I can find my way back to my mate in another life. I close my eyes and ride the drug-induced tsunami of my demise.

* * *

I honestly can't say how long I have been here. It may still be the same day. There is no perception of time for me at the moment. As a wolf, I can metabolize drugs quicker than a human so the comedown would be much faster as well. But being pumped with drugs consistently is weakening my ability to metabolize the drug. Hugo also knows the right timing for the dosages he is giving me because every time I begin to feel lucid again, he comes and administers another dose. That asshole already jabbed my arm in so many places that I can't feel the pain from the aggressiveness he uses with the needle anymore. Footsteps stomp down the stairs in a menacing echo of my demise.

Right on time, asshole.

Never a moment long enough to think of a way to escape. Only enough time to remember that this is how I die.

"You must really like this shit, huh? Your body takes it like a champ. How about I let you do this one yourself?"

Hugo unlocks the cell and walks in waving the needle with a higher dose than before. The syringe looks full, and the liquid is darker than the other ones. Even the size of the needle is slightly off.

My body leans in towards him instantly, anticipating the next hit. I don't want to crave the drug the way that I do. Nonetheless, here I am jonesing for it. I already surrendered to the pleasure of the evil concoction and if I am going to be held hostage by this asshole, I'd rather be numb to it all. Hugo laughs at me and uncuffs my hands that had hung over my head all this time. There isn't an ounce of strength left in my body to move, let alone attack him. My arms fall to my sides heavy and useless. I am a mess, swimming at rock bottom along with my pride.

"I'll leave this right here." Hugo sets the full syringe on the floor just out of reach. The bastard wants to see me struggle for it, I'm sure. "Use it when you're ready. I need to run errands real quick, but don't worry, I'll be back in time for your next dose." He steps away but turns back and places the syringe in my hand instead.

He leaves me alone without bothering to lock the cell. He is fully aware of how far gone I am. That man is the devil incarnate, and I regret the day I didn't kill him when I had the chance. So many times, I could have poisoned his dinner, stabbed him while he slept, or shot him during the battle with Iris' father, Liber. Yet, because he is my father, I spared him while I, in turn, suffered.

Lo odio.

The needle he left in my hand stares at me dripping with anticipation. Tears roll down my cheeks. All I have to do to end the pain is inject myself as I have done so many times before. The years I spent swimming in this pool of drug induced ecstasy chasing dreams that got further away the more I used. No matter how much I'd understood that I could die or forever stay dependent, it never bothered me. It meant I was away from home. I had nothing to live for back then.

That is no longer the case. I don't want to be here. I don't want to die. The last thing I want to do is shoot up again because I want my mate instead. I want happiness. But maybe it is too late. My father made sure of that in the form of a needle.

My heart cries as I sit there wanting to scream but with no strength left to do so.

I went through so much to make sure I never lived through this hell again, just to end up right back here. My month in rehab, down the drain. Tires peeling off the gravel from above gives me momentary relief from his presence. Just knowing I am free from Hugo for a few hours lets me breathe just a little easier. His looming dark passenger is finally gone and here I am with the opportunity to escape. Yet, I'm unable to move. My will to fight is nothing but a far-fetched thought. One that I struggle to maintain at the forefront of my mind.

I take a deep breath in. The pull to use the drug is strong. It looks a bit darker than what Hugo has been giving me, but I don't care. I need to take the edge off. My fingers twitch around the syringe, the desire to use it tries its best to claw its way out. But I don't need the drug. Honestly, no one does? At this point, I want it just because it feels out of this world and that simple fact scares me.

Maybe if I only do a little bit to take the edge off, I can manage to escape.

The thought doesn't seem too bad, but I know that it's just me trying to rationalize taking the hit. I've done it before—injecting just enough of the drug to numb out the world but remain functional. Numb to my inner thoughts. Numb to my emotions. Despite all that, something still nags at the back of my mind. Who's to say that this time will be the same as the last? Is it worth the risk? Nothing justifies using the needle, but who am I kidding?

I am broken. Unrepairable. Unworthy. A disappointment.

Okay, half a dose then.

With a heavy sigh of resignation, I press the needle into my arm. I don't even feel the sharp metal pierce my skin. Time slows as I sit and stare at the needle protruding from my arm. I don't push the syringe's contents into my vein just yet. I know this may be my last high. A sob escapes.

I'm stronger than this. I could get up and leave right now. This could all be over. But making that decision seems nearly impossible to accomplish. It's why Hugo mocks me. It's why he left the door open. My sobs soften into whimpers as I stare at the liquid waiting to enter my system. The dark purple liquid mocks me with its silver tinge reflecting off the light.

"Fuck. This. I need Demi," I say out loud.

Demi is my only drug. The only one that I will willingly inject myself with over and over because I love him.

I do my best to get up from the floor, but with my weakened legs and arms, I slip and tumble over to my side. I slide back down the wall and topple over on top of my arm. The action pushes a small amount of the drug into my arm. I exhale when only a few units are injected. If anymore had gone in, it could have been game over.

Shit! Something is different.

The small dose burns something fierce as it courses into my veins. Hugo must have laced it with extra wolfsbane or something else altogether. He's probably counting on me taking the full dose, essentially finishing myself off.

Fuck, fuck fuck! I'm gonna die. Demirius. I won't see my mate ever again. I want to live. Goddess, I want to live. I… want… to…

My eyelids droop and I drift off into another dreamland of false hope.

6

Demetrius

I wake up to a cold empty bed. With a loud yawn, the immediate stretch that activates is unavoidable. I let it out with a squeal and thwomp my hand on the bed to rub the vacant space beside me. Frowning, I reach further into the space since he could have rolled out of my reach. Still, there's nothing there. I look over to his side of the bed and the revelation of his complete absence has me wide awake. I scan the room looking for signs of him. I thought by now Alex would have come back from the kitchen and by the looks of it, he isn't in his bathroom either. The sun creeps up into the room and it settles my nerves a bit. Maybe Alex started his day early. I didn't even realize I fell back asleep when Alex took too long to return to bed last night. My exhaustion had me in a chokehold.

The digital clock on the nightstand changes to six-thirty in the morning, but it doesn't sit right with me. Alex never wakes up this early, so it must be that he never came back to bed. I would hate it if he were thinking about his father and crying in the living room so I can't hear him. That is something he would definitely do. Now concerned, I use my link to call out to him. I listen to the silence getting nothing in return and it only turns my concerns to worry. It's like my call to him is bouncing back to me unable to find its destination. For that to happen, either the person is too far for the link to reach, they disconnected the link, or they are intoxicated.

I try one more time for good measure, but, again, I get no response. The pit of my stomach clenches at the thought of something not being right. Especially with the kind of thoughts that Alex had last night. The situation is everything but okay.

Where are you, Alex?

I toss the blanket off me, making it fly to the other side of the bed. It falls to the floor, but I leave it as I find some pants and forgo the shirt. I hurry over to the chair where Alex stacks his clothes and borrow a pair of socks. My mind races in circles of the endless possibilities of what might have happened. Hopping on one foot I put on the socks and then the boots. The conversation I had with Kristofer about there being a snitch within the pack lingers on my mind. Someone was listening in on us and it's no coincidence that now my Alex isn't responding to me.

With hurried feet, I run through the house, my breathing growing harder with each passing moment I don't find Alex. Kristofer isn't in his room nor anywhere else in the house and for a second, I allow myself to believe that Alex may be with him.

In hopes that I may be right, I run out the back door to look for them on the training grounds. Halfway towards the woods to the left of the house, I see the training grounds. I run a bit and spot Kristofer and Iris among the others that were training. But in the mix of everyone there, Alex is not among them. From the distance, I link.

Kris, come here. He looks my way, sensing the unease spilling into the link.

Everything okay?

No, it's Alex.

Kristofer speed runs to me with a swoosh, allowing Iris to continue the training on her own.

"What's wrong?" he asks.

I stop the tears wanting to push through as a bit of dizziness creeps in. The fact that I may very well be overreacting does dawn on me, but my gut is telling me otherwise. "I think something happened to Alex. I don't think he ever came back to bed last night and now I can't sense him anywhere or the link."

I pace back and forth chewing on the inside of my lip.

"What do you mean he never came to bed?" Kristofer concentrates on the ground with that look he does when he is trying to mind link. He could be trying to reach out to Alex.

"He woke up last night. I felt him when he got off the bed and left the room. I just thought he was getting something to drink because he does that sometimes. I ended up falling back asleep and when I woke up this morning, I realized he never came back."

My hands tremble, my palms are sweating, and my breathing is rapid, making me lightheaded. The anxiety from not knowing his whereabouts or what happened is killing me.

Kristofer eyes me with concern and runs inside the house. I follow him, ending up in the kitchen as Kristofer stares at Alex's mug still in the sink. This is something he never does. Ever since I convinced Cecile to let Alex keep the mug, he makes sure it is never out in plain sight. If he ever uses it, he will quickly wash it and put it away.

This isn't good.

"Have you tried his cell?" Kristofer looks at me expecting me to say yes right away, but I hadn't even thought of that. "Dear Goddess, call his cell before freaking out you moron." Kristofer palms his forehead then mumbles under his breath.

He's right. I can call him and clear all of this up and laugh about it later. A call is all I need. I pull out my cell and select his name from my favorites. His phone starts to ring loud and clear from his room playing the jingle from one of his favorite shows. My heart sinks and I turn back into the giant disaster of a man that I let go for the few seconds it took me to dial his number.

"Okay, now I think you should use your special tracking skills. I couldn't sense him either." Kristofer whispers as he holds the mug and places it on the counter with newfound concern.

"I can't. I haven't used it in years, and I used to get sick afterwards, remember?" There's no telling if I can even do it anymore. It is a skill that was passed down to me, but I haven't had a need for it in years. I wouldn't be surprised if I lost my ability track.

"Demetrius, this is your mate we are talking about. Sick or not, you need to try. If not, then there's nothing that can tell us where he is or what happened. His scent is already naturally faint, and right now its barely in the kitchen."

"I know that!"

Kristofer scratches the back of his head as he looks around hoping to find something. Anything. If I have to go through the gates of hell for Alex, then I will. There's only one place for him and that is safe in my arms.

I shake out my body and take a deep breath. It takes every bit of concentration from me to do this sort of tracking technique. Filling my lungs and exhaling slowly, I focus on slowing my heart as best I can and listen through my senses. My vision, hearing, and smell, all heighten. The sweet smell of the donuts on the counter fills my nose. Iris grunting with each strike all the way across the training field, the light bulb in the kitchen above my head becomes brighter making me squint, and for a second it feels as if the world slowed down around me. A wave of nausea flows through me, and I wobble in place ready to vomit.

"I can't do it," I whisper with a pang of guilt in my heart.

Yes, you can, but you might need Shoneah to help you. My wolf, Alcide, chimes in.

What do you mean?

Your own fear and doubts are what's stopping you. You need to break free of that and Shoneah will help. It makes sense but what if it still doesn't work.

But...

THIS IS OUR MATE. GROW A FUCKING PAIR AND GET SHONEAH NOW.

My wolf bellows into my mind, causing my breath to shake and my chest to squeeze. He's angry and afraid and here I stand a coward, unable to do something out of fear of getting sick.

"Alcide said Shoneah can help me," I look up to Kristofer and his eyes focus on calling out to Cassius.

"He will be here soon. Go wash up while he arrives. We will leave as soon as we find out what happened. I'll go tell Iris and the others."

Kristofer leaves me in the kitchen feeling ashamed and useless. My mate is out there somewhere possibly hurt, and I am doing everything besides acting like the Beta I am. I scoff at myself and march to my room to shower and change.

By the time I am done showering and changing in my room, someone knocks on my door. I call out to come in and Cassius strolls into the room wearing sweats and a hoodie, holding a coffee thermal between both hands. He still looks a bit sleepy-eyed, but all that changed when he wrinkled his nose getting a whiff of something. He loses all color in his face and runs out of the room and to the bathroom, dropping the thermal in the process. Thankfully the lid is closed, and nothing spills in the process.

Cassius pukes his guts out into the porcelain bowl and all I can do is thank the Goddess that he made it to the bathroom in time. I can only assume it is the body wash or the candle in my room that triggered it for him. Poor Luna Cassius is a month and a half pregnant, and his morning sickness is intense.

I make my way downstairs to the kitchen. I figured the last place Cassius will want to be in is my room. No point in making him walk back up the stairs to come retrieve me. Seeing the mug still on the counter makes me choke up again. How could I have not heard if there was a struggle? But what if Alex simply left? The kitchen is spotless, rid of anything that can give me a clue or hint of what might have happened. Only his mug sits there, out of place.

"Okay so, I am going to let Shoneah take over okay," Cassius speaks up from behind me, scaring the hell out of my soul, forcing a little yelp out of me. He chuckles and it begins. His body changes into the image we all have grown accustomed to as of recently. His hair turns silver-white, but the tattoos that usually cover his body didn't manifest as usual. Maybe that only happens when Cassius remains in control, but I'm not too sure.

"Hello, Demetrius and Alcide." Shoneah's voice is very deep compared to Cassius'.

"Hello, Shoneah," I bow my head in respect and so does my wolf internally. Although no one could see the gesture, I think Shoneah senses it from Alcide.

"What is it that scares you so? Not many wolves can track like you do. It's a gift. So, what binds you in fear?" Shoneah walks up to me and places a hand on my chest.

The cold of his fingers makes me shiver slightly, but as I open my mouth to answer him, my eyes grow heavy, and a flutter emerges in the back of my mind. The odd feeling as if someone is flipping through my mind becomes more intense and then I am thrust into a flood of memories. They move around in small images and encircle me until one in particular stop and plays out like a movie reel at a drive in.

I'm back as my ten-year-old self. My mother stood before me wearing the blue dress she loved so much. She was panicking because she sensed something was wrong with Dad, and she needed to find him. I sensed it too, but I couldn't say how. Mother hugged me telling me to stay close to her, but the tears and the shaking in her hands scared me. The smell of flowers in her hair did little to soothe the fear I felt. I nodded my head to what my mother said and watched her close her eyes, sniffing the air. I tried doing the same as her but all I got was the anxiety from her pheromones leaking out of her.

Mothers head darted from side to side, and I realized she was tracking. It was different from how other wolves' track. My mother had a gift. She walked around as if following someone's steps and said out loud the scents that surrounded us. I worried my lip as I watched and then bit it when mother screamed. It was as if she felt whatever might have happened to father.

She shifted into her wolf and before I could register what I felt, I shifted and ran after her. My wolf, Alcide, gave chase as best he could, and we ended up in a clearing at the edge of the woods by our home. A hunter killed my father and stood over his body laughing in triumph. That must have been what my mother felt. We watched, unsure if there were others around. All we could do was stand there waiting for the hunter to leave. But he never did. My mother refused to give up on rescuing my father even if it only meant recovering his body, so we hid and waited. After some time went by, she fell asleep from exhaustion and so did I. By the time we woke up, we found that father was gone and so was the hunter. My mother closed her eyes again and tracked them doing the same thing she did before.

Locking in on a scent, Mom went in full sprint. This time I could smell the hunter as well. Blood dripped out of her nose as we ran but she kept going. My wolf, Alcide, called out to her, wondering if she was okay but she ignored us.

By the time we reached the hunter, it was too late. The hunter was skinning my father in a shed. This time, mother didn't wait and in a fit of rage, she shredded the hunter apart. Mother changed back to her human form, taking my father off the butcher's block, and bringing him back to the pack house where we buried him. My Mom was never the same after that and eventually went mad. Mother inevitably died from a broken heart not long after.

Shoneah removes his hand from my chest, and I open my eyes not realizing how wet my face is from reliving that memory.

"That is a lot to see as a child. I can understand the fear of you going mad as well, but you won't." Shoneah looks through me as if staring at my soul instead of me.

How can he say that so easily after witnessing my memory?

"You don't know that" I whisper, unable to form any other words. My eyes water further and the emotions inside me turn into a storm of anger and hurt. That memory was so tightly locked away and now I relived it more vividly than I cared for.

"My child, I do know. You have used it before and walked away fine each time. Just because this situation is similar to that of your mother's, it doesn't mean it will have the same outcome. If you won't believe me then listen to Sheila instead." Shoneah smiles which confuses me.

Sheila is the name of my mother's wolf. How does he expect me to listen to a dead wolf?

He extends his hand and white flames form in his palm. "Give me your hand. It won't burn."

Trusting that it wouldn't harm me, I reach out and place my hand on his. Instantly, Alcide stirs. An odd sensation grips me. Alcide emerges from my body in a white, smoke-like form, standing tall next to me. Then the same thing happens to Shoneah but the wolf that stands before him is not Wolfie. I recognize the red eyes staring at me anywhere.

It's Sheila in the same smoke-like form as Alcide. If only I could see her soft black fur once more.

"How is that possible?"

The excitement I feel from seeing my mother's wolf after so many years struggles against the fear and anxiety from moments ago. It has been nineteen long years without my parents. My heart squeezes as she looks at me.

"Her wolf hasn't reincarnated yet, so I brought her here to speak with you."

I don't even look his way as he speaks. My eyes are fixed on Sheila. If only I could run my fingers through her fur, but I know that is not possible. This whole situation should be impossible. Yet, here I stand. Here we stand.

"Sheila, do you remember me?" I know it's a stupid question, but I am at a loss for words.

"Yes, Dem Dem. I do. My, how you have grown." Her voice is as gentle as ever.

My heart floods with emotion. I haven't heard that nickname in ages. Sheila and my mother were the only ones allowed to call me that.

"I've missed both of you so much." I sob like the child she once knew, letting everything building inside me to break free.

"We miss you too, but we have never left you. Your father's wolf recently reincarnated, but he was by your side until the very last second. You need to let go, Dem Dem. You have used the gift before and are extraordinary just like your mother. You getting sick afterward is simply your fear hindering you."

While I hear what she is telling me, I am stuck on the fact that they are watching over me. They never left me. All this time I thought I was alone, but they were there all along.

"How? How do I let go?" I barely manage between my shallow breaths as I try to calm down.

"You need to realize that the gift isn't what killed your mother. The loss of her greatest love did. If your mother never used her gift, then we wouldn't have had a body to bury. It is thanks to your mother that his wolf was saved. Had she not found them and not done a proper burial, then his wolf's soul would have died completely along with your father."

Sheila comes closer. We are almost eye to eye with her size. She is massive in her spirit form. So is Alcide.

"This isn't a gift." I shake my head. "Every time I've used it I've gotten so sick that I would throw up for hours after. I couldn't hold anything down."

"Oh, but it is," Alcide finally speaks. It is the first time I've ever heard him outside of my head. It's weird.

"How? I can't even use it without bleeding just like Mom did. I get dizzy and nauseous to the point I'd taste bile in my throat. I can barely last long enough to gather any kind of tracking information that's useful." I blink away the new tears that are forming.

Alcide continues. "You are projecting your fears. Instead, give in to the gift, and hone it. You are letting your demons control you instead and it's manifesting as the symptoms your mother had. When you'd use it every other time during a rabbit hunt, you never got sick. It was only when you had to track a person. Your mother was exhausted that day and was already sick with worry over your father missing. Her body was stressed which is why it wore her down."

Alcide looked back to Sheila and so did I.

"Accept what has happened," Sheila says to me. "Allow yourself to heal Dem Dem. Remove the shackles you've placed on yourself. You are strong, you just need to believe that as well."

I close my eyes and take a deep breath. When I opened them again, Alcide and Sheila are gone.

I sigh and squeeze Shoneah's hand.

"If I panic, can you help calm me down?" I ask Shoneah.

He agrees with a smile. I close my eyes once more and concentrate. I will scorch the earth if it means I can save my mate. It's time I fight my demons with all I've got. I hold both Shoneah's hands and get to work.

7

Demetrius

Shoneah holds onto my hands and walks with me to Alex's room so I can breathe in my surroundings and begin tracking. Kristofer and Iris join us to watch, curious if this will work. Kristofer knows how I used to fail and how hard it was on me mentally. But I'm willing to do anything to get Alex back.

Gripping Shoneah's hand tightly, I stand in the middle of the room, close my eyes, and relax my shoulders. I concentrate on the smells around me. My scent along with Alex's forms in my mind's eye. The sweet coconut in his pheromones and the sweat of our sex swirls recalling the memory of our passion. With deep steady breaths, I fill my lungs and just like my mother once taught me, I allow the way the scents mingle with one another and attach themselves to items around them, forming a picture in my mind's eye.

Mother always told me that the gift we possessed was different from any other kind of tracking a person could learn. She told me stories about how all scents had a memory, but the only ones that could tell a story are those of living things. Because of this, it is especially easy to see the room around me without having to open my eyes.

Every inch of the room is covered with me and Alex. The scent from fragrances registers faintly, revealing where objects are on the nightstand. The same with the candles and air fresheners plugged into the wall. While I find them to be strong, considering that Alex never developed his sense of smell like the rest of us, he enjoys his air fresheners. While they won't paint a picture the way pheromones do from humans, wolves, or other living creatures. However, they act as a great way to know what is stationary and how an area is laid out.

I turn my head, following the trails of our scents and with another deep breath, I sway as I fall deeper into a state of focus that is needed to capture the memory of our scents. Things begin to unfold before me, just as they happened.

The visual of Alex and me before he woke, materializing before me, forming in smoke-like swirls of magenta and browns. He wakes and lingers, looking around confused. Either he had a bad dream, or something caught his attention and he's trying to figure out what. My mind follows him like eyes on a muted screen and I watch as he gets up out of the bed to walk out of the room. With my eyes still closed, I follow Alex's scented figure. In hazy swirls, as the scents form images in my mind, I can see everything around me perfectly as if a second sight through smell.

A bout of nausea threatens my throat with its bitter taste of bile ghosting my tongue, but I push it back. My nostrils flare a bit, but I swallow a second time and exhale. My hands clam up and the speed at which my heart rate increases, makes my mind blur, pulling me out of the deep state I need to be in. Shoneah squeezes my hands to either calm me down or to encourage me to keep going. Either way, I relax just enough to slip back into my focused state. The reassurance that I am not alone helps me remember that it isn't going to end the same way it did for my mother, although that fear is creeping into the back of my mind.

Alex's scent leads me to the kitchen where I take in more smells deeply through my nose. With each exhale, the kitchen forms in my mind's eye with Alex filling his mug with water from the tap. The potted succulents on the window come into view with Cecile's scent lingering as well. She must have been in the kitchen a bit before Alex was.

The smell of dish soap by the sink and the fresh baked goods on the table mark the spaces of the kitchen for me to know where I stand relative to it all. I can see Cecile come and go in the kitchen as memories of the scents form all at once in a jumbled mess, but I pluck the scent I want with my nose and lean into it.

Cecile vanishes from the smokey vision and only Alex stands there, drinking from his mug. A faint scent then appears from behind me. Alex seems to know the person with how he stiffens. When the mystery scent thickens, no longer attempting to suppress itself, I recognize it as Hugo. Anger swells inside me, almost distorting the images in my mind. I grasp onto them before they can slip away again. His father has already done so much to hurt my Alex and here he is again, front and center. Shoneah squeezes my hand again, bringing me back to focus. My anger and fear are out of control, and they alone would be my undoing if I don't learn to handle them.

The smell of silver and possibly the sweet smell of something lingered briefly as it mixed with Hugo. Alex's father pounces him, and Alex grabs his father's arms trying to pull them away from his face but it's futile. He is weaker than his father and is dragged out of the kitchen unconscious. The sweet scent could possibly be chloroform since it knocked out Alex. Following my mate who is taken out the front door, my veins turn cold when I stop short of the entrance to the house. I can't hold back the tears. The strength that I thought I had, is gone. My mate was taken from me and all I did was sleep right through it.

The weight of my body becomes too much for my knees to bear or maybe it is the guilt that weighs me down. I drop. The pain I felt as a child, my mother unable to save my father, and now my mate being kidnapped, storms in my chest in a violent wrath of emotions banging against my ribs.

The desperation and pain in my heart must be what my mother felt all those years ago. It might have been even worse since the ones that took my father were hunters. Even then, history is repeating itself and I am left once again to look for someone I love.

I can barely move with a face full of tears, a heart full of pain, and a mind tormented by the fear of what I might find.

"Demetrius, you need to be strong for Alex," Shoneah places a warm hand on my shoulder breaking up the thoughts suffocating my mind.

"I can't. I can't do this! I... I am not strong enough," my words stammer between my sobs while my nose drips as it did many times before.

I wipe my nose. My hand comes back with blood smeared across the back. I gulp at the sight of it. It's happening again. My hands shake and my breathing becomes haggard. Flashes of my mother finding my father plays before me like a memory on a projector. His body, half skinned, hanging from a hook, and blood pooling on the floor.

"Demetrius, you are no longer that little boy. You are no longer helpless to the situation before you. You can do this. You are a Beta to this pack and rightfully so. Stand up and find your mate the best way you know how." Shoneah offers his hand to me to help me stand.

Through salty tears, I look at the faces around me and calm my nerves by swallowing everything that is pouring out of me. I say that I am strong, and I will walk through fire, but my fear of ending up like my mother, broken and alone, cripples me. Yet, before me, I have a family that keeps me strong. They stand here to remind me that I am no longer that little boy. I am a Beta and a mate, a friend and a brother. As scared as I still am, I have a chance to make a difference this time and I don't have to do it alone.

My nose guides me out of the door, away from the house, and into the woods, picking up the scent of the trees and grass around me. I can smell the way pollen lingers in the air, traveling to another area before it falls with its seed. Small animals take form as they skitter by or around bushes.

Then, I stop.

The scents become obscure. I can no longer distinguish in which direction Hugo and Alex might have gone. With another deep breath, the bits of berries around me from the bushes invade my senses and the spores from the mushrooms on the ground lay out a picture of the dense area.

A couple of minutes go by. In an attempt to determine which direction they went, I take a step forward in each direction to see where Alex's scent is the strongest.

There.

My mate's scent forms again, but as I reach our territory lines, I pick up two more wolves. The two wolves form in my mind but vanish just as the memory begins to fade. My heart is pounding. Like a fuzz on the TV screen or the white noise of a radio creeping in from the loss of connection. The memory becomes harder to discern. Nausea threatens me again, but I am able to keep it at bay and focus on the vague number of pheromones lingering.

I barely make out Alex being placed in something, a vehicle maybe. Then the three other scents fade along with him. The memory blurs and turns into a thin line of hope that travels southward.

I choke on the thick air of the truth that he is gone. Sweat beads on my face as I gasp for breath. I claw at my neck struggling to expand my lungs with relief, but it is useless. Blood drips again from my nose and then everything goes quiet.

Shoneah calls my name and in a split second, all the sounds and scents come rushing into me all at once.

I open my eyes, realizing I am actually in the woods surrounded by everything I had been seeing with my eyes closed. It was like I never closed my eyes to begin with. I am panting and trembling down to my core. Despite this being the longest tracking session I have ever had; I am still too weak to track. I lack all the skills to do what I must. At least without the help of someone else. I only got this far because Shoneah is with me.

Right behind me, Kristofer and Iris wait eagerly for me to regain composure and explain what I saw. Shoneah wiped the sweat and blood from my face. He pats my back in comfort and offers a sympathetic smile before transforming back into Luna Cassius.

I finally find my voice. "It was Hugo. That asshole used silver-laced chloroform to knock Alex out and drag him here. He continued up there," I point to a spot in the distance, "where two other wolves waited by territory lines with a vehicle. They stuffed him in the trunk and drove off, but the car must have been wiped or a burner. Their scents were not as strong as they should have been. It becomes so faint that it will be nearly impossible for me to follow long enough to see where it might have gone."

I don't want to admit that my not being able to follow the memory is due to my struggle to maintain composure and focus during the tracking. They already know this but voicing it out loud is just too much right now. Cassius is back to his normal self and quickly turns around to puke again, but this time I have no idea what could have been the trigger. Iris rushes to her brother-in-law's side and rubs his back while he continues to retch. I would hate to be pregnant. I don't know how women do it. I wouldn't be surprised if it is the smell of deer poop that isn't too far from where we stand that's turning his stomach.

"Okay, that's a start. Let's get ready and go." I clap my hands.

8
Councilman

Watching Kristofer, Demetrius, and the other two from a distance, I remove my hood and suck my teeth.

"That damned wolf must have the same ability as his useless mother."

"Who does, sir?" the young councilman to my left asks in hushed whispers. Still too wet behind the ears but perfect to wrap around my finger.

"Never you mind that. We need to hurry our plans. Hugo is no longer of use with how sloppy he is being. All he will do is bring us down."

With a weave of my hands, I cast a spell for us to teleport back home but before we vanish, we are spotted.

9

Demetrius

I snap my head to the left. The back of my neck pricks. Someone is out there. Someone is watching us. Kristofer turns as well and narrows his eyes in the same direction as me.

"What's wrong?" Iris asks.

I scan the surrounding trees and in a fraction of a second, I see three figures in cloaks disappear.

"What the hell?" I snarl between my teeth.

"We are being watched now?!" Kristofer clicks his teeth.

He must have seen the cloaked figures too. They have to be the council. They are the only ones that walk around in cloaks like in ancient times. But just as quickly as we see them, they disappear.

We all head back inside the house feeling a dread that hasn't been there before. Things just went up a few notches.

"I knew it. Hugo is up to something with the council, why else would they show up?" Kristofer balls his fist until they are white knuckled. "Fuck!"

"They didn't approach us though. So, either they didn't expect to be caught, or they purposely waited for us to notice so we would know they were keeping an eye on us," I hit the wall with my fist as we walk into the living room.

"But why?" Kristofer questions.

"Babe, calm down. Keep a clear mind," Iris opens her arms to Kristofer who is pacing. He folds into his mate like a child taking a deep breath. I would find it almost comical with their size difference if it weren't for the dread hanging over me. She is Kris's anchor, the same way Alex is mine.

"I'm going home, I don't feel well." Cassius waves goodbye and leaves with a pale face. His pregnancy is truly taking a toll on him, but he did well. He hung in there for me.

***

Kristofer and I head back to the training grounds and grab a few men to join us for a rescue mission. One of them, John, is an excellent tracker, but in a more traditional sense when it comes to reading tracks in the wild. He can tell the weight, size, and direction of an animal. Or he can tell if it has bad or good intentions just by surveying the area. His skill is purely through observation while mine is in scent memory. Since Alex's disappearance occurred in the house where everyone's scent is intertwined, it would have been hard for him to know exactly who did what, whereas I can separate the scents and trace them individually.

However, now that we need to track outside and the scents cut off from me, a physical tracker would be best to aid in the rescue. I am sure I can pick up traces here and there, but it will take too long to make informed decisions. John's tracking skills will be able to pick up where I'd lack in direction. To aid us in numbers in case we end up needing to fight, we also bring with us Fred and Oscar. They are great warriors and excel in stealth.

Iris hands me a syringe filled with a sedative she grabbed from the first aid kit. I just hope I won't need it for Alex.

"Let's start with the territory lines. We will travel in wolf form and keep within the lands of our allies. John and Demetrius, lead the way," Kristofer directs.

Then we all shift. I let go of my body as if detaching my soul from its physical body and recede into the body of the wolf as Alcide takes over. I lose all my senses and simply exist without existing. While my senses are gone, I can still feel here and see but only as a spectator through Alcide.

From the depths of Alcide's mind, I watch John's wolf, Keokuk, sniff the area and inspect the dirt for footprints and tire marks, and the direction they lead. We all follow and every time he loses his tracking, I guide Alcide in helping with what I can while Keokuk stops and re-examines the area. I would be lying if I said I was truly any help. The feeling in the pit of Alcides stomach and the fear wanting to grab hold, is one I sympathize with.

Like the reel of a silent film, the scenery passes by me as Alcide runs. Before I know it, a few hours have rolled. We end up by the river with the intention of following it. Considering the scent seems to follow the direction of the river, it would be easier to travel along the bank as the sound of rushing water helps mask the sound of us running.

Alcide tries to reach out to Alex through our link, but all he gets in return is a wall. Nothing responds but it feels more like the call is bouncing back as opposed to an echo in a void. An echo is a definite sign that the person is too far to reach but the feeling of thoughts bouncing back is more of a wolf guarding their mind. Sometimes it even means they're under the influence. Hope finally welcomes Alcide and I within the darkness of our despair.

While staying hidden from the main road, we continue to follow the river. We must be close to where Alex is being held since this time my bond to him is beginning to strengthen. I could almost feel him but it's faint. The need to see my mate safe and in my arms gnaws at the guilt that grips my consciousness. I pray to the moon Goddess that he is safe. I pray he is not being broken into the small pieces of his past. He has been doing so well putting himself back together after the disastrous life he had before me. My heart pangs at the thought of what my Alex could be going through. My thoughts are so potent, they distract Alcide enough for him to bump into Keokuk which makes me snap out of my thoughts.

What's wrong? Zeus, Kristofer's wolf, links to all of us, but directs it to Keokuk.

The sun is getting low and it's becoming harder to track.

We need to hurry then, Zeus responds.

We all nod our heads, but the truth is, the sun is setting too fast.

It isn't until another two hours before we come across a small cabin.

This ain't right. I don't smell him here at all, my wolf Alcide calls out to the others.

I think I might have lost the trail, Keokuk admits and then turns around sniffing in the direction we just came from. Maybe trying to double back.

You are supposed to be the best, how do you lose track?! My wolf Alcide snaps with flared lips and snarling teeth at Keokuk. Spit flies from his mouth.

Don't you dare pin this on me! I can smell the way your emotions are fighting one another. You are supposed to be helping me, yet you are letting your fear and guilt cloud your ability while your mate is out there suffering. I am doing my best with diminishing daylight. What are *you* **doing outside wallowing in your self-pity?**

No one says a word but the rage filling inside Alcide and me at the truth of his words has Alcide clawing at the dirt. This is one truth pill I do not want to swallow.

Fuck you! If you had a mate, you'd know how hard this is. If you watched your father skinned alive and your mother succumb to her despair, then you'd understand. But you don't know, do you. You fu-

ENOUGH! Zeus steps in between my wolf and Keokuk snarling at us. **We'll get nowhere like this. You are my Beta, mate or not, get your shit together. And you are my finest tracker, get us back on track and respect your Beta.**

Keokuk stares at Alcide and huffs. With a nod of his head, he returns to sniffing the ground and observing his surroundings while I take deep breaths to help Alcide retrace our steps. Both of us find our paths realigning and eventually we regain our course.

After a few hours, we reach a house that looks rather abandoned, but the light from the windows tells us otherwise. We are several miles outside of our territory away from home. We get low to the ground and survey the house. The ground is covered in gravel by the front where the car is parked and off to the side. However, the area behind the home is still covered in grass. Aside from the two guards in front who were chatting and smoking, the area is vacant.

I take a deep breath and there it is. A faint scent lingers in the air. I can smell Alex which means this is the right place. Relief washes over Alcide and I, but I reserve that excitement until I have him in my arms. Alcide spots a small window on the side of the house by the foundation of the old home. He must be in there. The barely noticeable shred of hope that's been hovering in my stomach spreads throughout my wolf. We suppress our scent to help conceal our presence before the wind gives us away.

Alcide looks over at Kristofer's wolf and mind-links with one another, agreeing that stealth might be the better option since we very well may be outnumbered. Kristofer, John, Fred, mine, and Oscar's wolves all carefully survey the home once more to be certain no one else is outside or hiding. If Fred and Oscar didn't stand next to Alcide, I would have forgotten they were with us. They remained silent the entire time in the back while Kristofer, John, and Alcide led the way here.

Alcide huffs. No matter how well we suppress our scent, we are still traceable to an extent. All hiding our scents does is minimize how strongly we smell and how far out the scent is detected.

We circle the house, keeping our bulking bodies low to the ground. **I will go around the front and keep watch, if they sense you, then I'll distract them.** Keokuk sneaks off towards the front of the house and Fred follows him.

Kristofer and Oscar quickly shift back into their human forms and enter through the back door of the house while Alcide and I are close behind. I peek around the door frame as the two sneak inside. There is a man sitting at the kitchen table with his feet up and sleeping. His head is tossed back, and his mouth is open.

This makes things easier.

A sound from the front of the cabin has the man flinching awake.

Or maybe not…

He sits up straight still not noticing us and draws a long breath into his lungs. Oscar and Kristofer may be in the shadows, but their scent can't be hidden for long in such a small space. He begins to stand but Oscar and Kristofer are on him before he gets the chance.

I shift back into my form as well and drop the clothes I had in my mouth. Quickly, I remove the syringe I have in the jeans pocket. While Kristofer holds the man down, I inject a strong sedative, putting him back in the same position on his chair. Anyone that sees him would think he is still asleep. The sedative was meant for Alex, just in case he is injured, but this works as well. I only inject half into the guard. The rest I save.

We hear another set of feet coming down the stairs and hurry to hide by the entrance of the kitchen, against the wall. I peak around the corner enough to see another guard traipsing down the stairs. I quickly hide again, holding my breath. He stops just before entering the kitchen and turns.

Movement at my side has my attention drawn to my pack mates. Oscar covers his mouth, and, at that moment, I knew it was going to get wild. Oscar sneezes and Kristofer lunges towards the man that comes charging into the kitchen. They wrestle onto the table, knocking their sedated comrade over. Oscar catches the unconscious man before he hits the floor preventing the loud thud and Kristofer manages to snap the neck of the man he is holding in a chokehold. We freeze waiting to see if anyone else heard and is coming towards us, but the house remains still.

I drag the dead body into a nearby closet as quietly as I can. Alpha signals with our sign language that he and Oscar are going to sweep the second floor. I give them a nod and watch as they walk up the stairs on nearly silent feet. Wolf skills at their finest. I stay behind and scout out what remains on the ground floor.

I follow the long hall that leads towards the front of the house and into a living room. The room is unkempt with empty food wrappers all over the floor, cracked windows, and peeling wallpaper. A long sofa sits to the side of the living room along with a lawn chair decorated with clothes. I scan the room and spot a person looking out one of the windows. He has headphones on loud enough that I can hear the beat. I step into the room to bring him down quietly.

The floor creaks louder than in a horror movie. The guy turns in surprise as he air drums to the music. Then he lunges toward me before I can register how quickly he's moving. I shift back into my wolf to fight my attacker. Alcide is more capable of handling this bastard than me. So, I gladly let him take over. Alcide releases a howl, alerting not only the guards outside, but my pack as well.

Keokuk begins to snarl and the fighting echoes throughout the house. He must have attacked the guards when Alcide alerted them of our presence.

Kristofer barrels down the stairs, fighting another man while Oscar is nowhere to be seen. Chaos surrounds me. There isn't time to think. Alcide swipes at the man before us as he jumps back fast enough to avoid injury. Kristofer yells in a horrifyingly painful roar when he is slashed with a switchblade. Oscar shifts mid-air down the stairs letting out a howl to knock the attacker off Kristofer, but Oscar himself doesn't look too good. He is bleeding from his face. Possibly his left eye.

I got this, go help Keokuk. Oscar's wolf links with Kristofer.

The attacker on Alcide shifts into a wolf as well and slashes his paws in our face. One of the claws narrowly misses the eye but draws blood quickly from Alcide's eyebrow. I growl internally in annoyance and so does Alcide. Neither of us have the time to waste fighting. Alcide leaps toward the wolf before him who is a tad smaller and sinks his power canines into his face. The wolf howls in pain but Alcide makes sure to not stop with a sickening crunch of bone.

With claws out, we slash the crying wolf beneath us before biting his leg and snapping it. Alcide shifts back into my human form, and I spit a mouthful of the guy's blood on the floor.

Huffing, I finish searching around the first floor. Blood drips from my brow down my cheek, but even so it is already beginning to close. It stings but trying to find Alex does wonders in helping me ignore the pain. The last door I check looks like it leads to a basement.

I yank the door open so hard it's ripped half off its hinges. To my relief I find my poor Alex unconscious on the floor with a needle sticking out of his arm on the crook of his elbow. His body is no longer healing from whatever he is injected with. Multiple puncture wounds track his skin highlighted by small, purple bruises. He looks lifeless lying there. If my guilt didn't weigh on me before, it definitely sits heavy on me now. Seeing him like this tears me open. I let this happen. I should have stayed up. Why didn't I stay awake?

I pick up my mate with trembling legs from the exhaustion of the continuous run through the woods. Alex groans and I pull him close to me and whisper in his ear that he is safe. With trembling lips, I adjust Alex better in my arms and meet up with the others upstairs. Kristofer is covered in blood and doing his best to wipe some of his from his face. He curses at the sight of Alex, but there is no time to fuss with the possibility of others showing up. We need to leave before we get caught by anyone else that might have been alerted from a mind link.

We all leave out the back door again. Instead of going back the way we came; we decided to cross the river first to place some much-needed distance between us and the house in a different direction before heading home. This should help with redirecting our trail if they have a tracker. The river is freezing but shallow enough to allow us safe passage across. The rushing water slices against my knees, but I make sure to take careful steps to keep Alex dry.

We reach a point where the house is no longer visible and turn North to make our way back to the pack house. Halfway through our journey my anxiety starts to kick in again. A sense of urgency begins to nag at my bones. We need to get home faster and have Alex checked by our healer. He is still unconscious, and I hope it is only the drugs that's keeping him under. Walking is only going to delay that. I shift into Alcide and Kristofer positions Alex across my back. He then removes my mate's pants and uses it to tie him to my body and then Oscar's pants to tie his hands around my neck.

Running in wolf form is faster than walking, although we can't run as fast as we'd like, for fear of Alex sliding from our back. The moon is rising, and the stars twinkle their way across the sky. I make the decision to continue past our home and straight to Atlas. He's the next closest Alpha to our pack house and someone we can trust. By going there, we avoid the possibility of Hugo turning up at our pack house to drag Alex away again. I mind-link to Atlas to let him know of our pending arrival.

Everyone else, aside from Kristofer and Oscar, returns to their home with instructions from our Alpha to report anything out of the ordinary. Oscar shifts into his human form revealing a gash going down and over his eye. He will most likely have some kind of optical damage.

Atlas' healer waits for us at the door and then guides us to the infirmary to give Alex a once-over. My throat clenches the entire time he is checked, because of how bad his arms look. I pray to the moon Goddess that he wasn't beaten. If there are bruises under his clothes, I will hunt Hugo down and rip him limb from limb and even then, I won't be satisfied. His current state is already enough for me to beat Hugo to a pulp. Alpha Kristopher grabs my arm most likely sensing how I am fuming and shakes his head to deter me from fulfilling my thoughts.

"He has been drugged over and over to keep him at a steady high. That's why you weren't able to link to him. Luckily you all arrived when you did. The syringe you brought me would have been his death." The healer, Sylvie, rubs her forehead. "There's so much in his system already. The contents of the syringe alone look fatal, but we would have to test it to learn what's in it."

"But he is okay now?" I ask, trembling at the thought of him dying.

"No. This is a very critical time. Although the needle is mostly full, Alex may have used a bit of it. He also might already be dependent by the looks of it. I'll know more once we analyze the cocktail in his bloodstream. But when he starts to detox, that's where the challenge begins. I'll do my best to wean him off the dependency with herbs but be prepared to see a very different side of Alex." Sylvie sighs with worry and offers a sympathetic pat to my forearm

"How bad?" Kristofer asks, pulling my attention back to her.

"Bad. If he lashes out, don't believe what he says. He will try tactics to get you to give him a fix, then damn you when you don't. He might become violent and even start self-harming. We just need to do what we can until his body can detox properly. Once it does, the process is fast unlike it is with humans."

Nodding at Sylvie I walk over to Alex and kiss his tired sleeping face.

My sweet Chiquito. I'm so sorry.

His body looks so battered with his face laced in sweat and dark circles under his eyes. Bruising covers his ankles and wrist which is most likely from being tied up. Luckily every other part of him seems fine. His lips quiver and small whines escape between them. My heart aches, but all I can do is help him pull through. I grab a chair with Sylvie and Kristofer leaving the room, I fall asleep to the sound of Alex's breathing.

10
Alex

The basement doesn't sound as hollow anymore. The humming of the water heater is gone, and the room feels cool. I wiggle slightly and the floor also feels soft, like a pillow almost but not quite. It would have been nice if I was this comfortable from the beginning. It would have made the whole thing a bit more bearable.

The air smells clean, no longer tainted by the mold that surrounds the walls or the musty corners of the room. I must really be in my dreamland to think all this feels nice. The drug has never brought me this much comfort before.

Someone sobbing beside me makes my fingers twitch. If my arms didn't feel so heavy, I would have flinched. My eyes glide open to see who is weeping beside me. But before I can make that discovery, I pause at my surroundings. Either I'm hallucinating, or I'm no longer in the basement. The bright overhead lights blind me for a second but as they adjust, the familiar overhead fixtures come into view. The white walls and picture frames of wolf anatomy hang around the room. The smell of disinfectant lingers in the air just enough to notice it. An IV pole stands next to the bed and on it is a bag of clear fluid that is about half empty. It's an infirmary but not mine.

Did I dream the whole thing?

A wave of nausea hits my throat, but I swallow it back.

Nope, not a dream. If it had been then I wouldn't suddenly feel sick. That only ever happens once the drug effects are wearing off.

The agonized whimper pulls my attention again. I glance down to find Demetrius holding my hand, crying in his sleep. The furled brows and dark circles paint a picture of anxiety while the pale salted streaks down his cheeks tell me a story of hurt in his face. It cuts through me like glass. But above all, he is real and holding my hand. He must have found me and saved me when I couldn't save myself. I let myself relax into the bed, knowing that I am safe with my mate. Exhaustion finally overcomes me, weighing me down. I'm ready to sleep away the nightmare that has been the last few days. Before I can slip into sleep however, the door opens. I don't have the energy to open my eyes again, so I stay quiet and listen.

"Demetrius, want dinner?" A whisper floats between the silence of the room.

Iris. I'd recognize my Luna's voice anywhere.

Demetrius stirs awake and mumbles a no. The door closes again, and Demetrius squeezes my hand with a shuttered breath. He inhales deeply and exhales, bringing my fingers to his trembling lips.

"Alex, wake up soon. I can't stand to see you like this for much longer." He presses his lips to the back of my hand. "I'm so sorry for letting this happen. I should've checked on you sooner," he sobs again.

My eyes almost open on their own accord when he continues. Now I'm fighting against the sleep I was so willing to fall into moments ago.

"I never told you that I've been in love with you way before I knew you were my mate. Before I knew what love truly was. By the time I did, the guilt I felt for loving someone so young had me hating myself. When you turned seventeen, that's when I realized the reason my eyes always followed you. I was attracted to you. I don't know if it was the fact that you always kept to yourself or how you always had this look of sadness behind your eyes. You were always trying to hide behind the smiles and laughter. But I always wanted to protect you from whatever pain you felt." Demetrius rubs his thumb over my hand before he continues.

"We would have random conversations and have the most interesting, theoretical arguments." Demitrius let out a small, sad laugh. "I was smitten by you. When I finally realized what I felt was nothing brotherly towards you, but instead romantic, I kept a distance. I made sure not to be in the same room alone with you and I stopped being affectionate. I was afraid of myself and my perverse thoughts."

I can't believe what I'm hearing. How is it that a man like him—sexy, strong, and smart—can find such a broken person like me attractive? I had noticed when Demitrius distanced himself from me, but I thought nothing of it. I enjoyed his company. However, he was not the center of my world yet. At that time of my life, I was distracted by my infatuation with Cassius. Then escaping my father. I never noticed Demetrius' true feelings.

Oh my god. wait. He said seventeen. I was so pimply then. Ew.

"Months went by and I wasn't able to let go of the thought of you—of us. I felt so disgusted with myself because you weren't even an adult. I'd started signing up on online dating sites. I was able to set aside my impure feelings because you were underage, and I couldn't accept that I was acting like a pedophile. Although no other person made me feel the way you did, no matter the age, I couldn't accept it. I refused to. By the time your eighteenth birthday rolled around, I was scared to go near you because those feelings crept up again. I was doing fine for months and went on a few amazing dates in hopes I would meet my mate. But, if I am honest, the thought of you finding someone and it not being me scared me as much as my love for you did. So, I stayed away so I wouldn't have the chance to smell you and realize you weren't mine." The words come out in choked sobs and my heart aches with him.

"One day, a few days after your birthday actually, I walked into the pack house after a morning run. I was hit by the most delectable scent of pineapple and coconut. The scent was faint, but it grabbed hold of me all the same. It was the scent of my mate.

"My heart did backflips because I thought to myself that I was free of my sin. I was given the chance to move on from you. Imagine my surprise when I walked into the kitchen and saw you there eating cereal. I didn't know you were in the kitchen. I had no idea you had just moved into the main house either." Demetrius chuckles at the memory. "The breath I'd been holding since the day I met you, the breath I hadn't known I was holding, rushed from my body. I stood there waiting for you to notice my scent, waiting for you to claim me as your mate so I could let go of my guilty past of unethical feelings and love you openly. It finally made sense that my attraction to you was because you were meant for me." The smile in Demitrius' voice is evident and tempts me to open my eyes. But I don't. I let him finish his story and unload this burden his carried.

"So, I waited. You looked at me and smiled but continued eating like nothing happened. But that is exactly what happened, you felt nothing. I left the kitchen and went to my room and cried in the shower cursing at the Goddess for her cruel, cruel joke. It was my punishment for loving someone so young." Demetrius stops talking and I peek one eye open.

A tear rolls down his eye. He was staring at an invisible point on the wall, not looking at me. I couldn't take it any longer. He truly feels the weight of his love for me having started so long ago. Even though to him it was a lot to harbor, I can't help but focus on the fact that he loved me not because of the bond but because it was me. It was always me for him. "It wasn't a punishment," I break the silence.

Demetrius snaps his head up to me wide-eyed.

"You're awake!" He shoots up from the chair sending it flying behind him and against the other bed.

"It's not your fault I didn't recognize you as my mate. It's mine. You weren't punished for loving me even though I was seventeen. You did nothing wrong. A pedophile doesn't care who it is as long as it's a child. They act on those desires without guilt or remorse. They don't try to forget and move on like you did. That is not you. You said nothing and did nothing. You distanced yourself and kept it all in your heart. You didn't fawn over other children or lust over anyone else either. You only had eyes for me and ignored it because of your morals. I never even felt an inkling of what you struggled with, and I doubt anyone else did either. Yes, it isn't okay to pine for someone who is also a minor, but I think you might have also felt that way because, at the end of it all, I am your mate. You wanted to protect me. You wanted me safe. So, it's okay to love me now." Demetrius folds me into his arms sobbing hysterically.

How long had he hated himself for feeling like he'd done something wrong when he was in fact the most honest and pure person I knew? I hug him tighter, rubbing his back in circles.

"Who is the one saving who here, hm?" he whispers, and I chuckle at how his voice cracks.

"I don't know what you mean," I whisper in reply.

I do understand what he means though. He may have saved me from certain death, but I think I just saved him from his guilt.

"Even though I pulled you out of that basement, you just freed me from my mental prison. Even though the Goddess gave you to me, I still felt guilty for loving you and being happy about it."

Demetrius pulls away, and I did for him what he has done for me countless times. I lift the blanket and wipe his nose that's dripping with snot. Then I rub my fingers on his cheek to wipe his tears.

"You love me?" I tease.

I don't think he has realized how much he threw that word around in the last few minutes. He looks at me with his puffy eyes and red nose, blushing as the word and emotion sink in.

"I love you, Alex Santos," he smiles and places his forehead on mine.

He finally said it properly.

"Well, I love you too, you old pervert," I whisper back, earning a huge gasp from him.

"Damn, kick me while I'm down huh," he pouts but when I laugh, so does he.

I missed him so much. This doesn't feel real yet. He leans into me and kisses me sweeter than he ever has before. No tongue. No lust. Just love. He sucks on my bottom lip and nibbles while I moan against his lips. He is my everything. This is better than any high in the world. We continue to kiss for what seems like an eternity, but something isn't right.

Demetrius pulls away, concern etched on his features.

"Chiquito, are you okay?" Demetrius asks but his voice is fading away.

My body goes stiff, and I then it starts. My body shakes uncontrollably, and I begin to convulse harder than ever before. The last thing I hear is my dear Demetrius calling out for help.

11

Demetrius

Alex convulses in my arms. His limbs go stiff as he thrashes against me. My heart is breaking as I do my best to quickly lay him down without hurting him, but the violent nature of the convulsion is terrifying. I've never dealt with something like this before, but I know that he may bite his tongue if I don't do something. You tend to learn a thing or two as a second in command with the number of rogues we have taken in temporarily. I shove my fingers in his mouth, wincing at the pain when he clamps down.

"Help! Someone, please help!" I call out to anyone who can hear me. The pain in my hand distracts me as Alex clenches his jaw tighter. "Anyone!" I scream louder.

Kristofer, Iris, and Sylvie rush through the door.

Kristofer helps hold down Alex's upper body while Iris grabs his legs. At the count of three, we roll Alex to his side to keep him from choking. Sylvie takes out a serum and injects it into the IV bag that is already attached to my mate's arm. Alex lessens his hold on my fingers, allowing me to slip them out as the medication takes effect. Eventually, the medication relaxes Alex's body into the bed. His arms and legs soften, losing all the stiffness in his joints. He remains still for a couple of minutes before he opens his eyes. Alex looks up at me for a moment before his eyes roll back and he is out.

"What happened, why did he convulse like that?" I move the hair away from his sweaty face.

His gentle features relax into a deep sleep.

"He was given the drug at steady intervals. He must have reached that time constraint and is now experiencing withdrawal from not having the next fix. It's only going to get worse before it gets better." Sylvie checks Alex's vitals and, once satisfied he's stable, walks out of the room.

"Demetrius, go eat something and take a bath. You haven't left this room since you got back. I'll stay here and watch him," Iris offers with a sad smile. Atlas stands by the door having arrived in the middle of us restraining Alex. I saw him approach from the corner of my eye, but I guess he stepped back as we had it covered. I shake my head at Iris and look back at Alex. I don't want to leave his side yet.

"Demetrius, go. You stink. Wouldn't it be better if you smelled fresh the next time Alex woke up?" Iris is slick but she is right.

"Don't make me have Kris use his alpha voice on you," Iris says.

"Fine," I pout.

I know she's right. I can't take care of my mate if I'm exhausted and hungry. He needs me at full strength.

"Come on," Atlas gestures to follow him while pinching his nose. I roll my eyes at his stupidity and take one last look at my sleeping mate before leaving to shower in the guest bathroom. The hot water runs over my tired body trying to soothe my aching muscles. Even with the shower, I still can't relax. I only see the image of Alex seizing, replaying in my mind. Never have I witnessed such a thing before. Flexing my back and then rolling my shoulders under the water, I adjust my position and lean to one side so the water can hit where my muscles are tense.

The last of the bite is healing but it still stings under the running water. I watch as the broken skin on my fingers slowly knits closed, becoming a faint scar before fading into non-existence. The bite wasn't deep, but it was enough to draw blood from the multiple spots the teeth punctured. With my fingers healed, I grab the shampoo and lather my hair. The shampoo works up into a nice fluff of white foam and bubbles with a soothing scent of lavender. My lungs fill with the calming notes, almost doing the trick in helping me relax.

Instead, my chest grows tighter trying to fathom what my mate thought about in those moments. He most likely felt like no one was going to find him and gave up on seeing another day. I grunt in frustration. If only I could rewind the clock. Shampoo drips down my face and right into my eye. I groan at the burning sting and shove my face under the water. The sting continues to work through my eye before I decide to put my entire head under water. The shampoo rinses out and I frantically rub my eye hoping it'll help relieve the fire from the shampoo.

The burn is intense, and the water isn't doing a damn thing to make it better, and I snap. I break down without a care in the world that someone can hear me crying. There's no way I will allow myself to lose him. I can't lose my other half this quickly. My reason for smiling my reason for wanting to be a better wolf. Yet, the pain I felt when he clamped down on me while I watched him convulse must have been nothing compared to what he is going through.

A shiver shakes my body from the water turned cold. I stop crying and dress with the pile of clothes Atlas must have set out for me. He must have placed them on the counter before he got me. Feeling more tired than before I sigh, slumping my shoulders. If the shower did anything, it gave me the alone time I needed to release everything I have been feeling to this point. The clothes that Atlas has out for me surprisingly fits and Atlas is sadly mistaken if he thinks he is getting them back. The shirt is super soft, and the jeans hug me perfectly.

I go to the kitchen that is at the end of the hall from where I am. The kitchen is empty, and it doesn't take me long to find the bread, some peanut butter and jelly, and a banana. It looks great but I taste nothing. The sandwich hits my tongue, but no flavor seems to register. It is bland and I sigh, this feeling of hopelessness ravages me from the inside out. If I ever see Hugo, castrating him before killing him wouldn't be enough to make him pay for his crimes against my mate. He is the lowest of the low and deserves a painful death. Even then, it would be too merciful for what he did to my Alex.

If only I hadn't fallen back asleep then this wouldn't have happened. The tears staining my face drip onto my plate. All the desire I had to eat leaves me. I place my dishes in the sink after tossing the food in the trash and go back to the infirmary to check on Alex. He's peacefully asleep, looking like my angel. Iris lifts her head from her phone and smiles at me in a way that's sympathetic to my appearance.

"Did you eat something?" she asks.

I nod and something like pity glints in her eyes. Everyone is doing their best to hide it, but it's painfully obvious. It's a terrifying situation no matter how we look at it.

Iris offers me my seat back so I can continue to watch over my love. It's all I can do to help him through this ordeal. Holding on to his hand, I pray to the Goddess that he will quickly detox everything out of his system and come back to me quickly. I want to begin our lives side by side. I won't leave him, not even for a moment. If I have to move mountains to make him feel safe and loved, I will.

Iris silently closes the door leaving me to care for Alex. I'm no longer afraid to show how much I love him and while the guilt of loving him for so long will take a bit to overcome, I'll love him no less.

Alex stirs in his sleep before finally opening his eyes. I was hoping he slept longer but it was only a couple hours. I hold my breath waiting to see what he will do. Will he thrash? Or yell at me while damning me to hell? My heart pounds and my palms dampen with anticipation.

Is he going to have another seizure?

"How do you feel?" I whisper a bit too scared to startle him if I speak loudly.

"Water please," Alex croaks.

I hand him a glass from the table side and watch him struggle to take a sip. The cup trembled within his shaking hands. The anger of what Hugo did wells up in the pit of my stomach as I reach over and steady his hand, helping him drink as much as he can. With a deep breath, I try to douse my fury.

"Thank you," he manages to croak out.

"I was scared," I mumble mostly to myself.

For some reason, Alex seems indifferent. Detached almost. I know he heard me by the way he tilts his head in response. His eyes are dilated, and he seems unfocused. His breathing is slow, and his dry cracked lips remain slightly parted.

"Hey, when will I get another dose?" Alex shivers suddenly, lifting his blanket a little to his mouth after he hands me back the glass.

"What do you mean? Like water? I have a pit-"

"No stupid. Drugs, I need more! Give. Me. MORE!" Alex screams at me. I grip the glass in my hand making it crack. The pit that formed in my stomach earlier grows but with fear. This isn't my Alex.

His eyes are bloodshot and full of rage when he finally fully turns my way. His cracked lips bleed from the yelling and the red contrasting against his pale skin paints a horrifying portrait of my mate. It is the addiction talking through him just like Sylvie said. He tosses the blanket to the side enraged while he continues to rampage over more drugs.

"No. You need to get clean. I will help you." I tried to soothe him by rubbing his hand, but he yanks it away and punches me instead.

"Give it to me, NOW!" Alex attacks me at full force landing on me in a straddle. He swings a few more times, managing to hit me again before I flip him over. I link to Kristofer for help as I hold him down, fighting the emotion stinging my eyes once again. It pains me seeing him beg for poison. I don't want to use force, but the strength he is displaying is beyond my understanding.

Kristofer runs into the room with a rope and ties him to the bed. It's the best way to stop him from hurting himself or anyone else for that matter. It will also stop him from shifting. Alex continues to thrash around, spitting profanities at me in between the moments that he calms down to sweet talk me for a fix.

If I had a penny for every curse word he hurls at me, I'd be a wealthy man right now. Satisfied that Alex can't move an inch from the bed, I pull my chair back toward the wall to watch him from a distance. I don't want to see him like this, but I can't leave him alone either. The need to see for myself that he is okay and not going into another seizure is greater than me being uncomfortable. I fall asleep for small stretches, but never for too long. I always end up waking when Alex goes into another episode of yelling and thrashing. I do my best to drown out the drug rage.

The number of times I had to step out of the room to take a deep breath is frightening. Despite being a strong Beta, experiencing first-hand what it is like to detox is no joke.

At one point, I woke up to him falling off the bed because I untied him out of pity. He ended up busting his lip open when he did that and now blames me for his violent antics.

He laughed like a madman when he saw the blood. And there I went, having to tie him again as he spat his blood and punched me for not giving him his dose. At least now, he is calm, but Goddess knows when the yelling will start again. Until he is out of the danger zone and has mostly detoxed, I will keep my chair as far from Alex as possible.

***

One Week Later

Alex has been asleep for the last six hours. It's the longest he's slept since I rescued him from his father. The exhaustion in my bones is indescribable at this point. I know it's nothing compared to what my mate has gone through the last seven days.

"Babe, are you awake?" Alex's voice sends my heart into a frenzy as I am already conditioned to his violent outbursts. They all started sweet before becoming violent and hurtful. I look up at Alex who is staring up at the ceiling. I can't tell anymore if this is another tactic or if he is finally lucid. So, I stay quiet and listen to the silence in the room, waiting for what he has to say. The sound of his breathing keeps me calm on the outside, but my mind is racing. I've already heard everything under the sun from him and nothing can surprise me anymore. Things I never thought I'd hear from his pretty lips. I remain silent, waiting, praying he remains calm for whatever it is.

"Well, if you're awake, I want to tell you why I was always a loner growing up."

I sit up straight in my chair but stay quiet.

"I was never going to tell anyone this but after everything that's happened, I think you deserve to know." Alex takes a deep breath and lets out a slow hiss like he's in pain.

"For as long as I can remember, Dad and I never had a good relationship. My mother left when I was young. I have no memory of her. I actually only recently found out she's still alive. I grew up thinking she had died. At some point, Dad started to treat me like his slave. I would clean instead of playing with other kids. I would cook and do laundry, just so he wouldn't get mad. If I forgot what he said or didn't do something when he asked, I wouldn't get dinner that night. He never hit me because he knew someone in the pack would notice, instead it was all mental abuse. He cursed at me and belittled me. He accused me of my mother's death, even though he knew she was alive, but since I didn't know, it was his favorite weapon against me."

I listen to Alex, wanting to comfort his pain, but I know if I stop him now, then he could possibly close up again. I'd never know his burdens. This is the most open he has ever been with me.

Alex sighs and sniffles a bit.

"When I turned fourteen, I realized I was gay, but I was too scared to admit it. I knew Hugo would punish me if he ever found out and I had already gone a couple of days with no real food. My survival depended on whatever I stole from whenever I visited the main house. I would eat it quickly, too scared to bring it to our cabin or leave evidence. I couldn't afford to get caught.

"I started getting extremely depressed. I got hooked on drugs that I'd find in the streets when I ran away at night to numb the pain. I would steal pills or buy some off of shady people in school from money I'd stolen. There wasn't anything I wouldn't do to get my hands on them. Eventually, I was dependent on the drugs and hit rock bottom."

Alex's voice cracked with his last word. The choked cry trying to break free. With a deep breath, he collects himself and continues.

"I was with fellow users all the time and we were all wasted on crack. Of course, I always had to lace mine since I am a wolf just so I could get a good high that lasted. One day, one of them shot up too much and died minutes after from an overdose and it freaked me out. The way he convulsed was terrifying. I told Dad my school was having a trip out of the country, and I left, but what I really did was go to rehab. He beat me, locked me up, berated me, and held food from me for three days before he agreed to let me go. I came back after a month since my werewolf genes allowed me to recover faster than humans. The rehab tried to keep me there as they didn't believe I was better, but I escaped once I had the strength to do so." My Alex's voice continues to tremble. My heart breaks for him as he continues.

"When I was sixteen, Hugo caught me flirting with Cassius and lost it. He waited for me to come home and stripped me of my clothes. It was the middle of winter, and he made me sleep outside in our backyard. I got so sick that he had no choice but to bring me to the doctor because other pack members noticed how ghastly I looked. I almost died that night.

"However, he brought me to an outside doctor he knew from another pack. That's when we found out that I had developed a condition. Since I was severely malnourished for so long, I had underdeveloped Lycan glands. It's why my wolf was always small, why I was never as strong as I should have been. It's why I never healed as fast as others. It's the real reason I never recognized you as my mate."

Alex's voice cracks as he weeps quietly. Tears fall onto my own shirt as I bear witness to the story of his tragic upbringing. My mate pulls himself mostly together and continues between huffing breaths.

"Because the doctor was a friend of Hugo's, he never told anyone what my father had done. The doctor told me that my condition was reversible with medication, but my father refused to let me take them. So, I ended up turning to drugs again a few months later.

"Luckily on the night, I did my first shot, the doctor just so happened to pass by the alley I was squatting in. He took me to his clinic and helped me flush the drugs out of my system. He apologized for not putting me first as a patient. He's been giving me the medication secretly ever since. Luckily, it's not something I need to keep taking forever but just until my hormones and glands reach normal levels and functionality. It's because of the medication that my wolf has grown larger and stronger, along with your training. It's also why I suddenly developed my full senses. Unfortunately, the timing sucked because that's when I shot you, but I am still grateful for it."

And Alex is right. The timing really did suck. We were right in the middle of the fight between Iris' eleven father and the undead he controlled and commanded to fight for him. Alex was sniping from a distance and taking those out from around me when he was hit with all his senses, including his ability to detect me as his mate. However, the onslaught of his senses almost cost me my life as it occurred the moment he pulled the trigger. Alex pulls from my thoughts as he carries on.

"I had fallen so deeply for you that I was going to leave so you could find your mate if I had never realized our bond." Alex takes a deep breath and whispers, "Please don't give up on me, Demi."

Those words break the last piece of my heart into a million shattered parts. I hurl myself out of my chair and untie my anguished mate. I hate that he hurts the way he does. I hate that his father put him through hell the majority of his life. I hate myself for not having noticed just how deep the sadness he hides behind those eyes goes. I think back as I embrace my mate tightly to see if I ever noticed any signs that he is suffering with this internal turmoil.

Were there signs? Did I miss anything?

Maybe if I hadn't pulled away, I would have saved him sooner.

I cry with no words, holding my mate against me. I hold his weak body not wanting to ever let go but too scared I will suffocate him if I don't. Even with all he went through, he is strong. However, I need him to be healthy, too. I need my feisty mate back so we can take on the world together. There is nothing I wouldn't do to help Alex become his true self.

"Mi Chiquito, I will never give up on you. Nothing will ever keep me from loving you more each day. You are my world. You're stuck with me, now and forever," I whisper, managing to calm down from my cries.

He whimpers in my arms, hugging me as tightly as he can. I can feel though he still isn't at full strength. That truth only hurts me more and I promise to make Hugo pay tenfold for what he has done.

"How do you feel?" I pull back a little to look at the dark sunken eyes of my beautiful Alex.

"I feel good actually, I think it's out of my system. I guess I was able to recover faster now that my wolf is stronger than before. Thank Goddess I never stopped my medication."

Alex gives me a tired smile. It tugs at my heart strings seeing his feeble state and yet strong will.

"Let's get some food in you and build up your strength." I carry him in my arms, determined to keep him there until my last breath.

12
Alex

With a mouth full of scrambled eggs and toast Demetrius prepared for me, I almost burst into moans at how good it tastes. The last week has been me slipping in and out of consciousness with only an IV for nourishment. I mostly slept or had moments I blacked out despite being awake. It mind-boggles me how Demetrius is still by my side. He has seen my worst and heard my dark past, yet he is happily watching me eat. If I had the strength, I would dominate him on this very table. Unfortunately, I barely have the strength to lift my fork, let alone a whip.

"You're going to burn a hole through my head," I chuckle at Demetrius, making him blush.

"Sorry, I just... I'm so happy that you're awake and eating." He places his hand on mine.

"Me too."

I thought I was a goner. But once again, Demetrius saved me. A happy tear rolls down my face.

"You're awake!" Kristofer enters the kitchen. "Good timing too because I need to talk to both of you." Kristofer pulls a chair from the table and turns it around to sit backwards. He smiles at us before continuing. "How are you feeling? I see you can eat now."

"Better. I have all of you to thank." I smile back and shove more eggs in my mouth.

"That's what family does. No need to thank us." Kristofer sticks his tongue out in jest, but I see the relief that washes over him.

I'm grateful for him through and through.

"What's wrong?" Demetrius asks, voicing my thoughts after a moment of silence.

"Well, a few days ago, Hugo was spotted going to his cabin in the middle of the night. It looked like he packed up his things and left town. I am assuming whatever plan he had fell through when we saved Alex. On the flip side, we managed to find out where the council is hiding Finn. Poor bastard has been missing for a few weeks or so now. Or at the very least since Christmas."

"The council?" I manage between the chews of my toast.

"Yea, I've been thinking. Flinch goes missing and his finger turns up during Christmas. Then that weird message underneath it. Now, Hugo turns out to be a mole for the council and kidnaps his own son. So, by logic, it had to be the council hiding Flynn to lure us into a trap. Alex must have just been a bargaining chip for whatever Hugo wanted. The real threat is the council, especially with how they showed up here. If my dream from before means anything, then it would be that the council must be planning some form of rebellion."

Kristofer grabs an apple from the center of the table and rubs it against his shirt before biting into it.

Kristofer's dream. I remember when he told us about it back then. The room was filled with most of the members of the council, and it was surrounded by chaos and death. It was crazy to think back then that the council might have something to do with all these attacks on us lately. But the more that I think about it and with how frequently the council comes up in conversation, I am inclined to think that it may be true.

"When will you ever get his name right? It's Finn." I roll my eyes, but I know full well why he does it. Pettiness. Kris purposely calls the postman by the wrong name just to get under his skin because he keeps losing his mail. Now Finn suffers the same fate because of how he disrespected Kristofers relationship with Iris.

"Whatever. I hate him," Kristofer shrugs unapologetically. "We need to come up with a way to rescue his dumbass. He is deep in Arlan Region. It's a two-day drive and it's nothing but vampires there." Kristofer gets up to toss the apple core in the trash.

Arlan Region is known to be heavily populated by vampires. Ever since the last great war of Gaea Cry, all of us species have kind of separated into groups within different territories. While we all pretty much live in peace with one another, we still have a few that hold that age old hatred.

"Well, I guess we round up the others and get ready for the trip,"

Demetrius manages to say.

Suddenly, a scream breaks from Iris' room.

Iris' voice echoes throughout the house, and Kristofer is already out of the kitchen and running upstairs to reach his mate. We all follow behind him to find Iris sitting on her bed. Her eyes are glazed over. Her skin damp in sweat. Her arms are bloody, and she is panting erratically.

"Iris what happened?" Kristofer hugs her to calm her down. I run to the bathroom, hoping to find a first aid kit and hand it to Kristofer.

"I-It was a dream?" Iris stumbles her words, still trying to differentiate between her dream and reality. "It was so vivid. It was similar to the dream we had last time" Iris looks at Kristofer and he nods in understanding.

"What was the dream about to make you do that to your arm?" Demetrius asks, walking up behind me wrapping his arms around my shoulders.

Oh, how I missed his embrace.

I lift my hands to hold onto him.

"I was in a weird place underground. I saw the council there but not all of them. In fact, it was the same few that came here when we were outside trying to track Alex in the woods. I saw Finn chained up being tortured and branded. He screamed so loud it was deafening but they just laughed. They were enjoying it, calling him filth and dirt-mutt."

Iris scoffs as she says the last word. It's such a disgusting word for those that are mixed breeds.

"While I watched, I saw a woman chained up as well. I don't know who she was, but they were taking turns raping her while others watched. She seemed unconscious and battered as they did what they wanted. A few of the onlookers were saying that since Hugo failed, they would need to finish the job themselves. Then Councilman William, came into view saying that they would draw Kristofer and Atlas' pack to incite a distraction. Then as if noticing my presence, he turned straight at me, partially shifted his hand and clawed at me. I raised my arms in defense and that's when I woke up."

Kristofer finishes up with the bandage I gave him and puts the first aid kit aside. For a moment, they look at each other, holding their gaze with one another as if forgetting Demetrius and I are in the room. I know that look all too well. It is similar to how Demetrius looked at me when I first woke up out of this mess. A longing to heal all the pain yet incapable of doing so.

Their facial expressions then change ever so slightly, and it dawns on me that they may be having a private conversation through their link. Demetrius coughs, breaking them out of their mental conversation. It earns a growl from Kristofer, but I roll my eyes in response.

"Before you forget, write down everything you remember of what the place looked like, the people, and the woman while it's still fresh." Demetrius takes charge and I can only assume it is because Kristofer seems too emotionally distracted over his mate's distress.

I rub my mates' arms wrapped around my shoulders, taking in a deep breath of his scent.

I missed this. I missed HIM.

Iris finishes typing up everything on her phone and looks up, signaling she's finished.

"What now?" I asked, breaking the silence.

"From what Iris said, Kristofer seems to be on the money with the council having Finn. Also, Iris, I don't think that was a dream. I think maybe you had a vision in real time or astro-projected somehow. I don't know, something of the sorts that would have allowed his attack to manifest on you," Demetrius says.

It makes sense. If it was just a dream, she shouldn't have gotten injured. Her powers as a half elf must be strengthening.

"I think we should break into two teams. We can send warriors out to rescue Finn and another team should go to the Elders." Demetrius adds when Kristofer just stares at him.

"Why the Elders?" I shift out of Demetrius' hold, starting to feel nauseous. Maybe I'm not as recovered as I thought.

"The Elders are ancient. They are pure blooded wolves that have powers we cannot fathom. They carry the history and answers of our past and have the ability to see the future. If we let them do a reading on Iris, maybe they can answer what we don't understand from my visions or whatever they are. We can also get backing if shit goes down." Iris shrugs prompting a proud smile from her mate. *Do I look that goofy when I'm looking at my mate?*

The urge to hurl slams into me. I smack my hand over my mouth and run to the bathroom. Demetrius is on my tail while I barely make it to the toilet. Everything I ate recently comes out of me as I bend over the porcelain bowl.

"I guess maybe we shouldn't do solids until your stomach can handle it." Demetrius rubs my back comforting me as another round came up.

This is so not sexy.

I roll my eyes at myself and hurl for a third time.

Demetrius helps me up and turns on the sink so I can rinse my mouth with water.

"I want to lay down. Can you take me home to my bed?"

Demetrius scoops me up in his arms. Completely unnecessary, but I have no strength to argue the point. I collapse into his scent, listening to his heart thump as loudly as mine. The bass in his chest from his voice booms as he tells Kristofer and Iris where we are going. It relaxes me further. This is home. His arms holding me, his body keeping me close, and his affection is my home. I drift into a deep sleep before we reach downstairs to go to our pack house.

13

Alex

My stomach wakes me up with a violent growl. I am famished but my stomach has no business screaming bloody murder, especially after throwing up so much. I give a good stretch with my arms while lying in bed until it moves through my body and down to my toes. Now I can say that I am feeling like I can take on the world but that can only be achieved after I eat. Or drink coffee. Glancing around, I notice Demetrius has brought me home after I fell asleep in his arms. It's a wonder how dead asleep I must have been to not notice him moving me around so much. I leave my room and make myself some lunch in the kitchen. The house is oddly quiet, especially for it being a little after two in the afternoon. My stomach growls again as I turn off the pot on the stove.

I couldn't cook fast enough apparently. I grab a spoon, sit at the table with my chicken noodle soup and hum when I take my first bite. The flavors on my taste buds explode and my stomach jumps for joy at the incoming food. This is the best soup I have ever made despite it coming from a can. Either the brand changed their recipe, or I am starving to the point of finding the soup something like gourmet. I practically lick the bowl clean.

As I return to my room, I notice again the eerie silence of the house, setting me on edge. It is rare to be in the kitchen and not have one person enter or steal the food being made. I can only assume they are all with Kristofer going over a game plan; or who knows, maybe they already left. I shrug my shoulders at the thought and grab my phone before heading to the bathroom. It wouldn't surprise me if they left me behind considering that I am still weak and recovering.

Happy to see my phone light up, I smile. Demetrius must have plugged it in to charge being that I haven't used it in weeks. He is always so attentive to the smallest things.

I turn on my shower to just above boiling and undress. My reflection is a painful reminder of what I went through. The bruises on my body are finally almost gone, but the fact that I can still see them only lends to how far I still have to get to peak condition. I stare at the figure in the mirror admiring how all the track marks in my arms are gone. Only the yellowing remained. But what bothers me most is how I look way too skinny. I lost so much weight I'd hate for my mate to see me this way.

If only I had a body like Demi.

I run my hand down my chest. Demetrius has the body of a god and here I am, a skeleton in comparison. Then a thought pokes through to the forefront of my mind.

"You are beautiful no matter how skinny you are. He loves you and I should start to love me too. I, Alex Santos Neverdeen, am enough!"

The bathroom is now the equivalent of a sauna, just the way that I like it. I step into the shower allowing the steam to wrap around me in its misty embrace. It hugs me as if accepting my proclamation in the mirror and telling me that I am okay. Supporting me and nudging me to keep moving forward. I know it's just the water that is thick in the air and clinging to me, but I think I am finally mentally ready. Ready to accept all that I am and all that I will be. The people around me are my real family and I wouldn't trade them for the world.

"Mmm, this is nice." I moan under the running water running my hands over my chest again but this time smiling because I know my mates adores me regardless.

I close my eyes, chasing the chills that's erupting on my skin with my fingers. The water is heavenly at its inferno temperature. Too bad I am alone. I would love to be turned into a mess by my mate and dance to the moans that would echo against the tiled walls.

You'd think with everything that went on I'd be put off by sex. Yet it is the opposite. I crave intimacy now more than ever and the need to feel Demetrius' skin on mine is intense. After going through that ordeal alone, I want comfort, companionship, and love. Most of all, I want to hear Demetrius moan my name after making him beg for punishment. Only then will I give it to him and reward myself with his massive flesh buried deep within me. I wonder if he ever gave thought to my exhibitionism question. I know a lot has happened since, but I'd love to show the world how he is mine. A moan slips from my lonely lips just from thinking of him when an electric tingle forms in my mind.

What are you doing, my love? I'm suddenly feeling hot and bothered? Demetrius links to me, questioning.

What do you mean, Demi? I'm in the shower.

Don't lie, Chiquito. Are you touching yourself? He responds.

If I didn't know any better, I'd say he's growling those words with anticipation of me saying yes.

I wasn't touching myself, at least I wasn't until now. Yet the thought of him feeling my arousal through our bond has a new feeling surging straight to my cock. It twitches a bit against my thigh, leaving me to squirm under the water seeking relief. I grab myself and stroke my length, allowing my arousal to intensify beneath my fingers. My breath quickens, adding to the ambience that surrounds me with its white noise of the shower. I don't know if it's the mind link, but it feels like Demitrius is here with me.

"Demi," I whisper with another moan echoing in the bathroom.

"Yes?" A husky lust-filled voice responds to my call. I smile because I was right. I'm not alone. He couldn't help himself. The moan that rips out of me again is louder as I stroke myself a bit faster.

"Demi," I whisper again to see if he will be patient or pull the curtain to jump in. I turn to face the curtain and just behind the frosted material, I can see Demitrius with his hands in a fist at either side of him.

"Master, please don't torture me. May I come in?" Demetrius asks in a strained tone. He sways from side to side and lifts his arms behind his head with strained impatience.

I've trained this man so well in our short time together. I'm proud of how he flips his switch for me.

"Strip," I command.

Within seconds, I hear his clothes ripping off and dropping to the floor.

He is adorable when he behaves like a good little pup.

I pull the curtain open, exposing my not-so-healthy body. But I don't care, because in these moments, I am in charge. It is my whip and mine alone that he obeys and turns him on.

"Sit!" I demand. Demetrius sits on his knees, but the hard-on he displays makes *me* impatient for a change.

"Has my Suga behaved today? You didn't go humping anyone else while I was sick, did you?" I lift a brow.

Demetrius shakes his head quickly.

Woof

"Good boy, you can lick, just once, then sit."

Demetrius crawls over to me and licks my erection teasingly slow from the base to the tip. The pure torture I am giving myself makes me question my sanity as precum pebbles on the crown of my dick. Demetrius sits back in his former position with his eyes locked on mine.

Woof My mate barks, doing well to not use his human words.

My Submissive pup whimpers and boy do I sympathize. My own wolf, Peyton, doesn't seem to want to wait either. However, for me, this just makes the sex after so much sweeter.

"Get up and clean me so I can scrub you as well."

Woof woof

My not-so-little Sub stands up painfully slow, giving me a nice long pause while I drink in every inch of his nakedness. His length dances when he stands up to his full height as if inviting me to play. Demetrius' abs ripple as he breathes heavily beneath my wandering eyes. He is carved to perfection, and I intend to enjoy every curve of his body. Every freckle splayed across his back. Every dip his abs, back, and his muscles take.

Before I can reach his eyes with my own, he steps into the tub and lathers his hands excruciatingly slow. His rough, calloused fingers then glide over me, making sure to clean every inch of my aroused, slender body. A groan chokes within my throat as he takes special care of my member in long languid strokes. My wolf howls inside as the connection between him and Demetrius' wolf, Alcide, strengthens through our touch. They haven't spent much time with one another, but the thought slips away as quickly as it comes. Demetrius whimpers with my dick throbbing between his fingers. I turn him around, allowing my member to slide out of his hand only to be met with the view of his plump ass. With excitement running rampant in my chest, I lather my hands and clean every inch of his wonderfully soft skin.

I knead him with my fingers, but this may not have been the best time to initiate play. I am desperate for him. Flipping him around, I bite my lip at the surprise in his face from the sudden action.

"Get down and open your mouth. No hands." I look down at his kneeling body with increasing hunger. It is moments like these that I thank the Goddess above for having a shower slightly larger than average. It fits us perfectly. Demetrius' head tilts back to face me as I gently slap him with my dick, then drag it across his lips. A smile curves at the corner of my mouth at how his eyes burn with a fire waiting to be set free. Demetrius twitches a bit, ready to jump me at any second.

"Stick out your tongue," I command and watch as he sticks out his tongue as far as he can for me to shove my dick in his mouth.

My head tosses back as I thrust into his awaiting wet mouth. The warmth of his tongue gliding on the underside of my dick.

Fuck, this is amazing.

I am ready to burst, but I want to make this last.

"Suck, you filthy Sub. And don't spill a drop."

My voice is husky and riddled with a lust that is unrelenting. It takes a lot of willpower to not come undone in his mouth. I grunt watching his hands work my length with his lips wrapped around my shaft creating a suction that can rival any porn star. His head bobs up and down, gagging when he goes too far. He works me up well and I am ready to release.

"You ready to swallow me like the obedient little shit you are?" I moan and grunt as the impending feel of spilling my seed into his throat grips my groin muscles tight.

Yes, feed me, master, Demetrius' mind-links still slobbering on my dick as if it is his favorite toy.

And it very well should be.

"Fuck!" I shout and spill all of me into my obedient Sub's throat. Coating his tongue with my milk. Demetrius chokes but swallows all of it. "Good boy. Ready to prep your master?" I tease, waving my still-hard erection in his face.

Woof

"You're free to speak."

"Thank you, master." Demetrius smiles with his swollen lips. making me want to suck them into my mouth.

Turning around, I bend over, slightly leaning against the wall. With my ass perked, I wait for my Sub. Demetrius spreads my cheeks and runs his tongue up to my rosebud. With a quiver, I lose it as the sensations jolt through my body from wherever his tongue touches. He stops at my entrance and sucks against it. My legs tremble from the onslaught of pleasure and gasp against the cold tiled wall.

Fuck, I missed this. This feeling with him, overpowers everything else.

"Master, I'm going to use my fingers now." He waits for my response, but I feel his finger waiting against my puckered hole. I remain quiet, earning an impatient whimper from him.

"Proceed," I try to say unbothered, but my quivering voice gives me away.

It betrays me, revealing how very much eager I am for him—any part of him—to penetrate me, fully and deeply.

His finger slides into my hole with slight resistance. It has been too long since I had had him inside me and the intrusion, although tight, is welcomed.

"Mmm." The width of his finger excites me more than anything that size ever should. The way my body is yearning betrays any self-control I try to maintain. "Right there my dirty little plaything."

My little Suga moans at those words like the good Submissive that he is. He loves dirty talk just as much as I like doing it. Demetrius stands up and presses his chest against my back. His hands move faster making my breath hitch from the pleasure building inside me.

Shit.

Another finger slides in and the sound of him thrusting into me, slamming against my cheeks, fills the room. I am coming undone faster than I hoped. If I don't have him fuck me soon, I'll finish against the wall with nothing but his fingers. A third digit slides into me, and I squeeze his fingers, sucking them all into me as the girth of them prove to push me closer to the edge.

"Master, my dick hurts. Can't I put it in now?" He whispers against my ear in a gravel far too sexy to comprehend.

A shiver races down my spine as his strong erection rubs my inner thighs, begging for entry. My ears ring hot from his breath, rendering me unable to speak. Of course, at that moment, my voice betrays me again. I nod my head in a silent command agreeing to his plea. My Sub happily teases my entrance but before he puts it in…

"Hold," I manage to command with the tip of his thick cock pressing against me.

My cute little Suga whimpers again. I have to remind him I am still in control and with a smile, I push myself back, spearing myself onto his waiting dick. He gasps as my hole swallows him inch by inch. I almost scream at his size, but I bite my tongue having forgotten how much he fills me up. Slowly my body remembers his length, his shape, and how suffocating it is. I will happily stop breathing if this is the prize. His girth stretches me to my limit, but I take a deep breath and hold myself steady as I reach his base. My little Submissive groans from the agonizingly slow pace.

"Master, please do something."

I look back at his eyes, which seem as if they are devoured by his irises. The glare lets me know he is struggling to maintain self-control.

I begin to move back and forth. His length runs ripples of pleasure through my body as I pick up my speed the best I can. The sound of his flesh clapping against mine is music to my ears.

"Does my dirty little slut want to play on his own?" I whisper a breathy moan.

"Fuck master, yes. I want to play." Demetrius groans still standing there, not moving an inch, obeying his master.

"Uh huh, where are your fucking manners?" I snap with a grin from ear to ear.

"Can this dirty little whore of a Sub play with the Master's hole, please?" Demetrius does his best to stay in control, but his dick betrays him. It throbs inside me growing a bit more.

"Good boy. Now play."

I barely get the words out before Demetrius takes control. His hands grab my hips, and he slams into me, turning me into a moaning mess. Over and over, he thrusts all of his pleasure, his need from the last couple weeks, his lust, his love, everything is filling me to the brim. We both moan desperately, like an opera choir against the acoustic bathroom walls. Our voices are loud, deep, and heavy.

"Master, I'm ready. May I?" My horny little Sub begs and who am I to deny him his little whimpers.

"Fill me up," I reply.

Demetrius pumps harder into me, making me scream into the stars and then I feel it. My release decorating the bathroom tile while his seed fills me up as if his life depends on it. We stand there panting.

Shit that was fucking godly...

The heat of the bathroom is getting to me, but I still feel him pumping himself dry into my hole. I can only imagine the mess inside me.

"You better clean me up." I turn to face my beast of a wolf and kiss him.

"Of course. Can't have my Master dripping for others to see." He smiles, giving me another kiss. "You're going to be the death of me, you know that Chiquito?"

I rub my nose against him with a chuckle. "Will I?"

"Yes, but at least I'll die with a smile and content." He gives me a little rumble.

"Not so fast Romeo, I expect us to become gray first, and even then, you can only die when your master says so."

We both laugh and finish up what I initially got in the shower to do... bathe.

14

Demetrius

DEMETRIUS! The sound of Kristofer and Atlas yelling blared into my mind through the link.

Demetrius: **What the hell, what?!**

Atlas: *Why did you cut off communica-*

Kristofer: *Never mind that, get your ass here now!*

My skin pricks with Kristofer Alpha's voice demanding my presence.

Shit!

After I just had some mind-blowing sex, too. But for both to be looking for me, something must have happened. I finish drying Alex off and kiss him on his forehead.

"Chiquito, I gotta go. Get some rest okay." I quickly throw on my clothes when a knock at the bedroom door filters into the bathroom.

I step out so Alex can change and open the bedroom door as another knock raps on the wood aggressively. One of the warriors stands there with a stoic face. His nose twitches and a slight smirk appears before quickly fading.

He smells the sex.

"Can I help you, Brian?"

"Alpha Kristofer sent me here to guard Alex," he answers. Before I can reply, his eyes look behind me as Alex appears along with the reappearance of Brian's smirk.

"Why?" Alex furrows his brows, crossing his arms in protest.

"We received a threat. Everyone is on home-bound orders. You are needed at Alpha Atlas' place. I'll stay here and make sure Alex is safe. There are two more men outside on guard."

Brian steps aside to let me pass but I turn to Alex first and kiss him.

"Link me if anything." I leave to make my way over to Kristofer.

Running to my truck, I floor it, rather annoyed at Brian and his smirk. I get why Kristofer would send him over as he is one of the best fighters we have but that man has always been a sleaze. He is cocky and knowing that he is the one guarding my man does not sit right with me. But I would be lying if I said that Alex wouldn't be well protected if we were attacked at this very moment.

I hit my steering wheel. As a Beta I know Alex is safe but as a mate, I do not trust Brian to not try and put the moves on Alex. With everything that Alex went through, I don't want him to have to fight off an advance. My Alex can handle himself, but he shouldn't have to. Especially not in his own home. I huff at the thought but now isn't the time for my jealousy. A threat was made, and it warranted Alex needing protection. *Why?*

My mind circles in thought of what the possibilities may be.

The house comes into view prompting my foot to go a bit faster feeling anxious. I throw my vehicle into park and take my key out of the ignition when something drops onto my truck. I jump at the sound, looking around to see if anyone is there. Cautiously, I step out of the truck and crouch a bit while linking to Kristofer. An unfamiliar smell hits me, but there is nothing in sight. Sniffing the air for anyone else that could be lurking, I close my eyes, and I strain my ears, but nothing is out there.

"What the fuck? Is that what I think it is?" Kristofer walks up to me and I turn to him but his eyes dart in every direction as if to make sure no one is around.

I follow his gaze to the roof of my vehicle and flinch at the sight.

"I think so." I gag at the rotting corpse that is laid in shambles. "Looks like a dead vampire."

Its body is falling apart and barely being held together by its clothes. It must be several days old already.

Atlas makes his way over, gagging worse than me. "Holy hell, why is that on your truck?"

Atlas holds his nose in an attempt to not smell the decaying vampire.

"I don't know. It literally dropped on my car when I parked just now. It just dropped out of nowhere."

I take a deep breath and remove the corpse. Kristofer grabs the tarp from the truck bed and helps me wrap the corps. Unfortunately, it keeps falling apart as we try to wrap it and each time a leg or arm falls off, I gag. "Let's keep it covered for now," Kris says.

"Great, so on top of another finger of Finn's being delivered, now we have a dead vamp on our property." Atlas sucks his teeth.

"Another finger? Damn, that's just cruel." I nod my head, and they hum in agreement.

We run inside to get away from the smell and discuss why I was summoned. Too much is unfolding, and I still can't see what the end game of it all is. None of the pieces make sense. I walk into the house and greet a few of the pack members. Most of them are warriors and the others are trusted recruits that I assume the Alpha's rounded up while they were trying to get a hold of me.

Kristofer kicks off the meeting. "Okay everyone, we will announce the two groups. One will be going up north to the Elders while the other will go save Flint."

"It's Finn!" Most of the people speak in unison.

Kristofer rolls his eyes. "Anyways, we need to be very vigilant no matter what team you are assigned to. I don't know what the council wants, but we can't let them have their way." Kristofer steps back, allowing Atlas to step forward.

"My top three warriors and Alpha Kristofer's top three will go to save Finn. We must be as stealthy as possible and only engage in combat if necessary. The rest of you will go up north to the Elders and escort Alex with you. Luna Cassius will remain here holding down the fort as best he can with Mavis."

Atlas looks around and the room grunts in unison.

"Okay, my Beta, Demetrius, will lead the team going up north along with Luna Iris. Atlas and I will lead the team to get Fl-Finn. After a certain distance we won't be able to communicate so always keep your phones on you. We will check in with each other every six hours. As soon as the mission is complete, rendezvous back at the vacation cabins. Once you know you haven't been followed, return here." Kristofer looks around as everyone nods in agreement.

We all break out into our teams and discuss the time of departure, the materials needed for the mission, and contingency plans in case something goes wrong.

"Demetrius!" Kristofer and Atlas call me over to the side.

I am about to get scolded; I just know it.

The looks on their faces says it all. I follow them to the backyard and no sooner said than done, one of them takes a whiff of me. Kristofer rolls his eyes into oblivion.

"You really couldn't keep it in your pants one whole day, could you?" Kristofer scolds me and it's like I'm caught with my hand in the cookie jar.

"He started it," I snap back like a toddler. "And it's been more than a week," I mumble under my breath."

"Are you a child? I need you to behave while you guys are up there with the Elders, understand me?" Kristofer eyes me, waiting for an answer.

"We need you focused. All this could go south really quick if you're distracted." Atlas adds.

"Oh please, you weren't any better with Luna Cass." Kristofer raises a brow at Atlas, reminding him of the antics at the lodge when we were looking for Atlas' mother around thanksgiving.

"We aren't talking about me here," Atlas snaps back, turning red as I am sure memories flood his mind.

"Guys, don't worry." I throw my hands in the air and walk away heading back inside.

"Everyone, we have one more issue to address." We all turn back to Atlas. "A vampire was just literally dropped at our doorstep. I am sure this will make the mission to rescue Finn in the Arlan region more dangerous. That's vampire land if you didn't know already. This is why I cannot emphasize enough the necessary stealth needed to make this mission successful." Atlas crosses his arms, and a few men grunt in agreement. We may be at peace with one another, but I am sure that a pack of wolves travelling into Vampire territory will raise alarms.

The team Iris and I will lead, all turn to me awaiting orders. "We leave in two hours. Gather everything you need and fill up the vans with gas. Iris and I will contact the Elders to announce our travel. We will also contact any allies we might have on the way in case we need help."

We all go our separate ways as the time counts down for what seems like the calm before the storm.

Before anything, I need to tell Alex the plan and get ready for departure. If things go south, then I at least want to tell him I love him one more time before I go.

Arriving at the house, I find the guard chatting it up with my mate at the kitchen table. I watch him, carefully hiding my scent as best I can. Brian must have felt very comfortable while I was gone. He laughs at something I can't quite make out because of the blood rushing to my ears. Brian then touches Alex on the shoulder and allows it to trail down his back. The wrath building inside me boils over but before I do anything, my mate slaps the warrior with all the strength he can muster.

The warrior shoots out of his seat huffing and puffing, but Alex stands up as well and holds his ground. For a person who looks so fragile, he has the personality of a lion. Brian growls at Alex, which only causes my mate to slap him across the face again. I almost laugh out loud because how can I not love my feisty little lobo.

"How dare you lay your hands on me. You should feel honored that a wolf like me shows you interest," Brian bellows at my mate.

I tilt my head at the audacity that he is willingly throwing himself at my mate knowing he is spoken for, marked or not. I ball my fist trying to decide if I will lose my place in this pack if I kill Brian where he stands or if I should at least disable him.

"Who said you're worth any honor? I only need one wolf, and he is more than you could ever amount to be. Me? Feel honored? You're lucky he isn't here to rip you limb from limb for disgracing my body with your disgusting hands." Alex turns around to walk away.

"You fucking whore. Do you think that Beta scares me? He's garbage. A useless wolf pitied by the Alpha. Just be an obedient wolf and open your l-"

I didn't think I could cross a room as fast as I did. As Alex growls at Brian baring his teeth, I wrap my hand around his throat lifting him from the ground and slam him against the wall.

"Care to say that to my face?" I squeeze tightly watching him struggle to breathe.

"Demetrius, what's going on?" Kristofer enters the room, but I ignore him. Nothing is registering at the moment.

"If you ever lay your hands on Alex again, it'll be the last time you'll see said hand attached to your body." I loosen my grip. I know I need to calm down and let Kristofer handle it or my anger will get the best of me.

"How badly does this whore have you whipped? I bet he does the same for Daddy before running to you," Brian manages to spout.

They will be the last words he'll ever utter.

"Shouldn't have said that," Alex says from beside me.

I smirk at my mate's comment and I catch the fear that flickers in Brian's eyes. I squeeze the prick's throat, watching his face turn a fun shade of purple. The feel of him unable to breathe is soothing the rage that he brought out of me. I faintly make out Kristofer yelling at me to stop. However, all my focus is on watching the life fade from the wolf before me. I grin when his eyes begin to roll back and snap his neck for good measure.

"Demetrius and Alex, in my office, now!" Kristofer orders.

I laugh, dropping the limp body and follow my Alpha without batting an eye. I sit down in Alpha Kristofer's office content that there was one less scum on this earth. Apparently, my Alpha sees things differently. Yet, I don't regret it. I may lose my place in this pack, but I will gladly do it again if it means protecting Alex.

"Explain," Kristofer barks.

"There's nothing to explain. He crossed a line with my mate. Even though Alex set him straight, he kept saying things that earned his untimely demise."

Alex gasps at how nonchalant I reply but not in a way I expected. A devilishly smile accompanies his gasp.

"You could have simply beat him up or came to me to handle it. You are a Beta. MY Beta. Not an executioner." Kristofer slams his hand on the table. "I am not saying what he said was right, but you can't just kill my warriors or anyone when the mood strikes."

"My apologies for not consulting you Alpha, but I am not sorry for removing that asshole from this house. The same way you are angry that I overstepped, I am angry that I was disrespected along with Alex. Brian undermined my authority, disregarded Alex, and tried to use his position as a means to do what he pleased. Who knows how many other wolves he has done that to. You would have done the same had it been Iris. And you can't tell me otherwise." I look over at Alex and I see something else I wasn't expecting.

Is he horny?

Kristofer tightens his lips. He knows I am right. "I will announce his death and stretch the truth a bit, but only this once. I will not cover for you again. Best friend or not, that is not how I want to run this pack." Kristofer looks from me to Alex and scrunches his nose. "Why are you aroused?"

Alex is too busy thoroughly fucking me with his eyes to pay attention to his alpha. Finally, he pries his eyes off of me. "Can I not be aroused by the man who defends my honor?"

It isn't really a question. Instead, he turns back to me and bites his lip. If Kristofer weren't here, I'd be balls deep in my mate right now, in whichever hole he preferred.

"Get out, both of you!" Kristofer bellows.

15
Demetrius

I can't tell how long we have been driving even if I tried. After trying to convince Alex to stay behind with Luna Cass and failing, I forgot my phone in Alex's room. I'd ask Alex for the time on his phone, but he fell asleep, and I don't want to bother him. The screen on the van's dashboard hasn't been fixed either ever since it crapped out last week. So that's a no go.

Spike is sitting shotgun but has not turned around once and Lenny has done nothing but snack on his giant family sized bag of chips. The other two recruits are sitting in the third-row seats of the van and the last time I looked back; one was sleeping, and the other was on his phone playing a game.

Now I'm sitting within an awkward silence. although I don't sense an ounce of hostility from anyone. Instead, it feels more like discomfort mixed with...relief, maybe? Ever since Kristofer announced Brian's death, my team hasn't said a word to me. They are avoiding the subject altogether and the tension within the awkward silence is becoming palpable. I don't blame them though for not knowing what to say if anything needs to be said at all, but it is not like Brian was honorable of a person either. Not that I am justifying killing him because at the end of the day he should have been dealt with by the Alpha and then tried. My skin pricks with a need to say something.

We took two vans and Atlas' pack went in the other van with Iris. In this van it is only my pack which consist of Lenny, Spike, Mark, Dan, and Alex right now.

"If anyone has something to say, say it now," I try to say calmly, but the gruffness in my voice says otherwise.

The warrior in front of me, Spike, begins to fidget a bit and then turns to me. "Beta, can I speak frankly?"

He tightens his lips. I nod in agreement. It's now or never. If we are going to be successful on this mission, we all need to have a clear mind and no animosity toward each other.

Spike glances at the others, then back at me. "Brian was a fucking asshole. He tried touching my sister when he was drunk one night and I almost killed him myself. He was even a jerk when sober. Even though I'm not sad about it, you shouldn't let your anger get the best of you. You're a great second, don't let some asshole ruin that. I sensed the Alpha wasn't telling the whole story, and I don't want to know, but if you don't want to lose everyone's respect, don't be so rash in the future."

Spike smiles at me.

Well, that wasn't what I expected to hear.

"Yeah, I agree with Spike. He tried hitting on me after I broke up with my girlfriend, saying he was better in the sack than she could ever be. When I turned him down, he grabbed my jewels, so I punched his tooth out that night and haven't spoken to him since. But you should've gone to Alpha with this," Mark adds from the back seat.

I guess Brian got around. Alex stirs from his sleep and wipes the drool from his mouth. No doubt woken up by our conversation.

Lenny, the one driving, peeks over his shoulder to Alex. "I'm sorry you had to experience his disgusting nature, Alex. No one should ever have to and now no one will. I 'third' the opinion of killing him was not the answer." Lenny smiles and reaches for another chip in the massive bag he has in the center console.

"Don't be. He clearly felt entitled. While I agree that killing him out of anger is not the smartest move, I think Dem knows now moving forward to be more rational. Emotions have been high lately and it clouded his judgment." Alex grabs my thigh and slides his hand towards my crotch before squeezing it. I have no idea what's got him so riled up this time, but I'm not complaining either. He has been giving me these naughty glares ever since we left Kristofer's office. Even his hormones are skyrocketing through our bond. While I don't need him defending my honor because I know what I did was foolish, his hand is distracting me from his words.

Hey, unless you want to get fucked right now, don't tempt me. I look at my mate who is turning all shades of red. He has never been this direct in front of others before.

And, if I do? Alex replies through our mind-link.

You naughty little shit. If you really want it, then go to the back seat. I tease, completely forgetting the conversation we were just having.

I know he doesn't have the balls to do it. At least not with people in the van.

A smile forms from ear to ear on his sexy little face. My little deviant turns around and whispers to the guys in the back, prompting some shrugs and grunts. The hairs on my arms stand at attention with the realization that my mate is freakier than I thought. I shouldn't have underestimated him. He switches seats with one of the men while the other looks at me, waiting to switch as well.

"Come sit," Alex flips his switch for the first time in front of others. This is too unexpected. I'm not sure if this is him upping his role as Master or if he is using this as a way to regain the control he lost when handling Brian.

I know sex is therapy for Alex sometimes, but I don't know how ready I may be for this. My heart beats a mile a minute as the thought of breaking down my wall in front of everyone rings loud and clear. They already view me in a certain light due to what I did to Brian. Now they are about to see me in my most vulnerable state. The guy's heads swivel to Alex then to me. They must have caught on to Alex's plan. The look of surprise on their faces tells me they can smell the arousal. I trust every man in this van, but I would be lying if I said I wasn't a bit nervous.

My Master remains unphased at the attention and focuses solely on me. If anything, he seems more confident and ready to spank me if I disobey his next command.

I let out my breath and fall into my role, submitting for him. Not out of fear of punishment but I want to please him just as much as he pleases me. If he can be vulnerable in front of others and still command the room, then it is the least I can do for him.

"Yes, master," I reply, earning wide eyes and shocked grins from the others.

I cannot believe I just said that in front of everyone.

My heart dives to my stomach but I switch seats quickly so I can sit next to my master.

"Everyone, I apologize for whatever you hear. You can turn up the radio if it's too distracting. Do I have everyone's consent to continue?" Alex calls out to everyone, and a few snickers erupt in response. They all grunted in agreement and my heart swells that even in this moment he seeks permission from the others to continue our play.

"Now then, why isn't my little Suga behaving?" Alex slaps me lightly across my cheek. I whimper and nuzzle against his chest. The guy's gasp in unison and embarrassment fills my face, but it oddly turns me on as well knowing that they are witness to my taming.

"Strip," My master commands, pulling me out of my daze.

I peel off my clothes without breaking eye contact.

Holy shit. This is happening.

"Oh my. Why are you already dripping your milk? Does exposing yourself in front of others excite my filthy little wolf?"

Alex is in full-on Dom mode, which only makes me leak more. He is calm and drunk in his power, not bothered one bit by our location. Instead, he wears it like a suit and wields his words as if they are the laws of the Goddess herself. His eyes never leave my body and ravish every inch of my skin as I sit exposed and erect.

Am I actually into exhibitionism?

My aching cock twitches excitedly. Master slaps my hard length, and I yelp a bit.

Woof

Holy shit, holy shit, I just barked.

A few more snickers pass around the van, but Alex keeps going. "You naughty little bitch. Come here and put my cock in your mouth."

Alex waves his member at me.

When did he take it out?

I look around to make sure no one is watching but I catch Lenny peeking through the mirror.

"Focus!" Alex reprimands me and yanks my chin to face him. I whimper again, reaching over to grab him. My Master smacks my hand away with a sting racing across my skin. "Did I say you could use hands?"

Woof

More snickering goes off but louder and filled with a bit of nerves. Either they are feeling the arousal floating in the air or they are uncomfortable with the whole thing and don't know how to react. Yet, knowing they can hear me sends a jolt of excitement through to the tip of my dick. I have discovered a fun, new kink. I like to be watched. I like the audience and attention and the reactions my pack mates give to my intimate moments with my lover. Not sure if it is because I trust the people around me or it's with people in general, but this new feeling is exhilarating.

Alex holds his cock straight as I bend over and take him into my mouth. The warmth of his thick cock spreads across my tongue, sending a moan to ripple in the base of my throat. I am so turned on that I couldn't care less if they hear me slobbering all over his delicious shaft. I wrap my tongue around his length letting his veins dance against my tastebuds. Moans fill the car with Alex being loud and carefree. His voice is a symphony of lust echoing through the cabin of the vehicle. I can't tell where my moans begin and his end.

The snickering from the others have switched to slightly heavy breathing. My master is commanding the attention of the van, and it makes him throb against my tongue. He is close.

"You suck my cock so well. Shall I reward you?" My master grabs my hair, making me look up. I whimper again in need. "Now, now. Don't speak with your mouth full. That's not good manners." Master pulls my hair again, forcing me to release his member from my mouth with a slight popping sound "Speak!" he commands.

"Please, aster. This horny bitch wants a reward."

My glorious Master smiles and shoves his cock back into my mouth. He pushes my head down, making me go deeper each time. I gag as I go down and slurp his crown when I ascend, making indecent sounds that will rival any porn star. My head is spinning. It's hard to fathom how aroused I am.

I'm a slut for Alex.

"I can hear your ragged breathing, Mark. It's easy to get excited when one has a little slut face down in his lap. Care to watch?" Alex pulls my head back, releasing his cock from my mouth again, and kisses me, allowing himself to taste his own cock on my lips.

The lust in his eyes has my wolf begging for more. I can see in my mind, Alcide lying on his back submitting to Peyton. Only just registering what he just said to Mark.

Watch?

"If Beta is okay with it?" Mark asks with a little excitement. Alex breaks the kiss to look at me, waiting for my answer with a glint in his eye. Up to this point in our relationship, Alex has taught me more about sex than my twenty-eight years I've been on this earth. Each new thing has only elevated my love and addiction to him. So, while this is new and I'm nervous, I trust my mate.

Alex wants it and the gleam in his eyes makes it obvious just how much. But I never thought of allowing anyone to see Alex in all his glory. Yet now, the thought is rather exciting despite my jealousy peeking through ever so slightly.

Fuck, should I let him watch?

Alcide growls in approval. Without another thought, I agree under Alex's hold. My head is stuck, cocked back in Alex's grip and only when he turns my head do I see when Mark faces us. His eyes grow wide taking in all of me—my position, my naked body, and Alex in complete control.

A growl forms in his throat. Alex chuckles while guiding my head back down onto his length slowly but stops just as my lips hover over his cock. I can hear the gasps from Mark's lips when suddenly Master shoves me down, forcing me to deep throat his cock. He moans while I squeeze my eyes. Master pulls me back up slightly and my eyes water from the intensity. If I didn't know any better, I would say that I felt him grow a bit more in my mouth. I continue to bob up and down.

I use my tongue to glide along the underside of his cock and flick off the tip. He whimpers and I tease circles with the tip of my tongue on his sensitive crown. He loves it when I focus there, and the whimpers drive me crazy. I go down again and this time I relax my throat to go deep. His length fills me up and I have no choice but to hold my breath while I take him all in. Alex grabs my throat and gives it a small squeeze. That alone makes his balls tighten against my chin.

"I'm coming," Alex grunts but his voice is strained as if he is doing all he can to keep himself from exploding down my throat. But I can't breathe and the pulsations in my throat are starting to make me gag. I try to moan but instead it makes a low deep growl-like sound that vibrates against him making Master shoot his load down my throat.

He pulls out and as I gasp for air, I swallow the thick salty essence of him and lick the tip of his cock for good measure.

"Good boy," he coos.

A sense of pride fills my chest.

I know what's coming next and after watching my Master spill his seed so quickly with Mark watching, I'm ready for anything. My master lets go of me and removes his pants.

"Ready for prep?" he whispers.

I nod eagerly. I want nothing more than to be inside him.

"What's prep?" Mark asks with pure lust and curiosity in his eyes as they bounce between Alex and me. He is now sitting on his knees completely facing both Alex and me.

Alex smirks, "It's when my naughty little Sub here fingers me until I'm ready to accept his cock in my tight little ass." My Master lifts a brow with the question. "Still, care to watch?"

Mark stares at Alex for a moment but then smiles in agreement with a slight nod of the head.

Master turns around and bends over, giving me full access to his plump ass. That damn thing looks juicier than ever, even with his slender than usual frame. My cock throbs at the sight. I look over at Mark who is facing me and undoing his pants with nervous fingers. The grin that tickles my lips spreads wide.

I cannot believe how much I'm into this.

With a wink at Mark, I shove my face between my master's cheeks and lick away at his quivering hole. Moans ripple through him over and over as I pleasure him with my tongue. The van is filled from door to door with sex.

With my face deep between my Master's cheeks, I can feel drips of excitement landing on my hand between his legs. His dick must already be excited and leaking for me. I continue to rim him with my tongue making it soft and ready, for me to slide in a finger. Accepting the invitation I've been given, I thrust into him, eliciting a hearty growl. The urge to touch myself is unbearable, but I refrain from doing so until I am given permission. Master doesn't like it if I touch myself without his say so.

Mark, on the other hand, is moaning softly as he jerks himself off. I didn't expect him to be this open either, but here he is, without a care in the world, going to town on himself. Everyone in the car is affected by the pheromones because at this point, the three of us are lusting for one another, making the air thick with sex. It is intoxicating and even the warrior sitting next to Mark is panting while staring at Mark's dick. Dan has not turned around since we all switched positions, but it has not stopped him from enjoying Mark's performance.

I take note of how soft Alex's hole has become and slide another finger. He squeezes around my digits and my breath hitches at his tightness.

"Dan? I hear you, too," Alex says in a husky voice.

I almost come with the erotic sound. Dan grunts without looking away from Mark.

"May I?" Dan finally peeks over his shoulder to Alex, biting his lip.

I nod in an affirmative to Dan which it takes and turns around. Dan, I know is gay, so I'm not surprised by his interest in joining us, but Mark is as straight as it gets. I'm shocked that Mark is still jerking his cock while looking me dead in the eye. He doesn't oppose Dan watching him either.

I slip a third finger into Alex, and he screams in pleasure when I hit the prostate.

"Fuck me," Alex commands.

His voice snaps me back into our role playing.

"Yes, master. As you wish." My words elicit a groan from both Dan and Mark.

I position Alex and shove my dick in his quaking hole in a single thrust. We both howl at the intense pleasure, and I hold him there squeezing his hips in a grip I know will bruise him later. The images of my fingerprints bruised into his pale flesh is almost enough to make me come. With long, languid movements I begin to move. Keeping myself in a steady pace, I rock against him, finding his sweet spot. Dan joins Mark in masturbating and moaning while they stare at us. Alex curses in a gasp as I find his sweet spot.

"Fuck. Right there."

His walls squeeze around my cock, sending my horniness into a fucking frenzy.

"Shit Master. Don't do that." It's too much pressure, but I would be lying if I said I didn't want more.

Master laughs. "Do what? This?" He squeezes me again.

"Shit," I pound into him and bend him over even more, pressing his face against the seat facing Mark and Dan. I climb further on top of him while I hold him down. I'm not going to last much longer but I want to fuck him long and hard while the other two watch.

"Yes!" Alex's scream of pleasure is muffled into the seat as I bury my cock into his ass in desperate thrusts.

A hushed curse echoes from the front seat, and I know that Lenny is probably jerking off as well while he drives.

I lift Alex so his back is against my chest now and continue thrusting deep into my master, holding him by the throat. He moans again, sending the vibrations flowing from his body to mine which only spurs me to pump faster. His half-hard dick flaps against his stomach, applauding our performance, as I have my way with him.

A grunt beside me pulls my attention. Mark and Dan are staring at Alex's waving dick with content. They both sit with a sticky mess that coats the seat. They're both panting with reddened cheeks. I continue to thrust into Alex, and I can tell the moment they look into Alex's eyes and see what I get to enjoy every time I have sex with my mate. The face that my Alex makes when he is about to orgasm is one you will never forget.

Their eyes flare and just as my and Alex's release erupts. He screams my name arching his back against my chest. With one last hurrah, I push myself further pumping all of me into Alex while Mark and Dan send ribbons of cum into their cupped hands to prevent a bigger mess. Alex slumps back against my chest. Slowly, Alex lifts his hand and swipes a bit of his cum with two fingers off his body. He holds his fingers out to Dan and Mark. Without missing a beat, they both lean in and each eagerly suck a finger clean. A small gasp escapes the lips of my master, "Good boys."

Where I thought I'd find jealousy, instead I find awe. The strength and command Alex has during sex can bring any man to his knees. A zipper closing brings my attention to the front seat to find Spike is straightening up and Lenny is looking back at him with a smile. That son of a bitch did not just drive while getting a blow job.

"Well, I never thought I'd ever drive a sex van, but here we are," Lenny breaks the lingering silence with the gravel in his voice.

What we did was something utterly insane, but I am glad that I discovered something new, and the people involved are people I can trust. I know good and well that these guys will never say a word to anyone. I also find the pairings rather interesting. While I can sort of understand Mark and Dan, I never pegged Lenny to be open to getting sucked off. Ever since he lost his wife to cancer years ago, he hasn't been with anyone else.

The windows are fogged, and the van is immensely hot. Dan and Mark are wiping off their dicks clean, while I am satisfied and spent, still holding my mate's throat.

Spike turns around from the passenger seat taking in our appearance. "You have one freaky mate, my friend." His face is flushed red, and he chuckles. "Hurry up and dress so we can roll down the windows. We need to air out the van. The smell is too strong in here, you fucking perv."

Spike laughs turning around in his seat again, but not before I catch how he eyes Lenny.

"Don't think I missed how it didn't stop you from giving Lenny a blowy." I quip which makes everyone break out laughing.

Alex finishes getting dressed, finally showing a bit of embarrassment on his cheeks. The van settles and we all take a breath of the fresh air streaming in from the open windows.

"This does not leave the car, got it?" Alex's Dom voice fills the van. "I tend to get a little carried away when I'm horny and that's all there is to it." Alex lifts a brow to everyone, pointing a finger at each of their faces.

"You got it, Master," Mark says while pretending to zip his lips.

Dan mimics the action as well and pretends to give the invisible key to Mark who accepts it and tosses it out the window. I chuckle at the two and shake my head at how well they obey.

Spike peeks over his shoulder. "Just don't make it a habit in public." He pauses a moment before saying, "Or at least only do it when we're around."

Spike winks and Lenny laughs and high-fives him. I can't tell if the men are simply that loyal or if I am surrounded by sex addicts who are banding together. Whatever the case, as long as they remain quiet about it, that is all that matters.

Alex lays his head on my lap and falls asleep while Lenny continues to demolish his bag of chips. The cold wind whips in the van, whisking the sex filled air and replacing it with the fresh scent of snow and pine. Now that we are further North, a light layer of snow covers everything. We all fall into a comfortable silence for the next few hours as the sound of the wind blowing by lulls the heat from our bodies and chases away the last remnants of what he had just done.

I have one crazy mate, and I love it.

16

Alex

Conversation in the van wakes me up from the best sleep I've ever had in a moving vehicle. They aren't loud per se, but I was already stirred awake earlier from a bump in the road and have been in and out of sleep since. The guys have been whispering about what they think the council is truly up to. I, for one, think they might be going for a coup d'état. It's the only thing that makes sense with their sudden involvement in so many 'incidents.' I hate that all of this is happening. But what I hate more is that in the midst of it all, I need to find Mom.

What if my mother was the one who is held captive with Finn? What does she have to do with it all if she isn't even in the council seat?

So much is happening that it's difficult to wrap my head around it all. Yet here I am, horny, every second of every moment, because of my mate's proximity. My newfound bond heightens every arousal. While I grew up well aware that an established bond makes mates hypersexual, I already am naturally. So, add the bond on top of that and you have me. It's like I turned into a succubus for crying out loud. Even at this moment, I am ready to go another round.

I know you're awake. Demetrius links into my mind.

I am.

Why are you feeling so confused but aroused again? He teases and rubs my stomach. I didn't even notice his hand there.

I won't start anything. I just can't help feeling this way when I'm around you.

Demetrius runs his hand up to my face and caresses my cheek. The tips of his fingers chase away the chill from my skin. He has the most beautiful, deep, dark eyes. The way they burrow deep into mine leaves me transfixed.

"I love you, Chiquito," Demetrius whispers and bends down to kiss me.

"I love you, too," I whisper back into his lips.

They taste divine. Everything about him tastes like the Goddess used the finest ingredients when making him for me. He calms my soul.

We continue in our own little world, taking in each other's presence. Sometimes I wish I could freeze these moments, but I can, and have to resort, to ingraining it into my heart. I imprint his perfect face in my memory and vow to never forget even the finest detail. I wish the world could fade away and leave us alone in each other's arms where I know happiness lives. My heart squeezes at the merriness that fills it, ever so grateful I didn't run away. If I had, then I would have missed all of this, all of him. The wolf before me gives me the confidence to accept myself in ways unimaginable. I feel worthy for once to be alive and not like the trash I was forced to see myself as by my abusive father. The dark past that haunts me becomes nothing but a faded scar because of the love Demetrius drowns me in. *I am in love with him.*

"Okay, guys we are almost there," Spike calls out as he rolls up the windows.

I sit up and straightened my clothes. I guess Spike took over the drive at some point. Lenny is sleeping in the passenger side and Mark is playing on his phone with Dan.

Spike signals a turn and pulls off the main road. The town we drive into is deep in the mountains and far from any other civilization. The trees are bare, and the ground looks frozen from the winter if the patches of ice glistening under the moon have anything to do with it. Huts are scattered around giving the village a small fairytale-like feel with thatches covered in snow and I almost expect a hobbit to pop out from the cottage nestled into a mound. We drive the van into a spot in front of one of the huts and wait for Iris and her pack as they park behind us.

Guard wolves approach us in full wolf form and sniff the vehicles for any kind of weapons. It is considered disrespectful to enter the Elders' territory armed. Only a fool with ill intentions will bring guns to a sacred area like this. These are the lands where the first tribe lived, and the first wolf was created. Spike and Lenny show their hands through the window and step out first. The wolves sniffed them to confirm our identity and howl alerting the others that it is safe.

I step out with everyone else and walk to one of the huts where a beautiful woman dressed in white, and shades of beige awaits—a magnificent beauty to behold. Her long hair is slicked back in variants of silver and white that glistens under the moon and lays straight down her back. Her eyes are a fierce blue that shines bright, and her smooth skin is contradictory to her age. As an Elder, I know she must be hundreds of years old but to the naked eye, she looks twenty-five. I have never seen a wolf as striking as her.

She walks up to me, smiling with a slight blush matching the rosy hue of her full lips. If she had not moved, I would think I was staring at a marble statue.

"Your praise flatters me, my son."

I blinked a few times, wondering if I said my thoughts out loud.

"You didn't, but I can still hear them all the same." She cups my cheeks as I blush into oblivion. "I like you, Alex."

She chuckles and walks around me to greet the others. The warmth of her hand lingers on my skin along with her words.

She likes me and she hasn't even met me yet. I wonder how much of my mind she can read without trying. I thought she had to do a ritual or something to read to someone. But I see that it's more of a natural gift.

A long time ago, I remember Cecile saying something about the Elders being able to read our minds without really trying. For some reason, even when we guard our thoughts, the Elders can still perceive bits and pieces of them, as if being fed a low frequency that they then decipher. That thought alone confirms that this lady is one of the Elders of the village.

Our host guides us inside and it only strikes me now that she never told us her name. We all file in to sit at the table in the center of the room while others stand around us unable to fit at the table.

The lot of us watch as the Elder commands the room with her presence. She finally introduces herself as Maya. Her voice and even her name sound angelic to my ears. I wonder if the others agree. The collective smile from everyone confirms my thought as I take in everyone's awed expression. Her aura is tranquil like that of a mother's love, yet strong with what I am sure comes from her age and wisdom. At least that is what I have come to learn love, strength, and wisdom would feel like through Demitrius. *Okay, I seriously need to stop gawking. But I don't think I have ever seen anyone so pretty.*

Maya's eyes dart to me and her grin tells me she heard my thoughts again. I cover my face, positive that I look like a tomato. My thoughts will be the death of me around Maya.

"Okay my children, I vaguely have an idea as to why you are all here. However, in your words, please tell me what has been going on. Why do you seek my counsel?"

Maya unwraps a cloth revealing bones, dried herbs, and a small ritualistic knife. A candle sits at the center of the table along with flower petals spread alongside it. The lights in the room are dim and yellow, giving the area a warm feel. Now that I take a better look around, the hut isn't exactly a living space. It has a more ceremonial-like feel. Paintings hang on the walls of different wolves in packs or howling into the night. Knitted dream catchers decorate above an altar that holds books, statues, and an urn. The intricate design of the dreamcatcher is one I have never seen, and it's woven in gold and red threads. The halo symbol of the Goddess is scattered around in various forms like the paintings or sculptures and even on the rug that this table sits on. The hut is sacred, and it dawns on me how honored we should be for being here.

While I'm admiring the room, Iris walks over to Maya, distracting me from my thoughts. "Maybe it's better if I show you," she tells Maya.

The Elder cuts her hand with the knife, chanting something to herself in a tongue I do not recognize. I wouldn't be surprised if it was the first language we spoke before we were wolves. A language that has been lost to many of us, including myself. Elder Maya squeezes her hand, allowing blood to drip onto the bones, sizzling as it falls as if reacting to the contact with air. The blood seeps into the bone and vanishes. This is my first time witnessing a ritual of any kind. It is interesting, to say the least. The candle that is lit in the center of the table crackles as the Elder Maya continues her chant and holds out her hand to Iris. They interlock their fingers which causes the air around us to shift.

The light in the hut goes out, giving way to the orange flames from the center candle which expands up into the air forming a sort of screen.

"Give me sight," Maya calls out.

Her voice resonates within the room in a thunderous tone controlling the flames. The flames, although large, don't give off any heat but the sheer size of it keeps me from believing it is safe. Shadows form and dance around the walls like a reel of humans and wolves mingling and living out their lives. A soft white glow then emits from Iris and swirls outward to encase her interlocked hand with Maya's. The Elder drops her head before rising up again with her eyes pure white. Her irises have rolled back causing her eyelids to flutter violently. Images appear in the flames above us as if from a projector. All of Iris' dreams and visions play like a video on fast forward. The unusual way the flames are behaving under Maya's command is scary.

Iris throws her head back with a howl-like shriek that escapes her tongue. Everyone jumps when Maya slams her hand on the table as a new vision emerges. The flames turn red with images appearing of dead bodies on the ground. The men in cloaks fall to their knees in front of a hooded figure. He holds the head of a woman in one hand and mine in the other. I jump out of my seat in shock, looking around at the others in the room. Everyone is focused on the flames. All but my Demi, who is looking at me with concern. I look back up to the flames and the image changes to a war breaking the peace treaty among all magical creatures—nothing but chaos and bloodshed.

The flames go out and Iris drops to the floor in a thud. The strain from projecting her dreams the way that she did with Maya must have wiped her out. I jump again from the swoosh sound the flames make going out along with the sound of her body hitting the floor. One of Atlas' warriors standing behind her, lifts Iris just as quickly as she falls and sits her down in her seat. She seems groggy and as she comes to, Maya regains her eye color and composure.

The Elder rubs her eyes and blinks a few times, waiting for her vision to clear before she checks on Iris to make sure she is okay.

Maya turns to us. "I see now. The council has been corrupted and has been for a very long time. Yet Isabella and Alex are the key to all this, but why?"

I turn to Elder Maya, bumping into the chair behind me. I rest my hands flat on the table and lean in a bit. "Isabella is my mother." Tears ran down my face. I am terrified. I only just found out her name and that she is alive. If it wasn't for her letter begging my father to let her see me, I would still not have known.

"Wait, you survived? You're a Neverdeen!? How am I not aware of this?" Maya walks over to me in disbelief. "Come here, my child." She places her forehead on mine. "Relax and let me see your wolf."

Her gentle fingers touch my temples and trace small circles against my skin. An odd sensation forms within my mind, but I take a deep breath and release the tension in my shoulders. Fluttering flows through my mind while she sifts through my brain like files on a

Rolodex. Then it stops. Peyton emerges at the front of my mind's eye and sits before Maya's presence. He rumbles, recognizing her somehow.

"Peyton, can you show me what happened in Alex's past before his mother left?" Maya speaks directly to my wolf and also out loud for all to hear.

It never occurred to me despite our wolves not presenting themselves to us until after our tenth birthdays, they are still born within us.

My mind swirls now and a memory plucks from my subconscious and forms like a movie on a reel but not one I remember. I see my mother laughing and holding me in her arms as a baby. She looks exhausted. Her smile is breathtaking. Was this the day I was born? Then the memory switches to her and my father arguing. He hits her. Pushes her out of the door of the house. She rushes back inside but he holds her back. She breaks free and runs to me. Mom lifts me from the sofa. She runs but my father yanks me away. She loses her balance and falls. I'm crying as he kicks my mother.

The memory shifts again. I'm in bed and mother sneaks in. I'm excited. Quietly, she carries me out of the house. She runs with me on her back. We don't get far though. My father tracks us down in his wolf form and almost kills her. He snatches me, leaving her to bleed on the floor for dead.

I open my eyes not, realizing how much I am crying. Maya wipes the tears and pulls me into a hug. In the safety of her arms, I break down.

I wasn't abandoned. My mother loved me. Why wouldn't my father let me go? He hates me; despises my very existence. He always told me that he blames me for my mother leaving him, so why?

Maya continues to hold me until I calm down enough to breathe properly. Demetrius must have gotten up at some point because he also stands behind me, rubbing my back. They guide me to where Elder Maya sat before.

"I have a suspicion." She pauses then picks up a knife from the ritual circle." If I'm correct, I think I now understand why some of the attacks may be happening." Maya presses the tip of the blade against my fingertip until a drop of blood pools. She puts it on one of the bones and then wraps up the cloth that holds the other bone fragments and herbs. With a rough shake of the cloth to mix up the bones within it, her eyes turn white again. The flames rise from the candle in a tall straight green line. Maya drops the bones on the table and hums quietly in thought. One of the bones turned black as if scorched. She lifts it and places it in the flame of the candle. The black hue from the bone fades revealing a mark I have never seen before.

Maya's eyes return to normal, and she gasps.

"What's wrong, what does it mean?" Demetrius asks in a panic. Her silence scares me more than the magic in her flames.

"What do you know to be your father's name?"

"Hugo. Hugo Santos."

"Hugo is not your father." Maya corrects while inspecting the bone.

She rotates the bone to show me the symbol. It's a triangle with a pedestal in the center, forming a scale. A paw print sits on each side of the scale with an X crossing it all out. My eyes flit up to Maya, confused as to what any of it means. "You, Alex Neverdeen, are pure blood. Your father was a Marquis. This is their family crest. It's crossed out because he is no longer alive."

I grip the edge of the table to steady myself. "Wait, back up. Hugo, isn't my father? How does that make sense? And who is Marquis?"

"Okay now the bits and pieces make sense. Your mother had told the Neverdeen family that you didn't survive the winter you were born. Everyone currently thinks you're dead. Your father was Jon Marquis and part of a pure-blooded family along with your mother. He was also the heir of the Marquis estate and was next in line for a seat on the council. During your mother's pregnancy, he vanished only to be found dead a month later in the river. The heartbreak forced your mother into early labor, and you were so little and fragile. It wasn't hard to believe you died when Isabella turned up without you one day." Maya took a deep breath.

"So how does Hugo fit into this?" Demetrius asks in my stead.

"Hugo is the bastard child of Frederick Marquis. Hugo is Jon's half-brother. The Marquis family never acknowledged him despite having been born first since he was born out of wedlock. Frederick only gave Hugo and his mother enough to survive, but he never gave Hugo his last name or any rights to the family money. Hugo also isn't pure-blooded because his mother is human. When Jon was born, everything changed, and Hugo was completely cut off. I can only assume he took you from Isabella to hurt the Marquis family by eliminating the only heir to the name and in turn gaining the seat of the council for himself." Maya gives me a consoling smile. "Only, he never got the seat, and now I see that he simply kept you to raise as his own as his last effort to hurt the Neverdeen's."

"I need some air."

I turn away from everyone and step out of the hut letting the cold hit my body in a gust of wind. It cools my anger but the pain I feel is suffocating.

I sit on the step that is in front of the hut. The anger from having to suffer my entire life due to someone's greed has me wanting to scream into the night. If I was home, I would have done so but I don't want to scare the other Elders into an early grave either. Hugo Santos is a murderer and a kidnapper, and I am shocked that I survived all this time. A shudder moves through me and with that I sob into my hands. I could have had loving parents but now my real father is dead, and I don't know what's happening to my mother. If she really was captured, then
she may as well be dead along with Finn.

17

ALEX

The entire fuckery that has been my life can all be explained by the simple fact that Hugo isn't my father. Instead, he is my uncle.

What in the mental-fuck?

He's treated me like crap, conditioned me to keep my mouth shut about the abuse, didn't let me know who my family is, and it was all part of his master plan to manipulate and hide the truth. For the longest time, I believed I was the root of all the problems we'd faced. It turns out I simply have an uncle with Daddy issues.

The door behind me opens with a creak revealing Maya wrapped in a warm shawl over her shoulders. Her body let out a slight shiver against the cold as she joins me. She wraps her purple and gold shawl around her body even tighter and sits on the step next to me. Her presence is enough to warm me up slightly. The bitter turn my mind was taking a minute ago lightens. Together we look up at the dark sky in silence watching our breath take form in the cold. The night is clear with brightly shining stars twinkling in the dark sea that lies still above us. No matter where I go or how much time passes, the night sky is the one constant in my life. Now I have Demi too. The night sky has borne witness to all of me and remained there still to watch over me, even until this day. Unchanged and forever accepting. Will Demi do the same now that my family history has come to light?

Maya shifts a bit, jerking my attention while I continue looking up with my mind wandering no further than her.

I'm not as angry as I was initially about Hugo being my uncle, at this point, all I have are more questions than answers. But one question continues to circle my head like the moon does the sun.

"Why weren't you able to tell I was alive if you knew about my mother?"

Okay maybe I am angry. Why didn't anyone come looking for me or help?

"My divinity works when I know the direct question or if I am actively seeking for something. If the need never arises, then I won't see it. I watch over so many wolves with the other Elders that if we were constantly bombarded with information, we would go insane. When your mother went home crying saying you had died, I just so happened to be visiting for something unrelated. She was so distraught that I took her word at face value and made it a point not to invade her thoughts in order to let a mother grieve the loss of her child in private. Everyone did. I wasn't about to pry and expose her for anything I might have found. She had already suffered the loss of Jon, her mate, that no one questioned her when she lost you."

I looked at Maya who was also looking up to the sky. She was leaning in closer to me. The tired lines of her eyes mixed with the sadness of my past.

I guess her burden is a lot greater than I thought. It never occurred to me the magnitude of her role until this very moment. Being an Elder is like being the parent to the entire werewolf race. The years they have lived are far beyond any of us. Since the Elders are of pure blood and three of the remaining original wolves in this area, they are sustained by the magic in their veins. Like the Shaman in Cassius, they are connected to all of us and guide us. There are only about thirteen Elders in the world, each in charge of a region where wolves reside.

I sigh, dipping my head into my lap and wrapping my arms around my legs, pulling them tight to my chest.

"So why has Mom kept it a secret?" I mumble, feeling the most confused I have ever felt in my life.

"I don't know. That is something only she can answer, my dear." Maya rubs the back of my head. The gesture almost feels motherly in nature. I sigh, again wishing it can just all be over. Not being able to control the situation and just make everything better again is exhausting. Ever since Cassius found his mate, we have all been non-stop fighting one battle after another and I am simply drained.

The door behind me opens and slams against the hut with the gust of wind pushing it. I jump at the loud bang, but I don't look back. I close my eyes and take a deep breath. Within that brief moment, Maya was replaced by someone else. I am pulled into a pair of strong arms. I stiffen but quickly relax when the smell of musk and rosewood fills my lungs.

"Mi Chiquito lobo, are you okay?" Demetrius' voice instantly soothes my aching heart.

He lifts me up and places me on his lap. So easily I melt into his arms molding into his body. His warmth is just as comforting as his arms around me. Nuzzling into his neck, I take in another dose of his scent, placing my palm on his chest. It's moments like these that I feel spoiled, but I don't care. He spoils me no matter what I do. The sound of his heartbeat allows mine to sync to his.

"I don't know. It's a lot of information to digest. I guess I feel like I have been living a lie my whole life. I feel lost, like I don't know who I am or where I belong anymore." The words roll off my tongue as quickly as they come to mind.

Demetrius hugs me tighter in his arms, giving me the support I need to go on.

"Babe, I don't want you feeling that way. Despite Hugo being the epitome of an asshat, you are the most amazing person in existence. You and Kristofer both know that you have been my weakness for a long time, but that's because I have always seen how exceptional you truly are. Yes, maybe you didn't know all the details about your family, but it doesn't change who you are as a person at this very moment. You're a fighter, a warrior in training, the love of my life, the man I want to spend the rest of my life with, and one badass sassy wolf."

Demetrius kisses my hair and places his chin on top of my head. He always knows what to say to me. I'm sure he also doesn't notice the little indirect proposal he made, so I smile because I'm not ready for that conversation. At least not at the moment.

"Kristofer knew about your feelings for me?" I blush at the thought.

"Yeah, he found out one night when I was drunk. It was a couple days after your eighteenth birthday. I got wasted by myself near the river. I'd just found out you were my mate, and I was pissed because you didn't reciprocate the same enthusiasm. In fact, you acted unbothered. Kristofer went looking for me because I'd closed our link. He'd started to panic thinking something had happened to me. We had a bad period of hunters scouting the area at the time. But by the time he found me I was a drunken mess and crying while looking at a picture of you Kristofer had sent me saying that I was missing your birthday. I ended up telling him everything except for me smelling you after your birthday and realizing you were my mate. He listened and gave me advice then helped me back home." Demetrius pulls back to look at me.

"Wait, why did he act all surprised about us then?"

"I asked him to. I wasn't sure if you were going to acknowledge us or not. However, you never did or said anything. I was convinced you didn't want our bond. Then one day, we had been in a pack meeting, and I stood across the room to give us as much distance as possible. While Kristofer spoke, I couldn't take my eyes off you. It was too hard for me to ignore our bond which made it hard for me to understand how you could. Then your scent got the best of me and my eyes shifted. I wanted to claim you right then and there. Kris noticed and linked me to get out and walk it off. That's when he suspected something else was up but since he promised not to interfere, he left it at that. I didn't admit to him that you were my mate until he caught us on the sofa one night."

My face falls into sheer horror at his words. "He caught us fooling around. And you didn't tell me?!" I slap Demetrius in the chest as he laughs at my unsuccessful attempt to be mad. I wasn't but he could have still told me. "So, do you still have the picture?"

"No because it was blurry, but I do have a photo I printed of a picture I took."

Demetrius shifts me to one side and reaches into his pocket pulling out his wallet. He gives it to me, and I stare at it for a moment. The wallet is worn and has definitely seen better days, but it suits him. I open the wallet and gasp at the picture of me tucked behind the plastic window of his wallet.

"I took that picture of you in the wee hours of your birthday. It was just after midnight. I'd spotted you standing outside on the back porch. I watched you from the kitchen window, smiling at how lost in thought you were. You were surrounded by the fairy lights of the porch and leaning against the support beam. I couldn't look away. I was transfixed with your fair skin exposed by your light summer clothes. Then the moon poked through the clouds and shined on you as if the Goddess were telling me 'Here is your gift'. My chest wanted to explode because I knew I could never claim you as mine. Just then, Cecile popped in front of me and asked me to take a picture of her to see if her foundation powder had flash back. She was going out with the girls and didn't want to look pale."

"Oh, I remember that actually. Cecile had bugged me so much that day because she hated every outfit she picked. I ended up dressing her for that night. It was funny actually." I giggle at the thought. It feels like so long ago.

"Yea, I remember that too. So, I pulled out my phone and took a picture of her. She kept moving in different spots of the kitchen, so the light hit just right with the flash. That picture is one of thirty she made me take but the only one I cared for. I somehow managed to catch you in it. I zoomed in and printed it the next day telling myself I would shred it if you weren't my mate."

I couldn't look away from the picture. I knew exactly what I was thinking in that moment. I was contemplating leaving that very night to find my mother before anyone woke up. I was ready to give up on life at Lunar River because I couldn't stand my father any longer. Yet, Demetrius was having his own internal battles. Living the guilt of forbidden love because I was too young still.

"How did you fall for someone so broken and young like me?" I genuinely ask because I still find it hard to believe that I am his everything.

"I never saw you as someone who was broken. I saw someone who had beautifully been putting the pieces back together. As for you being young...I don't understand that either. I am ten years older than you. Not once had I found anyone younger than me attractive. In fact, I had a preference for older partners." He kisses my forehead. "The only thing I can honestly say is that I was attracted to that beautiful mind of yours, how persistent you are, and your laugh that fills the room. The fact that you became my mate is a bonus and only confirms for me that I wasn't crazy to love you. I just didn't recognize it as love until last year. My heart knew before the bond could tell me that you were my mate."

Fuck what I thought earlier. I'm gonna marry him right now if he asks.

I blush harder than I did when Maya read my mind as my heart raced with his words. I'm sure he can hear it.

"Feeling better?"

"Yeah, thank you." I kiss him softly, sucking on his plump bottom lip.

"Let's go to bed. We'll head back to the house tomorrow before sunrise. The Elders gave us their support. Just promise not to tempt me while we sleep. I don't want to have sex with the Elders around. Freaks me out."

We both laugh, but I understand what he means. It's like having sex with your parents in the next room. Exciting because you might get caught, but not ideal.

Demetrius lifts me in one swift motion.

***

My group and Iris' make it to the vacation cabins we own by late morning. It is the rendezvous point for our teams and those that went down to Arlan. I barely got any sleep because Demetrius kept pressing his boner against my back. He told me to ignore it, but how could I? The small amount of sleep I did manage to get was full of wet dreams. I woke tired and frustrated while Demi was well rested.

We contacted Kristofer to let him know we are at the cabin and are waiting to make sure we weren't followed. He and his team still had a few more hours of travel before reaching the Arlan Region. At this point, it's a waiting game for Finn to be rescued and then for all of us to meet at the summit where we will put a stop to the council before war breaks loose.

Demetrius speaks up. "Guys, change of plan. I relayed everything to Kristofer and Atlas. They want us to head south to meet with the Neverdeen family. Then go to a selected few on the council and ask for their help once Kristofer and Atlas meet us there. We will rest and head out tonight."

Demetrius scans the room to see if there are any questions. Everyone understands and goes back to whatever they are doing.

"I'm meeting my family?" My voice comes out shaky.

This is happening too fast.

"It seems so, but don't worry. I'll be right there with you." Demetrius kisses me before gathering everyone to go over our routes for travel.

I excuse myself and lean against the window, looking out into the trees. I went from having only an abusive father, to having a living mother, to being fatherless, and now a whole family.

I have a family!

The sudden reality check makes me nauseous. I always wanted a family. People I am related to by blood. Cousins to joke with and grandparents that spoil me and now that it is a possibility, I feel sick.

What if they don't like me? Or they have a problem with me being gay? Or what if they actually do like me and expect me to leave my pack?

I don't want the council seat or whatever.

"Ugh!" I punch the window, cracking it, earning everyone's attention.

I roll my eyes at the blood on my knuckles for being stupid and walk away, locking myself in the bathroom.

Nothing seems to be easy. Everything comes at a cost. Filling the tub with the hottest temperature I can tolerate, I put some music on my phone and turn off the light.

Perfect.

My body needs comfort. It needs to release its tensions. Losing myself in the darkness of the bathroom, I fall asleep to the instrumental sounds bouncing off the walls.

***

Shivering, I open my eyes wondering when the water turned cold. All the comforts of soaking in a hot tub are gone. I am left with no choice but to get out and dry myself so I can dress quickly for warmth. My teeth clatter as I shiver, and I grab my phone to turn off the music. The tub makes a few gurgling sounds as it drains, and I stare at it lost in thought. Sucks not being able to regulate my temperature as well as the other wolves. I am getting better as I take my medications, but my Lycan gland is taking forever.

Finally warming up a bit, I open the door, halting when the quiet of the cabin puts me on guard. It shouldn't be this quiet. Actually, it shouldn't be quiet at all. No one is around and it dawns on me that I am alone. The thought that something happened flickers through my mind, making my heart race expecting the danger I may be in. The heartbeat in my chest is so forceful I can hear the blood pumping in my ears.

As I cross into the living room and near the windows, howling and barking filters through from outside. I run to the window I'd cracked earlier and stiffen at the sight before me.

Bile rises up in my throat at the scene playing out before me. Several of my pack mates are fighting while others are dead on the ground. I scan the scene and notice Demetrius and Iris cornered but I can't tell by who. I try to scream, but my voice won't come out. Again and again, I yell as hard as I can, but my voice is mute. In frustration and anger, I bang on the window, cracking it beneath my fist, but nothing seems to work.

Wait, didn't I already crack this window?

I run to the front door and step out into the cold with bare feet only to find no one outside. No blood. No howls. Nothing.

What the hell is going on?

I turn around to head back inside, but the cabin has disappeared as well.

"Demi?" I call out as loud as I can, but I struggle to get my voice above a whisper. It's hard to breathe.

"Dem," I try again.

What is happening? My chest tightens. It hurts. My knees buckle as I struggle for air. The pain and burning in my chest choke me, and water begins to pool out from my mouth. Clawing at my throat, the world around me begins to tunnel.

"Alex! Baby, wake up. Please... don't leave me. Wake up!"

I open my eyes and projectile vomit water. My body is turned over and more water spills out of me. I gasp for air, groaning as my lungs struggle to expand properly in my chest. My chest burns up to my throat trying to work, but water must still be trapped inside my lungs.

"Alex, oh my god, baby, can you hear me?"

Demetrius' voice finally registers. My eyes find him and for a split second, I see the moment hope enters his eyes. He's a complete mess. His clothes are soaked, and his face is flushed from color. The whole thing must have been a dream, and I could have died in the tub.

I try to speak, but nothing comes out. At least nothing was audible, so I opened my arms to him instead.

My mate picks me up, holding me against his chest like I am the most fragile porcelain he's ever held. Demetrius rocks with me, back and forth.

"I was terrified. I thought I'd lost you again. I felt your anxiety coming through our bond and by the time I came in here, you were under water. I tried giving you CPR, but you weren't breathing. Alex I I-" Demetrius begins to sob uncontrollably into my neck, and I join him. "Don't leave me, Alex. Please. I love you so much."

My heart breaks into a trillion pieces at those words. He thinks I did it intentionally. My Goddess, I would never purposely drown myself, but he needs to hear it from me. I find my voice in order to sooth his heart. He needs to know I am here to stay. He needs to know that my heart is his forever more.

"Demi, nunca te dejare," I manage with my voice raspy and raw.

He continues to sob, squeezing me again but this time softly. We stay there in each other's arms, and I am left with no words to explain what just happened.

None.

18

DEMETRIUS
(Before finding Alex in the tub)

My heart is racing like a faulty metronome, ricking at an accelerated pace but I can't seem to understand why. I scan the area and listen to see if maybe there is danger approaching, but nothing stands out. Then panic. Pure fear and raw alarm grip me like a bat out of hell. My body turns cold, and I realize that everything I am feeling is coming from Alex. All his despair is coming through our bond like a radio signal with an antenna lifted high enough to signal a command tower.

I call out to him but there was no response.

"I think he is still in the bathroom. It's been a while," Lenny calls out from the kitchen after a moment of silence.

If anything, learning he hasn't come out from the bathroom frightens me more than if they had told me he stepped out. I run to the bathroom door, hitting my forehead against the wood, thinking it was unlocked. I bang on the door, but the only thing I hear is classical music. With a deep breath, I step back and kick in the door. The lock breaks off the hinges and to my horror Alex is under water without a single bubble coming to the surface. I pull him from the freezing water. His body is limp in my arms and he's unresponsive. Immediately, I begin pumping his chest to perform CPR.

Please don't leave me. Please come back.

I blow inside his mouth two times to fill his lungs and do a few more chest compressions. A little bit of water comes out, but still no response. I continue pumping his chest until I hit thirty compressions and administer another two breaths.

"What's going on?" Lenny rushes into the bathroom.

"GET OUT!!" I scream at the top of my lungs, desperately trying to keep it together. "One, two, three, four…"

I pump Alex's chest, using my weight with straight locked elbows to make sure I am doing it correctly.

My love, my soul, my everything isn't breathing. It's already been a few minutes and still nothing. But I repeat the process. I blew into his mouth again and again. Tears sting my eyes and drip onto Alex's chest. My vision blurs. My own breathing becomes haggard. I can't lose him.

Did he try killing himself? Was he really not okay after we talked yesterday? Why is this happening?

I can't continue like this; I have to think straight. There has to be a reason. He is a fighter. MY fighter.

Again, I need to keep trying, again.

I blow two more deep breaths and with tired arms, proceed with more compressions.

"ALEX! Baby, wake up, please… don't leave me. Wake up!" I pound his chest hard with my fist, spilling all my emotions into the action— frustration, anger, pain, and sadness.

Alex chokes up water like a fountain. A breath escapes my lips at the sight. A breath I have been holding for myself, making me feel guilty like I'd stolen it from him. I roll him over and more water chokes out of him and onto the floor.

Then, the best sound I could hear fills my ears as Alex takes his first breath, barely filling his lungs.

"Alex, oh my Goddess, baby, can you hear me?"

He turns over looking at me with blue lips and impossibly pale skin, still slightly gasping for breath. It still isn't registering that he's okay. I freeze. Shocked. Scared. And relieved. The look in his eyes is dazed and his slightly parted mouth attempts to speak something inaudible. He then throws his arms open for me and I gladly scoop him up and cry, rocking us back and forth.

"I was so scared. I thought I'd lost you again. I felt your anxiety coming through our bond and by the time I came in here, you were under water. I tried giving you CPR, but you weren't breathing. Alex I I -,"

I break down. I sob into his arms, a complete mess.

He is breathing. He is alive and breathing. I didn't lose him. I saved him in time.

"Don't leave me Alex, please. I love you so much," I continue crying.

My heart hurts so much at the thought of him wanting to die. After all that he went through. I want to help him and be his support. He is strong, I know that, but I will still be there if he falters like I am now.

"Demi, nunca te dejare," Alex's voice is raspy and weak but it is still music to my ears.

My body relaxes a little against him.

He won't leave.

I pant softly against him still crying quietly.

My sweet, sweet Alex.

I can never let go of you. We sit there in each other's arms hoping my body will warm up his. I am soaking wet from pulling him onto my lap. I finally have my baby back.

"Is everything okay now?" Lenny whispers from the door. I didn't even realize he was still there.

"Yes, I'm sorry. I wasn't in my right mind at the moment," I say.

I hate that I snapped how I did. I really do feel bad for screaming at him.

"It's okay, I understand. Anything we can do to help? Should we still get a healer?" Lenny offers and behind those words is nothing but sincerity in his voice.

"Yes please, and can you bring our bags to the room and maybe something I can wrap Alex in?"

"You got it." Lenny walks away to do me the favor as I turn my attention back to my mate.

"Chiquito, can you get up on your own?" I whisper into his ear. He shakes his head no. "Okay."

Lenny returns with a fluffy pink towel and shrugs, but I don't care that it's pink. I cover Alex and carefully carry him out of the bathroom. We enter the bedroom, and Lenny reaches for the door behind me, "I'll be in the kitchen if you need anything." He closes the door, and I walk over to the bed. Alex shivers in my arms still looking a bit pale but much better than he did a few minutes ago.

Quickly, I sit Alex on the edge of the bed and help dry him the best I can. His chest is riddled with bruising from my compressions. Thank Goddess for wolf-healing capabilities because the way his chest is seven shades of black and blue looks painful. I am sure I cracked a rib or two. The bags Lenny brought over earlier sit next to the bed open. I pull out a fresh set of clothes and dress Alex, making sure to double up in layers. The color is creeping back into his skin as his body warms up. His lips are plump and pink again and his pale skin has its peach hue underneath it.

My future husband is beautiful.

I help Alex under the covers and begin stripping my wet clothes next.

"Demi?" Alex's weak voice grips my heart.

"Yes, babe?" I turn to him, half naked, holding my wet shirt.

"Don't get dressed. Just lay with me like that." Alex tries to smile, but he looks more tired than anything else.

"Okay, but let the healer check you first." I slip on my sweats but before I can grab a dry shirt, a knock taps on our bedroom door.

The healer comes in and gives Alex a once over. She confirms he has a couple broken ribs, but he's on track to healing. The healer gives him a tea of sorts that will help raise his body temperature and heal faster. We thank her and close the door. All Alex has to do is give me his puppy eyes and I already know what he means.

I didn't even bother asking why either. It's what he wants. I slip out of my sweat while Alex lifts the blanket for me. Under the covers I go and snuggle with him. I pull him into my arms carefully, letting our bodies warm one another under the thin blanket and in seconds, he is fast asleep.

Alex's breathing is soft and a bit labored, but it's to be expected considering what he went through. I listen for a while and soon it becomes leveled and slow. Deep, slow, and steady breaths rise and fall against my body. His heartbeat is strong again assuring me he is okay. I close my eyes and allow myself to drift into a tired slumber.

***

I wake up with Alex still sleeping soundly in my arms. We managed to stay in the same position, and I can only assume it is due to how exhausted he is. I noticed the room's very dark, which can only mean that the night has fallen. I mind link with Spike and am informed we leave in an hour, but they encourage me to rest as much as possible.

"You know I wasn't trying to kill myself, right?" Alex's voice sounds much stronger now.

I hadn't noticed he was awake.

"Then what happened?" I ask, curious, but scared of what I might hear.

"All I know is that I went in the tub and put music on because I was anxious about meeting my family. I fell asleep and had a crazy dream. Next thing I know, I'm spewing water and you're crying. It took me a minute to realize what exactly was happening." Alex turned around in my arms, digging his face into the pillow. "I really don't know how I fell asleep. Por favor, believe me Demi," Alex chokes a little on a cry threatening to break free.

"Then no more sleeping in the tub. I nearly followed you to the grave with the panic attack I was having." I turn him towards me again and lifted his head up to kiss his nose.

"I'm sorry, mi amor." His words are sad and soft. He tries to look away, but I pull his chin back up to me.

"You don't need to apologize. You did nothing wrong. I was just scared out of my mind, that's all."

I place a gentle kiss on his lips, and he returns it in kind. His lips taste even sweeter this time. I now know for a fact his loss would kill me. I wouldn't survive. With that confirmation, his lips right now taste like sweet coconut on a hot summer morning. I hope I never get used to this feeling because I want to feel it new, every time I kiss him. Alex moans into my lips and pulls away.

"When this is over, can we go on a trip?" Alex has his sassy look back in his eyes. It feels so good to see it again.

"You got it." I kiss him again, giving him little pecks over and over. "Okay let's go eat something and get ready. That is if Lenny hasn't eaten everything in the fridge." I flip over the covers forgetting I am completely naked. Alex's eyes grow wide looking at my body with a newfound hunger. "Down boy. There's no time for play," I scold and Alex whimpers. "Nope, that's not going to work."

Alex pouts instead and I laugh at how adorable he is. He literally just came back to life from nearly drowning and already wants to jump my bones.

I wouldn't have him any other way though.

I get dressed with him still pouting and drag him to the kitchen for sustenance. What I wouldn't give to eat him instead.

19

ALEX

It has been two hours now, driving towards the Neverdeen residence. Demetrius and I are in the back seat making out like lovesick honeymooners. His lips devour me whole and all I want to do is bend him over.

I wonder...

"Hey, Demi?" I interrupt in between kisses.

"Yes, my love?" Demetrius runs his tongue across my lips.

"Will you let me fuck you?" Demetrius' eyes pop open stunned. Gasps and snickering fill the van. These men are worse than children.

"Ummmm...."

Demetrius clearly never considers me being on top. Not that I blame him. I'm this scrawny little thing next to him, but my dick is still decent in size. He is only a little bigger and thicker, but not by much. I could rock his world if I wanted to. I can definitely choke him with it.

"Oh, come on. That should have been a quick yes." Mark turns to us smiling. We basically are in the same seating arrangement as before. Dan turns around as well.

"I agree. Nothing wrong with bottoming every now and then. You'll be surprised how good it feels." Dan wiggles his eyebrows. I guess the experience we all shared made them a bit more comfortable around me and Demetrius…and joining in on our sex life discussion.

"Does it really feel that good?" Mark turns to Dan.

"Fuck yea it does," Dan replies while eyeing Mark for a little too long before looking away.

Mark blushes.

Something is up between those two. I wonder if Mark is becoming curious in men or at least curious in Dan. That look he just gave him is very suggestive. Demetrius turns to me, looking like a tomato.

"Okay," he says and buries his face in my neck, sucking on me and giving me kisses.

"So–are you going to try it now?" Dan faces me again and lifts a brow. This man is relentless. But I am curious about Demetrius' answer. I mean, I wouldn't be opposed to trying it here. It wouldn't be ideal, but the idea does excite me.

"No, not now. Maybe when this is all over. I would rather be home and comfortable."

"And here I thought we were going to get another show." Spike chimes in from the front seat.

"What do you think this is, a moulin rouge?" Demetrius narrows his eyes at Spike.

"Oh shit, it isn't?" Lenny quips and winks through the rear-view mirror.

"Ha ha, very funny. Don't you have a bag of chips to annihilate?" Demetrius snaps but his voice is still teasing.

"Calmate mi amor. I won't touch your ass until you are ready." I give my mate a kiss while the van in unison sighs in disappointment.

***

We finally arrive at the address we received from Elder Maya for the Neverdeen residence. The guards stop us at the gate, eyeing us, but let us in eventually with a few stunned faces after they catch a glimpse of me. The road leading to the house is long with well-manicured grass on either side. Despite the cold weather the grass is green and thriving. Trees line the edges almost as if welcoming us down the dirt road that leads to the house. As we approach the house, a large roundabout brings our car to the front. Pointed hedges decorate the exterior of the large beige home with windows that are framed with fitted black shutters matching the black door at the entrance. In the center of the roundabout, a wolf statue carved in stone and marble stood with water flowing beneath it.

A butler comes out of the double black doors and meet us with a blank expression, primed clothing, and one hand behind his back. One would say he looks the role of a stereotypical Alfred, and I will die laughing if that is how he is introduced. He extends his other white gloved hand towards the house so we may follow. I left the vehicle shaking, now regretting not putting more thought in my outfit. My feet barely manage to carry me inside the foyer and the sudden feeling of being underdressed lingers heavily. Standing before me is an Elderly woman almost identical to my mother's picture. If she didn't look so much like my mother, then I would have confused her for another guest or maybe the help.

She must be my grandmother.

Her eyes take in my appearance. A range of emotions flicker between the lines of her face.

"Oh, my Goddess, it can't be," she utters to herself.

Her hands cover her mouth in a gasp, trembling as she walks towards me. The rest of my pack files in behind me, but she pays them no mind. Her hand reaches for me, but I flinch away. The hesitation makes her pause but she places her hand on my cheek regardless. I stiffen against her warmth, closing my eyes at the feel.

"You are their exact image. This isn't possible." Her words come out in tears. "Who is your mother my dear?"

I open my eyes and smile wearily. "Isabella Neverdeen." My voice comes out a broken whisper, but it is loud enough for her to pull me into her arms.

"I thought... we all thought you died, ho-" her words are cut off by someone else who enters the room.

The sound of his shoes echo in the vast space of the foyer. A tall man, late in his years, but strong and well maintained comes towards us. Behind him and clutching the old man's arm is a younger guy that couldn't be any older than I am. He is also tall but slender like me. In fact, if it wasn't for his strawberry red hair and freckles across his nose and cheeks, I'd say we are twins. It is almost like looking in a mirror. I blink away my thoughts when the lady speaks to the older man now standing with his arm around her. My doppelganger however remains back a little with his eyes wide and staring directly at me.

"Honey! Look, it's a miracle!"

The lady hugs the man she called honey as he gets a better look at me. He pulls out his glasses, walks up to me, and stops with a gasp.

"Oh, my Goddess, it can't be," he runs up to me, hugging me, then pulls back to give me another once over. "Alex? Your name is Alex, right?" He suddenly loses all the tension and dominance he asserted when he walked in. Now he looks more like a child that just opened his gift on Christmas.

I nod and then both of them engulf me in hugs and tears. I stand there at a loss, mentally freaking out. I am not used to this. I am not used to happy hugs and tears of joy, not towards me anyways. The only time I've felt comfortable with such affection is with my mate but now these two strangers, although family, are showering me with foreign affection. They manage to pull away from me, smiling ear to ear.

"So, I'm guessing you're my grandparents?" I fidget with my fingers looking down at the floor.

"Yes," they say in unison.

I look up to see my grandfather hugging my grandmother. "Can we find somewhere to talk? We have a lot to tell you all." I gesture to the men and Iris awkwardly standing behind me.

"Of course, but before we go, I want you to meet someone. Riley, come here son." My grandmother calls over the guy that has been standing there quietly looking shocked. "Alex, I would like you to meet your little brother Riley, you're twins."

20
Alex

The boy—my brother—and I look at my grandmother in disbelief and then at each other in bewilderment. We look so much alike, but it's our eyes that are the undeniable, dead giveaway. Bright green eyes.

Is this why I always felt so broken?

"You told me he died when he was born?!" Riley suddenly develops a quivering lip with his words faltering upon them. He turns back to me, "I knew it. I knew you were alive. I felt it, my wolf felt it, but no one believed me and Mom refused to talk about it." Riley steps up to me crying but stops just inches away wanting to do something but hesitating. "Can I hug you?" he asks, unlike his…I mean our grandparents.

He opens his arms and waits for me to accept him. The warmth and smile that spreads through me plasters onto my lips and I gladly step into his waiting arms. A weird sense of belonging fills my soul as if recognizing I am finally home. A rush of happiness floods my body, healing the wounds that festered for so many years

A weird jolt sparks between us. We both jump back.

"What the hell was that?" Demetrius is instantly by my side pulling me behind him, protecting me from whatever happened. He must have felt it through our bond because everyone else looks confused by his sudden reaction.

"Babe you, okay?" Demetrius whispers and I chuckle, stepping out from behind him and caressing his cheek in appreciation.

"Yes, it was just a bizarre electric shock I felt, is all. "

"It's your twin bond. It probably reconnected. It's not just the two of you who are twins, so are your wolves."

My grandmother giggles with delight. She turns to my mate, who is still on guard.

He's gay!

The words float into my mind, and I suck in a shocked breath. What just happened? That wasn't my thought nor a mind link. I looked at Demi and then back to my twin. Then understanding grabbed hold. I immediately grew defensive.

"Is that a problem?" I snap at Riley furrowing my brows. He looks at me wide-eyed, shaking his head. Everyone else stands in silence, confused at my sudden outburst.

But it isn't sudden. I reacted to Riley. Demi leans into me to offer support, but he also looks puzzled as to what is happening.

"Did you just read my mind?" Riley asks, biting his lip nervously while his eyes skitter across the room. I guess we have the same habit of biting our lips out of nerves.

Maybe I did read his mind. Thinking back, I don't think I actually heard it. It's more like the words were suddenly there.

I guess you heard me thinking you're gay. So, to answer your question, I don't have a problem with it. I'm bisexual, so I was just excited that we are so similar even though we have been apart since birth.

I immediately take a breath in relief. Riley smiles and shrugs his shoulders. The nonchalant explanation and gesture have me thinking to myself how I should have followed my initial impression of him, but I'm not going to tell him just yet.

We collectively follow my grandparents into the family room. The room is large but lacks the seating necessary to accommodate all of us. I sit down first on the large sofa and Demetrius sits to one side of me while Riley sits on the other. Mark sits next to Riley and Dan stands next to him. The others stand alongside the sofa.

My grandmother stares at me with such longing and affection that the longer she stares the more uncomfortable I become. It's extremely weird to me to be showered with so much adoration so quickly from people I barely even know yet. We only just met and the way they accept me is still awkward. Then again, I'm not sure what I expected but it most certainly isn't this and a long-lost brother.

My grandparents finally break the silence and introduce themselves as Ida and Paul Neverdeen. We dive in for the next two hours catching them up on everything that's happened and what we learned from the Elders. They are mortified to hear their daughter is being held captive as they thought she was on a business trip. Had Iris not seen this and then it confirmed by Maya, we wouldn't be here. Yet, they claim that not long ago they got a call from her saying she was out of the country.

Maybe she was blackmailed into making the call.

"So can I ask something that's been bothering me?" I face Grandma Ida feeling my anger rising as the words form on my tongue. "Why didn't my mother look for me if she knew I was alive? Also, how do I have a twin?"

The room fills with an uncomfortable silence, but with a collective curiosity to the answer.

"I don't know why your mother hid you from the world. I can't imagine what the circumstances must have been for her to make that decision. And as far as we knew, you had died. But with Riley, she didn't know she was pregnant with twins. Due to her wanting everything to be natural, she never had a check up with a doctor. She only had our healer give her a once over every month. It wasn't until she came home one night crying that she ended up going into labor with Riley. She had bruises on her face and stomach with a couple of broken ribs. She said she was attacked by a rogue. You see, when you were born, it was a premature labor. Yet somehow, she was able to hold onto Riley's pregnancy for a bit longer. I wonder if it had anything to do with the magical abilities of your father."

"It wasn't a rogue that attacked Mom, Grandma. That night, Mom tried taking me back from Hugo. He snatched me from her and started kicking her on the ground. Then she tried taking me again in the middle of the night. We managed to run away into the woods while she carried me. He attacked her in his wolf form leaving her mangled. That is the last memory my wolf has of her." I push back the tears.

I'm tired of crying. I'm tired of feeling sorry for myself.

Why didn't my mother try harder? Did she not want me enough since she had Riley?

"That son of a bitch. He is as selfish as they come. He always wanted to take your father down. Goddess, rest his soul." Grandpa Paul shakes his head and sucks his teeth.

"Wait, my father had magic?" I sit up straight, curious to this revelation.

"Yes, he had an affinity for healing. All he had to do was touch whatever it was, but it demanded a lot from him, so he didn't use it often. Your mother, on the other hand, could astro project. What about you?" Grandma Ida lifted a brow at me in question.

"I don't think I have any powers." I shrink in my seat and wonder if life would have been different had I manifested any of my abilities. I might have been able to stand my own against Hugo a lot sooner. Did Hugo's starvation and abuse cause my powers to not develop just as my Lycan gland?

"Maybe there's still a chance. You're only now just becoming healthy," Demetrius coos softly by my ear and a smile form on my lips.

I realize with Demi's body close to mine; it wouldn't even matter anymore if I had powers. I am happy with who I am.

A hand reaches for mine from Riley, looks with tears threatening to trail his face. "Is it okay that I'm your brother?" Riley puts his head down like a small child looking for approval. The way I looked when I used to cower from Hugo. His voice is filled with hurt and loneliness and need. It must have been just as hard for him growing up knowing I was a part of him but being told that I'm dead.

"Of course, Riley. I wouldn't trade your existence for the world. I'm just hurt. Hurt because I grew up abused and unwanted. Hurt that I was lied to my whole life and not once was I saved from the hell I endured. Yes, Mom tried to save me as a baby, but why not after she regained her strength? Why not ask for help from someone to track me down? If I had known you existed, I would have tried finding you a long time ago, but even that was robbed from me." I hug my brother.

Riley hugs me in return and we stay in the comfort of each other's arms, letting our twin bond grow and strengthen between us. Yet even this hug saddens me. The difference in the way he feels compared to my body is like night and day. I am all skin and bones and my twin is healthy and strong. He may still be slender, but unlike me, he doesn't look sick.

Demetrius rubs his hand up and down my back, sending me comfort through his touch. It reminds me to stop falling back so easily to my belittling thoughts.

We pull away from each other and in that moment, a loud bang booms from outside. Some of the windows shatter inward spreading glass in every direction. We all jump at the sight of a can spinning on the floor letting out smoke of some kind, filling the room rapidly. I grab Riley's hand and Demetrius grabs my other, pulling us out of the living room along with him. The chaos that ensues makes every second that passes seem like an eternity. Demetrius leads us down a long hallway where it is easier to breathe.

"Run and hide," Demetrius' voice fills me to my core but I can barely move.

I'm not sure what is happening, but everything tells me not to leave my mate behind. Screams and fighting erupts through the home quickly and Riley takes the opportunity to lead. He pulls me down the hallway and I reluctantly follow. The last entryway opens up into a kitchen.

"Let's go to the basement," Riley suggests.

I couldn't agree more that it would be the safest place to be. The back door of the kitchen busts open, forcing Riley and I to back away from the door which leads down to the basement. Two wolves walk in snarling as they block our way of escape. A slow clapping sound emerges from the men blocking the door and a man cuts through between them. A man that I recognize all too well. Hugo stands before us dressed in tactical gear.

"Well, this is a lovely surprise?" Hugo rubs his hands together as he approached us with slow calculated steps. We mimic his pace and take steps backward, stopping when our backs hit the center kitchen island. "I have two queen nephews instead of one."

My stomach turns upside down. I want to throw up from hearing him call me nephew and no longer hiding the fact he isn't my father. But I need to be strong. My brother has no idea the kind of psycho this man is, but what else could I do? I place my arm in front of my brother and push him back slightly.

"Now that's precious. You think you can stand up to me since you have a new family? You're nothing but a cock-sucking worthless piece of shit. I am the rightful heir to this money and council, not you or your pathetically dead father." Hugo laughs. His boisterous volume thumps into my ears, deafening the fear that has taken hold. "You know, I came here with the intention of using your whore of a mother as a bargaining chip. But I think the both of you will do just fine. Boys, take them!"

Hugo quickly slides down his mask and tosses another can. The smoke fills the room just as quickly as the first. The wolves run out the door and two other men come into view before I lose consciousness.

***

Pain throbs in my head and the sound of Riley calling out to me forces my eyes to open along with a kick to my leg.

"Wake up you idiot," Riley yells with a shrill sound.

It makes my head hurt more but not more than what I see. We are in the field behind the house and tied to a post. Underneath us is a platform with a pile of wood stacked up like a pyre of sorts. If anything, we more closely resembled captive witches about to be burned for crimes we never committed. Out in the field are howls and screams from the fighting and the stench of blood of freshly slaughtered kin. My pack and Atlas' are all fighting Hugo and his rogues in a blood bath that is a scene out of the underworld.

All this for what? A seat on the council? Money that isn't his? My chest coils at the thought that all of this is happening due to the selfish nature and greed of one man. Hugo. A strike of lightning hits the ground before me, sending dirt to erupt from the ground. A group of witches join the fight along with some councilmen led by Councilman William. Sparks of the lightning fly in our direction and light embers in the wood beneath us. The fire quickly catches, starting the countdown to our death. What do they have to gain from having Hugo in a seat?

The platform beneath us heats, igniting panic within Riley and me. We struggle against our constraints to try and break free, but the ropes are too tight. They only chafe at my skin. My wrist burns with how raw they feel as I yank and wiggle to find a loose spot I can work on, but nothing. Riley whimpers as he struggles against the ropes and so do I from my arms and the rising heat beneath us. It won't be long before the fire engulfs us both.

Cackling and chants grow within the chaos of the fight surrounding us, as the witches stand alongside Hugo, outnumbering us and fighting with their magic. Ironic really, the ones about to burn alive are us while the witches fight freely. Not that they deserve it instead but ironic, nonetheless. The flames creep up to our bodies and Riley shrieks in pain unable to escape our inferno. I can see the fire reach his side first and is now burning his leg because he doesn't have the space to move away.

He cries as the burns worsen but the relief in his eyes as we both hear a wolf running up behind us and it scares me. He is giving up but I'm not ready, I can't die yet but even I know there is no way out of the situation we are in, and I brace myself for the attack. Neither of us can tell who the wolf is so I can only assume he is an enemy ready to finish us off. With a bark in a rather high pitch to let us know he means no harm, he shifts. I can hear his bones shifting into his human form. He unties Riley first, placing him away from the fire as the part where he sat collapses. Tears fall free when I see my brother safe, and the man runs back for me.

"I'm Ronan. The Elders sent for us. How can we help?" he asks as he finishes untying me. I look behind him into the tree line spotting a bunch of glowing eyes hidden within them. All of them are allies waiting for instruction.

"Take down Hugo, the rogues, the witches, and the council. The Neverdeen family and the Lunar River pack are on our side," I huff, and Ronan turns to his pack.

He howls in signal, and they all charge to the battlefield.

Riley limps a little but the burn that takes up his entire left leg is already healing. If only my healing abilities were as fast as his, I wouldn't be in as much pain as I am in right now. Then I remember our father was a healer and thought maybe Riley takes after him. We shift once Riley is mostly healed and run to my pack mates. The mayhem surrounding us is making me dizzy as blood and magic flies in every direction. The last thing I am good at is close combat and the anxiety it produces has me searching for high ground. If I can get my hands on my rifle, then I can help from afar. I just had to leave my weapons at home.

"Riley, do you have any weapons?"

"Yea, grandpa uses them to scare off hunters."

"Okay, can you link grandpa and see if he is okay. Then ask him to bring me a bag with a long-range rifle and ammo and meet us by the van."

I link to Mark and Lenny that I am getting some weapons since Demetrius is fighting and I don't want to distract him. I run with all I have alongside my brother to the grandpa running out of a basement door from the side of the house and towards the van. I shift back into my human form and thank my grandfather for being so fast. I look through the bag content with everything inside and put a pair of pants he kindly added for me and Riley as well. I turn to my brother to guide me to the roof of the house. and run

My legs are shaking with each step we take up the stairs. The house furnishings are destroyed and the smoke that settled on the floor and walls is leaving a gray residue clinging to everything. We reach the rooftop, and I set up on a small flat area that is the overhead of a balcony below. Riley's eyes go wide when I unzip the bag and pull-out parts of a rifle with familiarity.

"You know how to use all this?" my brother asks me.

I give him a smug smirk, letting him know I do indeed know and am proud. My brother watches in awe as I assemble the rifle and stand it in position. I can see the battlefield clearly from our vantage point. The moment from when I previously shot Demetrius fills my vision briefly, making me choke on air. I take a deep breath to fill my lungs and exhale slowly to clear my mind. With my steady breath, I exhale and shoot, taking out a rogue with a head shot. I have to be careful to only take out those I recognize. It's hard to tell who is an enemy and who is part of the pack sent by the Elders.

With another deep breath, I look through my scope and find another target. A second rogue is down. I search through my scope again but this time they are aware that someone is taking them out. A few of them look around trying to find the source of the shots. Riley and I lay down completely flat and wait as the adrenaline kicks up into high gear. After a few minutes, I peek back up and reposition my rifle to look through my scope once more. Down goes another and another. Four rogues down and plenty more to go.

"Alex, something isn't right," Riley whispers.

"What do you mean?" I reply while scanning the field.

"Weren't there fifteen of them? You killed four so that's eleven left but there's only nine in the field." I look over at Riley who is using the binoculars he found in my bag.

I look back through my scope and he's right. Two of the men are missing. As I scan the area again, goblins and shifters pour out from the tree line. Unlike the ones we fought against with Liber de Beur, these are very much alive and take our side in the fight. This is the tipping edge we need to gain an upper hand. I'm not sure why the shifters decided to help considering what happened with Liber not long ago, but we can use all the help we can get. Maybe they understand that what happened wasn't because of us, but because of a madman instead.

Riley and I pick up our stuff to head down a level to look for a different angle. Being half naked in the cold didn't help the ache in my bones from the position we were in on the roof either but that is the price for having to shift. We head back into the house crawling through the attic window and push the trap door down so it could open into a hallway below us.

With the rush of air that comes from opening the trap door, so does the scent of wolves. There they are. The two missing rogues waiting for
us to make our appearance.

21

Demetrius
(Back to when the attack started)

The thick smoke fills the room faster than I thought possible. Everyone jumps up ready for what is to come of this, but I for one can't wait to see what this is. I pull Alex and his brother out of the living room hoping they can escape from the danger or at least hide. Alex hesitates to let me go. As much as I don't want to leave him, I need to make sure he is safe. The gray smoke in the air begins to dissipate enough I can spot some wolves coming in through the broken windows. We fight to take them out one by one. However, I can't help but feel this is all a distraction. The rogues are too easy to get rid of and one willingly backed away as if told to leave.

My wolf, Alcide, stirs inside, only confirming my instincts that something is off. I run in the direction Alex and Riley went, but I don't see them in any one of the rooms I pass. Instead, at the end of the hall and through the threshold, a can similar to the one from the living room, is on the floor of the kitchen. The back door is broken in and drag marks lead out the door. I pick up the can hoping it wasn't anything toxic. The last thing I want is for the can to have any silver mixed in. The label seems to suggest sleeping gas, which doesn't make it any better."

"Shit," I curse out loud.

I throw the can across the room but the relief I feel that he isn't poisoned only helps ease but a smidgen of my worry.

My heart pumps a mile a minute. All of the worst-case scenarios are playing in my head like a broken record stuck in a loop.

I seriously need to teach Alex better hand-to-hand combat.

Alex needs to be able to protect himself in close combat for moments where he needs to fend someone off. Although with this many wolves, he would still be overpowered even if he tried. I race out the door spotting my pack mates chasing after a wolf to a field behind the house. There is nothing I wouldn't do to save my mate even if it means continuing to save him for the rest of my life. With as much speed as I can muster, I run through the bushes and pass a small clearing. I gasp at the amount of rogues Hugo has behind him.

When did he gather so many followers?

Off to the side, I spot Alex and Riley tied up to a post. My gut twists inside. Riley is kicking Alex to wake up and every fiber within me fires a signal to burst into a sprint but before I can, Hugo and other wolves' attack. Swiftly I dodge Hugo's hits, but he is too slow to land a good hook. Evading and ducking, I elude his attacks trying to not lose sight of Alex in the process. But it is an uneven fight that can spell death for me.

"Why are you so distracted? Should I have killed him first?" Hugo taunts, forcing my eyes to meet his with rage.

The blood in my ears is pumping loudly, drowning out the screams and howls of the fight around me. My vision goes red, and I accept the fact that this man needs to die. Knowing what he has done to my mate growing up and the things he has done now helps dig a grave so deep that Hugo can sit comfortably in the pits of hell.

I shift into Alcide. My spine elongates protruding under my skin as my back expands. Hair's sprout over my body forming my coat. My hands crack and break as my fingers fuse until I have paws. I howl as my face reshapes and my nose and jaw elongate into a snout. I land on all fours with a growl.

Alcide

Seeing everything through the eyes of Demetrius is nothing compared to seeing it for myself. Hugo shifts into his wolf, Czar, and circles me as if sizing me up. He must feel that he can easily take me with the confidence he exudes. He is sadly mistaken. Even with the enormity of his wolf, he doesn't train everyday like I do, nor is he as young. Czar growls, baring his yellow, unkempt teeth. His upper lip quivers with drool dribbling down between his canines, but I am no prey to the wolf before me.

My gaze shifts over to my humans' mate and notice he is finally awake and saying something to Riley. A calming wave of relief washes over me, allowing my mind to refocus. Demetrius also settles inside, knowing his mate is awake and breathing. I shift my attention back on Czar and pounce, clawing at his side. He evades the brunt of the hit by transferring his weight to dodge me. My claws barely graze him, only enough to slightly draw blood. But with how shallow the wound is, he can heal quickly without slowing down.

Czar tries to do the same by swiping at me and while I can easily avoid his slow movements, I allow him to hit his mark. This way I can close the gap between us. If I am to finish this quickly, I need to take a hit in order to do so. In turn, I bite into his front leg and snap it as I tug it roughly in the opposite direction. The way his stench fills my nostrils, and his matted fur coats my tongue makes me want to hurl. He yelps as my teeth sink in, jumping back on his three legs while holding up his fourth leg when I let go. He stands there trying to heal but I will not give him the chance. I want to finish him off.

I charge at him and slide underneath him at the last minute. With all of my body and strength under him, I push up and fling him into the air. He lands on his side, essentially slamming the broken leg on the ground. He shrieks in pain as the sound of his leg breaking again filters to my ears. This won't do. His pain is not enough. I step back, ready to pounce again when a lightning strikes, blinding me and others around me.

Witches appear from within that light, charging like Spartans through the field. They join in on the fight against us and increase the odds in favor of these bastards.

Well, this is just perfect.

With heavy breaths, I look around realizing that Czar used my distraction to give me the slip. The bastard couldn't even finish what he started. Fear rears its ugly head within me, but it isn't my own emotions filling my chest with darkness and regret. It has to be Alex, but what I find has Demetrius fighting me for control. A fire is lit beneath Alex and it's growing quickly.

I run towards him and yelp when I am tackled to the ground, hitting a large rock against my ribs. The break of my ribs creates a searing pain that overtakes my senses. Czar used the slip to heal himself enough to continue our fight. He quickly stands on his hind legs and stomps on me in the same spot where my ribs broke. We howl in pain with two more of my ribs caving under the pressure and his leg not as healed as he thought. Hugo limps back a bit as I see stars from the pain. I clench my jaw as I get up. Czar isn't going to let me save Alex or his brother Riley. I'm running out of time.

Behind Czar, Hugo's minions keep guard, watching us. Either they want to make sure I don't run or that anyone else interferes. They laugh at me, knowing I am struggling to breathe with how I gasp for breath. My ribs fortunately are mending so I fake a limp to not let them in on how much I am recovering. Czar eyes me in almost a mocking sort of way. He must be proud of the damage he inflicted on me. The sick bastard enjoys torture no matter what form he is in. Czar is just as sick as his human host Hugo. They deserve each other as well as their fate. A shot rings out and a wolf behind Czar drops dead. Someone must have finally gotten a hold of guns and is carefully taking out the wolves around me. This is my chance. The opening that I need and with no hesitation I attack.

I lunge towards Czar the moment he looks back at his fallen comrade. I part-shift my hands mid-air and land on his back. He howls at my weight on him and ferociously shakes his body to get me off of him, but my human hands grip his fur. It's like being a Jinete on a bull at a rodeo in Mexico. Goddess knows I used to enjoy watching rodeos. But this isn't enjoyable. It is only then that I notice our numbers have increased. A large pack of wolves is joining us in battle. Wolves I have never seen before. Although I have no idea where they came from, I am grateful.

I bite the back of his neck and sink my teeth into his thick fur and then into his neck. The metallic taste of blood pools into my mouth just before he howls again, and I lose my balance. My bite isn't deep enough to cause significant damage, so I let go of him. At least he is injured again. A second shot rings out and another wolf drops.

It has to be Alex. My eyes search for him but I know I am right. He is nowhere to be seen and is sniping these idiots one by one like a pro. Alex makes me and Demetrius so proud with his skills.

Oh, he is getting some tonight, Demetrius whispers to me, as if I need to know how his mate turns him on.

Czar's neck is drenched with blood but not as much as I'd like. Not enough to make him choke on it. He huffs a few times with his breathing shallow, but he still stands with enough strength to fight. Two more wolves drop dead around us. Thank the Goddess for his sniper skills. Even amid all the commotion, he is able to take down his enemy with precision. Czar, panics, shooting a look at his wolves, which sends two of them off to most likely find Alex. I attack him before he fully heals again, but as if the universe has something against me trying to kill this man, a witch steps in. She hits me with a blast of something cold before Iris cleans the floor with her on my behalf. I collapse to the ground, panting but all the icy blast did was knock me off my feet and maybe some air out of my lungs. At least that's what I thought until the glowing blue fire she hit me with burned brightly, singeing off my fur. I struggle to catch my breath when Czar walks up to me and shifts back to Hugo.

"Enjoy dying without saying goodbye to your little mate." He kicks me in the face knocking me out cold.

***

Demetrius

Waking up still on the floor, I shiver in my human form from exposure. My naked body is covered in dirt and blood from the fight and the chaos around me has more or less died out. Some of the wolves we fought are dead, along with a couple of the councilmen. The remaining councilmen are tied up with the bit of the wolves we captured. The wolves are being given a serum that will force their shift back to their human form so we can bind them properly. The witches that had joined the opposition must have given up, seeing as this is losing battle for them. Many of them fled while some of the witches seem to be helping us. I am not sure what they are planning but we will use their help in the meantime. I turn over to push myself up but fall when my elbow buckles under my weight. I try again and groan at the ache in my muscles. Standing up, I take in everything that transpired and search the surrounding faces hoping to find Alex or Riley, but neither are anywhere to be seen.

That's right! The two wolves went after them.

I try to mind link with Alex but am coming up short. I'm not sure if it's from mental or physical fatigue or if he is simply too far for me to reach. I wave at Lenny and Scott to come with me since they are the second strongest here from our pack. We run to the house and begin searching every room.

Third floor. Lenny links to me and I bolt like a madman up the stairs.

There is blood all over the floor and smeared on the walls. I take a good whiff. Hugo was here and I am praying that the blood is his.

Alex, can you hear me? I try again.

Oh, my Goddess, babe! Please come save us. I was trying to call out to you. We are running about 15 minutes North, but I don't know how much strength I have left. Alex replies and I am relieved to hear him.

You're doing great Chiquito. I'm on my way.

I tell Scott and Lenny and link with my pack to tell the others while Scott links with his. We shift again and run in the direction Alex gives me. We run like hell on wheels in hopes to get to him on time.

Alcide

Babe hurry, Czar is now chasing us as well.

I pick up Peyton's, Alex's wolf, scent as his words fuel my soul to run faster. I would rather die than let Hugo or Czar have him. The scent is getting stronger the closer I get to where they must be. They have to be close. I have to believe that. Spotting the wolves chasing Peyton and Riley's wolf, I sprint faster, pushing past my muscle's limit. Pushing myself further than I ever have before. My legs burn and scream at me to stop. They are going to give out any second if I don't stop. But I can't. I won't. My heart accelerates, working double time to help me reach my goal, forcing my chest to constrict. My vision almost gives out, but I blink it away and sprint on. I have to stay focused. I must reach them.

The first within my reach is the wolf furthest back chasing my mate. I snap at his hind leg and drag him down. The other wolf stops to help him, but it is too late. After breaking the leg, I bite his exposed throat cleanly through and drop the chunk of flesh on the ground.

Lenny's wolf flies past me and attacks the other rogue wolf, bringing him down while Scott's wolf and I ran after Czar next.

Almost there, I tell Demetrius.

In the distance, Czar swipes at Riley's wolf who is slightly slower than Peyton's. He trips and tumbles. His whimpering filters back to me. Czar's growl is guttural and violent as he charges to pounce on Riley's wolf, but Peyton turns around and heads full force into Czar in a head butt. Czar hits a nearby tree with his back and yips on impact.

Peyton bares his teeth, standing over his brother, growling and panting, already protective of his twin. My heart swells at the sight. Scott's wolf, Elu, walks up beside Peyton, and I stop behind the limping power-obsessed piece of shit uncle's wolf. He doesn't acknowledge my presence though. Instead, he zeroes in on Peyton with a murderous look worse than before. I growl deep and strong, taking a few steps forward. I'll be damned if this goes on any longer. Czar finally turns to me, and I don't miss how he flinched seeing how close I am to him. There is a hint of fear as he takes in my beast-like growl and stance.

He pounces on me, and we tumble onto the ground. I fall on my back but with my hind legs up, I take all his weight and push him off me, flinging him against the same tree he hit before. He yelps loudly and gets up limping worse than before. He is tired but so am I at this point. His old wolf is ready to give out and I am running on fumes. I swipe at him, but he somehow catches me first. He throws his weight on me to pin me down and begins to swipe his claws at my face. Blow after blow against my face he rips through my flesh. His barrage of attacks makes it hard to breathe and I can't wiggle free. Still a bit dizzy from over-exerting myself when running, darkness tries to take hold as my world begins to spin. I glare through the blood that covers my eyes at the wolf who tortured my mate for eighteen years.

Czar stops and opens his jaw, ready for my throat, but before I feel any piercing pain, a loud howl cuts through my ears.

Peyton.

It is a war cry.

Czar looks back and the next thing I know, blood is dripping on my face, followed by a loud snap. The wolf's head cocks sideways in an unnatural way staring back down at me. The life fades from his eyes and he drops.

Just like that, it's over.

My eyes re-focus enough to see Peyton standing above me with Czar's blood painting his mouth. He is panting heavily but I can feel how his legs shake at my side. Peyton shifts back into Alex and his beautiful body lowers to lift my head into his arms, blood staining his perfectly pale skin.

Demetrius

My eyes flutter open, and I am inside a dark place. A room, maybe? I am in a soft bed covered in the softest sheets. I need to find out what they are made of to buy some for Alex.

After a minute or so, my eyes finally adjust to the dark and I have no idea what room I am in. The only logical conclusion is that I am in a room at the Neverdeen residence. I move my body to sit up and groan at the aches exploding throughout my muscles. Everything screams overexertion.

"Hey, take it easy," Alex walks in through the door with a tray with what looks like food. "Here, I figured you would wake up not feeling too great. Abuela said this works wonders."

I chuckle at how cute he is already calling Ida, grandma. I must admit, they are nice people. To be fair, they didn't know he was alive either. I guess they would be easier to forgive than his mother. I take the medicine and drink the water offered.

"Gracias, Chiquito."

"You know, you're lucky I love you. I technically am *not* Chiquito," Alex giggles.

I love his giggles.

"I know, but to me you're Chiquito. Besides grandote doesn't have the same ring to it."

We both laugh a little harder than we should, but man it feels good to do so. We manage to stop a catastrophe that would've been his uncle taking over the council. We saved so many lives and snuffed his evil out of this world. I can finally be at peace with my mate. Now it is just his family matter that we need to attend to. Or, at least, Alex needs to. Then again, I still don't understand what the council had to gain with having Hugo in a seat. Or with anything they have done lately.

"Go wash up, dinner will be ready soon. We will be downstairs in the dining hall." Alex gives me a kiss, humming when he pulls away.

"Have you heard from Kristofer?" I ask, pulling the blankets off me.

"Yes. They just called a few minutes ago. They got Finn and Isabella. They should be here by tomorrow afternoon. So, Abuela said we can stay here and rest." Alex gets up and puts out his hand. "Come. I'll show you the bathroom then you can meet us downstairs."

We exit the room, and he shows me a bathroom that can easily be another guest bedroom. A set of clothes is folded on a lounge with a towel hanging on a hook by the glass walk-in shower. Alex closes the door leaving me to my naughty thoughts, but the seductive look on his face suggests he is having them too. I should have made him shower with me. He would have looked great against the glass, moaning my name.

Smiling at my thoughts, I undress and observe my battered body in the mirror. Everything has healed for the most part, but I still have slight bruising on my torso. My face on the other hand is wrapped in bandages.

This is not an attractive look by any means. I took some really hard hits to the face, and I know Czar tore through some of my flesh. I can't imagine the care I was given to make sure my face healed properly. I unwrap the bandage and flinch at the sight. Very fine lines of scars riddle my cheeks and forehead. I didn't look horrible but ugly isn't too far off. At least these will eventually fade. Tingling flares up around the scars and right before my eyes, they fade slightly. Whatever Alex gave me is already working. Thank Goddess for Abuela Ida.

The shower is something out of this world. I am surrounded by multiple shower heads at various height levels. When I turn the nozzle, they all burst to life which scares me half to death at first. The hot water hits my skin, massaging me from head to toe. *Damn, I need a shower like this at home.*

If it wasn't for Alex waiting for me, I wouldn't leave this bathroom. With a sigh, I scrub my body taking special care of scrubbing my jewels. I'm not saying anything will happen but with Alex, sex is never off the table. The suds roll down my body under the water and a thought comes to mind.

Should I clean really good back there?

I still don't know how I feel about Alex being on top, despite already agreeing. But I want him to do what he likes as well.

I mean, if it is Alex then I'm fine with anything but like Alex said, he isn't small either. For a guy so slender, his manhood is above average. He kills my jaw whenever I suck him off so imagine my poor virgin butt hole.

I sigh again but this time ashamed of myself. I only now see things from his perspective. I am his first so he must have gone through these same thoughts when we had sex. On top of it all, I'm bigger than he is so he must have lied when I asked him if it hurt our first time, and he said no.

Alcide chirps in. *Demetrius, you agreed. Stop being a wimp.*

Alcide, who even asked you?

No one, which is why I'm telling you to suck it up.

You just want it up the ass, don't you?

...no

Yeah right. You'll do anything Peyton asks you to.

Shut up. So will you. So let him fuck you, you little bitch.

Psh, who you calling a bitch?

You...duh.

I'm pretty sure that's what you are. You four-legged arse.

...

That's what I thought.

I turn off the water and get myself dressed in the clean clothes Alex left me. My wolf can be annoying sometimes, even when he is right. Can't believe he's calling me a bitch, although he isn't wrong either. If

Alex asked me to jump, I'd ask how high. There is no doubt about it. I take one last look in the mirror and try to slick my hair back as best I can, given I don't have any hair product. My baby is waiting for me, and I am starving. With a thumbs up to myself in the mirror and Alcide snorting at my reflection I head downstairs and join everyone for a well-deserved feast.

22

Alex

Demetrius finally makes it downstairs just in time for dinner. He looks nervous for some reason and scans the room wide-eyed when it lands on the table before him. There are fifteen of us, but the table can easily fit another five. I wave at him, and he practically runs towards me with excitement. Honestly, I'm not hard to miss since I am the only one with my practically platinum hair and impossibly pale almost translucent skin. You wouldn't think I come from Spanish descent. If anything, some may say I look more like a vampire. Yet, his adorable face when he spots me makes me melt, and vampire-looking or not, I am glad I look how I do if it means he looks at me that way.

"You liked the shower?" I ask while pulling his chin in for a kiss.

"Yes, but it was missing something," Demetrius pouts.

"What?"

"You," he teases. My cheeks turn a few shades of red and I slap him on the shoulder.

My grandmother stands up and so does my grandfather. For a second, I think they heard what Demetrius said to me, and I panic, but then Abuela speaks. "May I have everyone's attention?" She clinks her glass with a knife pulling everyone from conversation. "I want to take this moment to say welcome and that despite the bloodshed today, and the unfortunate circumstances onto which we have all come to know one another, I am still happy that we are sharing this moment. I would've never guessed that I had another grandson out there. One I thought was dead."

Grandma Ida chokes on a sob, pauses to wipe a tear, but then decides she can't continue so Abuelo takes over.

"We are not sure why our daughter hid Alex from us but believe us when we say that we have loved you since the day you were born. Alex, your real name is Alejandro Massimo Neverdeen, but we have called you Alex for short while you were in your mother's tummy. If you'll allow us, will you accept us in your life as your grandparents and grant us the opportunity to make up for lost time?" My grandfather raises his glass waiting for my response with a tear of his own trailing his cheek.

I stand up and raise my glass. "Only if you accept me as your grandson and my pack as an extension of yours. I don't know where I would be had they not taken me in and protected me."

"Done," Abuelo responds. We all raise our glasses and salute. With a small sip, I set down my drink before walking over to my grandparents. We hug each other in a small huddle of three.

I finally have my family.

A server comes out of the kitchen with the roast and a few other dishes. We pull apart from one another to allow the servers to set the food on the table. My Abuelo makes the first cut into the roast and the server takes it back to finish it up for the rest of us. In the meantime, we are served salads and appetizers while topping off our wine.

The dinner goes on while we talk and laugh with one another. Abuelo informs us two on the council that suspected the treachery of their sworn brothers, arrived while Demetrius and I were upstairs. They took in the members that were still alive for trial, one of which was William, and the others were collected for burial. Those who rallied with the council's bad eggs were also taken in by the leaders of their kind to trial as well. William admitted to plotting to reform the council with the intention to wipe out anyone who wasn't pure no matter the species.

It was a mess and the success of it all banked on Hugo being able to acquire the Neverdeen wealth. Their idea to start a supreme society was a seed planted by Liber de Beur when he first reached out to William for assistance. It is no wonder that they initially helped Liber since he held the same ideology. Thankfully, not all the council members were corrupted.

After we swapped stories and enjoyed the warm atmosphere that good food and company provides, I breathe in the moment and sit back truly grateful that I never gave up on life. If I had run away or taken the selfish way out, then I wouldn't be here. I would have robbed myself of the opportunity to share this moment with all the people I love.

"Chiquito, you alright?" Demetrius squeezes my thigh while stuffing his face with mashed potatoes.

"Yeah, I'm great. Guess I'm kinda soaking it all in," I reply as he smiles, unable to speak with a full mouth, but nods in understanding.

We finish the main course, and our plates are taken away as if on cue. We stay seated, rubbing our full tummies, and chatting about Riley's childhood. He is so embarrassed, and I finally get a good look at how I appear when I turn into a tomato since it is like looking in the mirror. Abuela laughs and announces dessert is coming out. We patiently wait for our last course. I'm not used to such a lavish dinner but anything to make this moment last longer, I will gladly accept.

"Demetrius, would you come here my dear," Abuela Ida calls out to my mate with a beckoning of her hand.

He turns to me freaking out and I chuckle although I have no idea why she is calling him over to her side of the table. He gets up, a bit nervous and sends me a mental SOS.

"Before dessert comes out and we all get that collective sleepy look in our eyes from overeating, I wanted to give you something." Abuela pulls out a box. "This has been in my family for many generations and after seeing the love and devotion you have for my grandson; I want to give it to you."

"Ida, it's okay. I love him more than life itself. The least I can do is give him all of me and more." Demetrius blushes and so do I. It feels like I shouldn't listen to what they are saying.

"And that's all the more reason to give it to you. It would do me a great honor. Please!" Abuela adds.

Demetrius smiles and accepts the box. With a tap of a finger on top of the box, it opens like a blooming flower, and his face goes from white to redder than the fourth of July.

"Ida, this is gorgeous. Are you sure? I mean, I haven't... we haven't... this-"

"My son, I am not asking you to do it now, but I want you to have it for when you both are ready."

Abuela stands up and hugs Demetrius.

"Thank you, Ida and Paul." Demetrius closes the box and puts it in his pocket. I know what it is based on the conversation, and I am super curious to see how the ring looks. I guess I'll have to wait though. You would think Abuela would have pulled him aside in private, but I guess being mates isn't a secret, and neither is getting married after finding one.

"Por favor, call me Abuela. Ya eres mi nieto," Abuela Ida smiles making Demetrius blush again.

"Bueno, nadamas si el dice que si," Demetrius replies, shocking both my grandparents.

They expected having to repeat in English thinking he didn't understand what they said. Instead, they get a full response which may have earned him more brownie points.

We finish up dessert and one by one leave the table. Some go to the den with my Abuelo while others turn in for the night. My brother Riley seems to really have taken a liking to Mark and Dan, but oddly enough Scott keeps following Riley with his eyes. I giggle at how obvious he is, but I keep that thought to myself. *I wonder why Riley hasn't acknowledged it yet.*

"Hey, let's go to our room." I place my head on Demetrius' shoulder.

"Would it be the same room I woke up in?"

I smile as my way of answering then lead him upstairs to the second floor.

The lights are dim, coming only from the bedside lamp when we enter the room. I walk straight to the bed and jump under the covers while Demetrius lights the fireplace. The room fills with a soft warm glow with the growing fire taking the bite out of the cool air. He joins me under the covers, pulling me into his arms with that sort of excited shimmy one does when going under a cold blanket.

"You know, when I first realized you actually were my mate, I knew this the path wouldn't be easy. I was ready to fight whatever demons you had hidden in that mind of yours. But babe, this was on a whole other level." Demetrius laughs and so do I because he's right. I entered this bond with baggage, but even I didn't expect all these skeletons to fall out of the closet when I opened the door. "However, I am over the moon right now. I am the happiest I have ever been in my life. And I owe all of that happiness to you Alejandro Massimo Neverdeen." Demetrius kisses the top of my head.

Hearing my real full name on his lips has me readjusting myself.

"I don't know if I'll ever get used to my full name, but I can't take all the credit for your happiness. You are an amazing person Demi. You should credit yourself as well. I love you, Demetrius Vos." I press my lips to his and feather my tongue between them until they part. He rumbles happily against his chest.

"I love the sound of my name on your lips. I love you, too."

"Really?!" I tease and kiss him deeper, moving my hands under his shirt and pinching an erect nipple.

"Oomph, babe, aren't you tired?" Demetrius moans, leaning into my touch.

"I am but never too tired to have you. I want to fall asleep with you inside me."

I lick my mate's enticing lips and witness the fire ignite in his eyes. My mate is just as much a horn dog as I am. I love it.

"Well, I was actually thinking…," Demetrius pauses, contemplating something.

My eyes flicker between his trying to figure out what he might be thinking.

"…Would you like to top?" His face turns a tinge of red as my eyes widen.

"Really? You're okay with it?"

Is he really going to let me top? ME?!

Demetrius chuckles a bit, making me bob a little on his chest. "Yes, I am okay with it."

"What if I suck? What if I am so bad at it that you're turned off?" I mumble. I know I am the one who asked first, but I am beyond nervous right now.

"Listen you are mine in every sense of the word and nothing you do will turn me off. I'm sure you dominating me and topping will have me wet for you. Besides if you'd like, I can guide you. Wouldn't you want me whimpering underneath you for a new reason?" Demetrius wiggles his brows with a cheesy smirk.

"Well, I guess I can't let my little Suga down, huh? Since it's your first time, why don't we come up with a safe word? If you don't like bottoming, then use your safe word and we can switch positions." I sit up on the bed beside him on my knees. I part them slightly in anticipation and watch his eyes trail me waiting for the moment they land on my stiffness so I can make it twitch for him.

"O–Okay, then how about... lobo?" Demetrius stumbles over his words as his eyes trail back up to mine.

"Okay, the Spanish word for wolf it is. Now my little Sub... strip!"

Demetrius grins at those words. The word 'strip' has become the word that initiates our plays. Once it's said we both know it is game time no matter what. While we do have other triggers, 'Strip' is our favorite initiation phase.

I spring up and off the bed. I watch him strip down to his birthday suit and sit on his knees on the bed like a good boy.

"Good boy. Did Suga wash up properly?" I walk up to the bed.

Woof

"Good, now come here and get on my lap." I sit down so he can lay across my thighs. My Sub crawls over to me and lays face down. I rub his juicy cheeks and slap his right side before doing the other. He gasps in a plethora of moans. I spank him until his cheeks are red with anticipation for me, loving the way it bounces back. His smooth flesh ripples under my hand while the sound echoes in the room.

"Flip over," I command, and he obeys.

He turns around with his massive hard-on waving at me. My mouth almost watering at the sight of it.

"Do you want me to touch it?" I ask.

If his now dripping dick wasn't enough of an answer, his nodding head and whimper tells me yes.

I grab his throbbing erection and stroke him painfully slow. His expression flickers between pleasure and need which sends a rush of arousal through to my core. I speed up my jerking movements making him moan as he rocks his hips before I realize what he is doing.

"Who said you could move your hips like a slut?" I stop stroking and slap his dick instead.

He yips.

Woof woof

"If you're sorry, then stand up."

My Suga gets off the bed and stands up before me in all his naked muscular hard glory. I grab his shirt from the bed, twist it up, and tie his hands behind his back with it. I then turn him, so he faces the bed.

"Spread your legs apart," I command and slap his ass one more time before I walk away.

This is his punishment.

He looks over at me confused, but I leave him alone in the room with the door half open providing a wonderful profile view of his body. Anyone passing by can see inside and find him standing there. But of course, I won't let that happen. I walk down the hall and then hide my scent before walking back towards the door. I stand by the entrance, keeping guard, and enjoying the rush of emotions coursing through me from Demetrius nerves. Everything is so heightened because of our mate bond.

I feel his slight panic mixed with horniness and anticipation. He is enjoying this all too well. He is excited at possibly getting caught and that's when it hits me. My mate likes to be watched and possibly as much as I do. I wait five painful minutes, but I am sure to him it is a lifetime of agony. However, I am just as impatient.

I walk into the room causing him to flinch. He almost attempts to move until he realizes it's me and relaxes. If I know my mate like I think I do, I'd say he is dripping right now. I close the door and walk over to the bed. My poor Sub eyes my every move still standing in the position I left him in. He's very obedient.

As seductively as possible, I slide onto the bed and roll onto my back to touch myself. Moans feather my lips as I run my hands all over my body making sure to not look his way. I remove my shirt and play with my nipples while I bite my lip. I arch my back with a rumble. Demetrius fidgets but I am determined to act like he isn't there. This is a two-part punishment and if he is to listen to his master then he needs to learn through punishment. I suck on my finger making it nice and wet and run it down my chin, neck, and nipple. I pinch myself and gasp at the sensation it brings.

The bond between us is sure to have him feeling my arousal, doubling our pleasure. It is one of my favorite perks of the bond so far. I remove my pants and briefs, tossing them to the side, making my erection bounce free from its tight captivity. With my long fingers, I stroke myself and continue playing with my erect nipple.

My breath labors and I whisper, "Demi," panting into the air.

The whispers of his name that roll off my tongue again and again, come out more like lustful pleas. Demetrius grunts and I know he is at his limit.

"Come here you horny little shit."

He climbs on top of the bed, and I undo the restraint. Moving myself up, I sit against the headboard and smile.

"Fuck my face," I command.

He stands on the bed to position himself in front of me with his hands pressed on the wall. I open my mouth and stick out my tongue, ready to receive his girth. Demetrius inserts himself and rocks, going deep each time. I moan at his warm flesh filling me completely and hitting the back of my mouth like a punching bag. His thick, long shaft picks up the pace and pushes down, thrusting. I lift a hand and grab him so that I don't take in his full length anymore as it is becoming harder to breathe. With my right hand, I jerk him to the rhythm of his hips and slobber him wet.

He grunts and grabs a fist full of my hair. He is close. I play with his balls, massaging them as I work my tongue on his shaft, causing his breath hitch. Another grunt and then a loud moan escape as his balls tightens in my hands. He pumps himself into me, almost making me swallow what he spills on my tongue. I hold his seed in my mouth and wait for him to finish before I spit it into my hand.

"Lay on your back and hold your legs open for me. You may also speak."

"Thank you, master," he lays down and positions himself like I asked. *What an amazing view.* He is panting and sweating but his eyes are droopy as if in a daze. His lips are plump and wet as he licks them under my gaze. He holds his legs open for me with his hands behind his knees showing me how his howl is twitching for me.

The load I spit in my hand is now the lube to prep my little Sub's ass. I slather it on his hole, and he flinches at the foreign touch. It is obvious that he's never been this intimate before, but the trust he is giving me has me rock hard.

"Relax, if you tense up it'll hurt, and you can tear." He instantly tightens every muscle in his body. I chuckle and coo, "I've got you Suga. Now relax."

He relaxes under my touch, and I slide a finger into his tight ring of muscle.

"Good Boy." I coo.

He squeezes me a bit, prompting me to stop moving. When his grip loosens, I continue as gently as I can until he is used to it. I pump my finger slowly and tuck my head between his legs to kiss his thighs to keep him distracted. He moans and releases any tension he still has.

A second finger slides in, and he quickly squeezes me again. Yet this time he relaxes his hold a lot quicker. I thrust a bit harder into him which has him building another erection. He is enjoying himself and it gives me the confidence I need to go further. My cute little Sub is moaning louder than he normally does, rocking into my thrusting fingers. I let his insubordination slide because it is the night he loses his ass-pussy virginity.

Any other night he rocks his hips without my say gets him a punishment and since he had one earlier for the same reason, I'll be lenient on this one. I slip a third finger, and he gasps arching his back. This time, I don't stop. Instead, I speed up and find his prostate when I push in further.

"Ah master, that feels... weird," he whispers, and I chuckle inside.

"No, that's just unknown pleasure. Ride with it. You trust me, don't you?" I bite his inner thigh and thrust harder.

"Master w-wait."

His body trembles, but I don't stop. I know what's happening. He knows his safe word. I pump harder into him, licking and biting his thighs trailing closer to his member.

"Fuck, master. I-" My sweet Sub comes in ribbons into the air and onto his stomach and chest.

"Seems like you're ready." I pull out my fingers and place myself at his entrance. I am so aroused from watching him writhe in his second orgasm that I have no space in my own nerves. I am eager and in that moment we both lose our virginities.

23

Alex

"Take a deep breath and exhale as I push in, okay?!" I whisper to my adorable Sub.

Demetrius takes a deep breath as I have done for him so many times before. I push myself into his now soft entrance. A wave of intense sensations washes over me as his body wraps around mine, my crown in its grip. His tight warmth encases me instantly.

"You need to relax. I can't go in further if you're this tight."

Nodding again, Demetrius closes his eyes. I pull out a little and push in again. I moan into high ceilings with how amazing he feels around me cock. My dick is halfway inside, and I am fighting everything in me to not pound away to chase the building orgasm. I push a little further and finally, the rest of myself in. *So, this is what it feels like.*

"Are you all in master?" My Suga opens his teary eyes taking deep breaths.

"Yes, I'll wait until you are ready for me to move."

I peck at his lips, sucking the bottom one into my mouth. His walls relax around me as I lavish him with my tongue, but I remain still, enjoying such an intimate moment with my mate. He moans into my mouth with his kisses becoming a little more aggressive.

"Master, I'm ready," he pants, looking at me with glossy eyes.

He is so aroused; his hard member is throbbing between us. His hips are beginning to thrust on their own volition.

I lift my weight from him and sit up holding on to the back of his thighs. Slowly I rock my hips, moving myself in and out in long steady strokes. Focused on his face and his reactions, I take in all the signals he gives me. One by one, I find spots he moans to and increase my pace.

"Shit, master," Demetrius moans out.

His sounds are so different from his usual ones. They are usually lusty and full of intensity but this time they are also needy. He bites his lip and grabs his dick to jerk off.

"You like it there, you horny little shit?" I thrust into him now, fast and hard. He arches his back moaning repeatedly at the sudden fast movement.

"Yes, right there. Fuck me there, Master," I lift both legs and close them, putting them over my right shoulder. Leaning forward to put my weight on my hands, I pound into him impossibly fast. The grunts rip out of me from the waves of pleasure rolling between us. Never did I think topping Demi would feel this good. The sound of our flesh smacking fills the room, accompanied by our voices and lustful whimpers.

I snap at the sudden increase in desire and lust between us.

"Flip over. Get on fours."

I pull out and watch him lift his ass for me. I smack it, earning a yip and then a moan. Again, and then again, I slap his ass before he starts to rock himself trying to find my dick.

"How bad do you want my cock in your ass?" I run a finger down his crack and shove my fingers in, smiling at the wet sounds coming from him.

"I want your cock," he whispers in a raspy voice.

Oh, my Goddess this is dangerous for me.

"You hear that? Those wet sounds are from your dirty, tight hole," I continue to tease him while he groans. "Say it again. What does my slut want?"

I continue thrusting my fingers and grab his swinging dick jerking him just as fast. His back dips and he buries his face into a pillow. Moan after moan he quivers against me.

"Master please, I want your cock inside me."

"Good boy," I pull out my fingers and shove my cock into his warm hole in one, swift movement. He lets out a scream into the pillow. I thrust into him holding on to his hips. I ram every inch of me into his quivering walls and I know he is almost ready with how he clamps down on my cock.

"Come for me you little slut. Come for master."

I pick up my pace, slapping against his bouncing ass cheeks.

"Fuck! I'm coming!" Demetrius shoots his load onto the bed shaking from his first major orgasm.

I pull out of him still hard as a rock. "What do we do about me, my little Suga?"

Demetrius turns to look at me waving my dick and slapping it against my thighs. His eyes are low, full of passion and the residual of his climax. His breath is heavy but becoming steady. A smile tugs at his sexy lips and without a word, he lays on his back and opens his legs for me again. He runs a hand up to his nipple and tugs one while the other hand begins to jerk his half-erect cock.

"Use me as you like, Master." He opens his legs wider.

"Would you like an audience then?" My heart races with my words. I took a gamble when I had Mark and Dan watch us, not expecting Demetrius to become so aroused. However, right now is the most vulnerable he has ever been during sex, but I find him so sexy, that I want to display how it's all mine. I might like dominating him a bit too much.

"If that's what Master wants?" he replies.

I blink out of my thoughts and look at my mate lying there masturbating and biting his lip. I smile because I expected the safe word 'lobo' to grace his lips. Instead, he is playing his role well.

"No, no. You must tell me what you want." I am so horny I might come just watching him squirm under me.

"Call Mark and Dan so they can watch Master fuck my lonely hole."

Demetrius smiles and I see something I haven't seen before. My little pet is fully into doing all my wishes. He is confident in himself and trusts me and his packmates enough to share this moment. I look down and my dick drips in anticipation.

"Good boy. Now *you* call them here."

Nodding, Demetrius grins ear to ear.

"Done."

"Good boy." I crawl on top of him and get into a sixty-nine position with him. "Suck me off until they get here."

I smile as I wrap my fingers around his length and take him into my mouth to lavish with my tongue. His breath hitches with my tongue circling around his crown allowing drool to fall over his length. Slobbering and stroking his length with my saliva letting my fingers glide over his pulsing veins, I apply pressure to his base and slurp his soft tip. Moans vibrate against my member like a toy I have back home. He is enjoying what I am doing, and my dick reaps the benefits with the sensation of his flexing throat around my girth.

I moan in turn, taking one of his testicles into my mouth, sucking, and letting it pop out with a loud sound before returning to his shaft. Demitrius jerks at the sensation and groans with his balls tightening.

A soft knock raps on the door just in time to save my mate from blowing his load too early. I link with them to come in quietly and lock the door behind them. This will be an experience I shall never forget. Mark and Dan enter the room quietly, locking the door behind them as instructed. They stare in fascination at the scene before them. Dan's eyes follow the movements of my finger as it slides into Demetrius. They walk closer, eliciting a moan from their Beta. I release his dick from my lips and look at the two wolves with approval at their reaction to the dense sex pheromones in the room.

"Both of you step back and kneel. Do as you wish, but no touching us. Understand?" I command the two and they kneel. "Answer! When in this room, you respond to your master with respect. Do. You. Understand?"

They both flinch at my tone but respond in unison. "Yes, Master."

My Sub's hole tightens around my finger, signaling that he finds what I just said arousing.

"Good boys," I smirk and return to sucking on my favorite dick in the world.

It pulsates in my mouth and for a second. I am sure it grew bigger. I slurp and pull away, turning around to face Demetrius. He is lost. His eyes are gone in the moment from the pleasure he is experiencing. It takes me with him.

"Ready to get fucked," I whisper loud enough for the boys to hear. They gasp with a smile so wide; I almost scold them.

"Yes, Master. Fuck me harder this time," he replies with a raspy deep voice.

"Good. Bend over the bed next to my other puppies."

Obediently he rolls off the bed.

"This time?" Dan whispers to Mark.

"Damn, I guess he tried it first before calling us." Mark whispers back.

"Did you have something to share?" I lift a brow at the two on the floor and they shake their heads no.

We walk over to the boys and Demetrius smiles at them fully enjoying being exposed. This Sub is going to need more training if we are going to add exhibitionism to our plays. He bends over and even dares to spread his cheeks for me with his head resting on the bed and turning sideways to face me.

Dan and Mark pant, watching us with building need. Demetrius seems to grow bold in front of the others. I will have to spank that out of him. It will have to be during another play because right now, I want to feel him around me. I position myself behind Demetrius and their eyes trail from their Beta to my cock that's standing at full mast.

"Oh, my Goddess. I didn't notice how big it was before." Mark whispers to Dan. He nods while staring at it with his jaw dropped low. The lustful eyes boring into me fuels the Dom in me and I feel Demetrius reacting to it as well. I rub my finger around the quivering hole and spit on it before shoving my full length inside my mate.

"Ah!" My sweet Sub moans in delight and squirms.

I remove his hands that are still gripping his cheeks and spank him while I thrust against his hips.

"You like it in your ass, don't you?" I slam my hips into him, tossing my head back and drowning in his tight warmth.

"Yes, Master. Give me more!" he begs in a growl that almost has me releasing.

Demitrius grips the sheets and pulls them toward him trying to find a way to control the waves of the orgasm building inside him. He pants into the bed, but the muffled cries continue to roll out of him like an encouraging cry to keep on going. I lift one of his legs giving the boys a perfect view of everything and pound away harder than before.

"Yes, Master. Right there." Demi lifts his head gasping for breath. I push in deep, and my cock stirs inside him, going crazy with how amazing it feels. Pulling out, I push him down, flipping him over and pulling his ass to the edge of the bed. Without a second thought, I reinsert myself and ram into him. Demetrius and I turn to look at the boys and catch Mark reaching over and grabbing Dan's thigh, digging his fingers. Dan looks down and then to Mark.

They're both sweating just from watching us, but unable to do anything to ease the pain of their growing erections. Dan reaches for Mark's face and turns him to face him. They stare at each other for a moment before Mark pulls Dan in first and kisses him. Seeing my pack mates turn their lust toward each other almost sends me over the edge for the millionth time. I guess watching others is something I'd like to explore, too.

Demetrius moans, gripping my arm. The sight of these two men has my hips going faster and harder and my poor Demi is about to come as a result. I don't know how he has anything left in him. I slow down and lay on top of him to kiss his plump lips. Demetrius tries to turn his face more towards me, but I push his face into the bed. I need to finish.

I want to be fucked too.

"Suga, I'm going to finish quickly. I want you to fuck me crazy," I whisper.

The color in his eyes shift slightly. Alcide is pushing through.

"No, no. Not tonight, Alcide. You can let Peyton fuck you when we get back home," I say to Alcide and Demetrius regains control as I pick up my speed. Demetrius clenches around me and I pull out, spurting cum all over his body.

Panting, I drop to the floor next to Mark and Dan. My thighs are on fire, and I've drained all my strength. I lay back on the floor and turn so my feet point toward Mark and Dan. They break their kiss and shift a little so they both can face me. While Demetrius wipes his chest, Mark and Dan have each other's dicks in their hands jerking off.

"That's fucking hot!" I say to them as I glance at their weeping dicks.

"What is, Master?" Demetrius walks around the bed and spots what his fellow packmates are doing.

"Don't you agree?" I open my legs, giving Mark and Dan a full view of all my assets. They growl slightly and I chuckle.

"Master, can I play now?"

My Sub gets in between my legs and begins to prep me after I give him a nod. The intrusion fills me with an electric feel of pleasure that rocks my hips against his fingers. Having him do this while being watched is a thrill out of this world. One I never knew I was into. My body continues to rock against his fingers, and I shift sideways a bit so both Demetrius and I can watch our pack mates have their fun.

"Are you guys going to play with one another a little more?" I ask, but Mark becomes visibly nervous.

"Well, I want to do whatever Mark is okay with. Since he is straight, I don't want to scare him away," Dan chuckles nervously and looks at Mark, almost pleading for something more than a hand job.

"I-I'm willing to try a few things." Mark fumbles his words.

Dan's eyes glint with a fire a bit mischievous and leans in to kiss Mark again. Mark's posture relaxes as his hand finds Dan's erection again and continues jerking him.

Demetrius turns to me smiling and then dips his head into my neck. "Master?" he whispers into my ear so low that I barely hear it.

"Yes?"

"I want to mark you," his breath brushes against my ear sending shivers down my spine.

This means so much more than any ring he can put on my finger. More than his I love you's and more than the amazing sex he gives me. I agree to marking me, too afraid that my voice will break if I speak.

Is it even possible to be any more turned on?

My mate pulls out his fingers and shoves his massive member into me. I gasp and lift my legs to give him more access inside me. My dick springs back to life, feeling full and complete. Him inside me is where he belongs. A loud moan grabs my attention, and Mark is panting while holding Dan's head. Dan is skillfully bobbing up and down on Mark, putting his experience with dick on display. I knew they would eventually play with each other. Their curiosity in the car was too open and natural with one another.

My skin shivers with the loss of Demetrius inside me but it doesn't take long for him to lift me into his arms. He hoists me up as if I am nothing and thrust into me again. I wrap my arms around his neck for support, bouncing on his cock. "Are you ready to mark your Master?"

Demetrius rams into me harder as if to give his answer. I am on the verge of releasing myself again.

"Yes, Master. Hold me tight because I want you to mark me too." I blink my surprise. He smiles and walks to the balcony doors. He manages to open it and walks over to the wall to push me against it.

"You're so deep," I moan as my weight settles on his dick.

"I love you, Master," Demetrius picks up his pace before I have a chance to reply. Over and over, he hits my spot and just before I climax, he bites my neck, sending me to the stars. His hard cock throbs inside me, signaling that his release is coming as well. I bite his neck in return. We both stand there pumping all of our seed and riding the tsunami of orgasms between us.

At the moment, I am drowning in our love. I can't breathe, nor do I want to with how intense I just came. This is the happiest I've ever been.

"You never used the safe word," I pant, smiling and licking the blood on my lips.

The satisfaction of marking Demi is immeasurable.

"I don't need one with you. I'll do anything my little lobo tells me to." Demetrius kisses me softly.

"Fuck! Dan!" I hear Mark call out.

Demetrius walks back to the doors, and we look over as Mark comes into Dan's mouth. Dan sits up swallowing the load and without hesitation, Mark clumsily pushes Dan down to the floor kissing him while stroking his dick. In seconds Dan erupts in ribbons into Mark's hand and onto their clothes. They stop kissing and remain pressed together, panting and smiling like idiots with their foreheads against one another. They definitely have a chemistry that neither of them expected and I hope they explore it more.

I slide off of Demetrius and walk over to the bed.

"Had fun?" I ask Mark and Dan while sitting on the bed. Both men turn to me, not having come down from their high, nodding yes. "That's not how you answer."

"Yes, Master," they reply in unison.

"Good. I suggest we stop here for tonight. You guys can pick up at home. Remember, this stays between us." I wait for their response.

"Of course, Master," Dan answers and Mark turns a new shade of red.

"Okay. Straighten your clothes and leave us. We will see you in the morning."

They do as I command and leave.

Demetrius hugs me from behind, kissing where he just bit my neck. "What did I do to get such a freak in bed?!"

"I don't know about you, but I'm happy you enjoy it."

We laugh and decide to race down the hall naked into the bathroom
before calling it a night.

24

Demetrius

The sound of Alex snoring softly on my chest stirs me from my sleep. It is rare to hear him snore like this, but I can only imagine it's from how tired he is. This level of rest only ever manifests after pure exhaustion. Last night was a bunch of crazy things for me—exciting, embarrassing, hot, and new.

Leaning my head back, I reminisce on everything that has happened until now. Growing up, I never thought my mate would be a man, but I knew it was a possibility. Mate bonds are rarely ever wrong. I wasn't sure what to think when I found myself head over heels for Alex. At first, I was distraught over our age difference. Alex being a man didn't bother me in comparison to our age.

After discovering Alex was indeed my mate, I was pleasantly surprised with his sexual appetite, and I just automatically assumed the top role. Never did I consider letting Alex have his turn. I don't know if it's because I can't see myself being that vulnerable, or if I simply take for granted how willingly he bottomed for me.

Whatever the case is, I'm glad I listened to Dan and Mark when they suggested I give it a go. My butt feels sore, but the experience was exhilarating. I've never had an orgasm before and to think my first one is through anal play. Alex stirs in his sleep, and I suddenly feel his wood on my leg. His size is delicious. I want to wrap my lips around him again.

Damn, it's turning me on again, but we can't…. Or can we?

I nudge Alex, but he whines and hugs me tighter.

"Chiquito, wake up. We need to get ready. The others will be here soon."

Alex stops snoring, so I know he is awake, but he doesn't move an inch. I flip him over with me on top and press myself against him growling.

"Now that's how I like to be woken up in the morning. Want to play?" Alex opens his eyes and licks his lips.

His erection twitched against mine.

Well, that doesn't help at all.

He knows how to get me going.

"As much as I want to roll around the sheets with you all day, we can't."

I lean down and nuzzle my face into the crook of his neck and trail soft kisses, nipping at his collarbone while rocking my hips. Grinding on him is giving my wood enough vigor to forget today's plans.

"Demi," Alex whispers, but before I lose all self-control, I push myself off of him and force myself out of bed. Looking over at him with my pants well-tented I'm determined to not do another round despite my obvious need. He looks so sexy laying there panting all hot and bothered. His eyes burn down my body and stop when he sees what he wants. His eyes call to it. A growl rises out of him, but I turn around to hide myself. I can't let myself get swept away.

"Let's go, Chiquito."

Images of pickle juice over pancakes has my erection in check. Usually, gross food combos do the trick for some reason, but I'm not complaining. We leave the room to start our day as it is also the last day in the Neverdeen house.

After brushing our teeth—and an inevitable hand job or two in the bathroom we—make it downstairs to the table with everyone already aware as to why we are late for breakfast. Can't say we were exactly quiet last night. Most of the pack is seated and servers are placing large plates of options for us to eat. The table practically looks like a buffet. I make a mental note to myself to make sure I pray extra hard for the Goddess to make me rich. One waiter steps out of the swinging door and walks over with a pot of coffee. I eagerly bounce in place for the liquid goodness and lift my cup for the first pour. I need the steaming elixir to fuel my veins and soul with its caffeinated magic. It's been too long without it.

We eat and talk about what the day will be like after Kristofer and Atlas arrive. During this part of the conversation, Alex remains quiet, and I'm sure it has to do with the idea that his mother will be joining them upon their return. I know he is worried about meeting his mother. I don't blame him either.

"Please excuse me, Atlas is calling." Scott announces to the table but squeezes Riley's hand before getting up to answer the call. *I wonder? Are they fooling around?*

Alex excuses himself as well and walks out towards the living room. The anxiety flows into me from him through our bond. He wants to run away. He's battling emotions that are almost overwhelming me through our mate bond—he's scared and angry, but mostly, sad. Knowing he will have to face his mother soon must be getting to him now.

Scott returns to the table a few minutes later as I get up to follow Alex. I tried giving Alex space, but I can't sit here and eat knowing he is hurting.

"They are thirty minutes away. They got here faster than expected," Scott says as he takes his seat next to Riley and continues eating.

I eventually find him outside on the veranda. "Hey, they're gonna be here in thirty minutes. You okay or do you not want to see her just yet?" I rub his back.

Alex turns to me burying his face in my chest. He's always so strong and self-assured on the outside, but it's moments like this, when he shows his vulnerability, I cherish. He can act in any way with me and it's okay. I want him to feel at home and safe in my arms until he takes his last breath.

"I'm just angry. I want to get this over with. I don't know why I feel this way, but I can't help it," he mumbles into my chest and takes a deep breath.

I love that my scent calms him down, but I feel like this time it isn't doing the trick like it usually does. Breathing me became a thing for him whenever he is stressed

"Okay. Want me to stay here with you until they arrive?" I hug him swaying side to side a bit.

"Stay with me, but not here. It's too cold."

Alex pulls me inside the living room. I sit by the fireplace and Alex plops right in my lap. I wrap my arms around his beautiful body, and we talk about what he wants to do for my birthday. At first, he tells me that he wants to rent out a restaurant and invite our family but then he decides he wants it to be intimate. He wants it to be special but all I want for my birthday is him by my side. I nod with a smile and agree with some of his ideas, especially the one with him dressed up for me in a red leather number he said he found online once. I teased him asking if he meant to buy that outfit for someone else since it has been a while since he found it online. The distraction works and he is relaxed in my arms.

Eventually, our conversation turns very sensual with just our lips. Not one of pure lust, but rather passion. A kiss telling me of his fears, his trust, his hopes, and his love.

A knock makes Alex stiffen in our hold.

Fuck, that thirty minutes flew by.

I hugged my mate tighter in order to break the ice already forming around his heart when it comes to his mother. We listen as everyone walks into the house excitedly greeting one another. They chat for a bit and introductions are exchanged. Alex pulls me back into another kiss. He is trying to avoid the situation, but it's too late. I feel Kristofer making his way over to where Alex and I are mouth to mouth, deprived of oxygen.

Kristofer clears his throat, making me chuckle. Alex pulls away panting slightly and looking over to our Alpha in a slight daze. He looks adorable with that love filled look in his eyes.

"Man, it's great to see you guys are okay. If I would have known everyone would have been here, I would have switched our teams. Getting Finn and Isabella was a piece of cake." Kristofer stops talking, taking in how quiet Alex is being.

"Where are they?" I ask while Alex remains silent, turning his attention to the crackling fire instead.

"Finns in bad shape. He's being looked at by Ida's healer and Isabella went to look for someone named Riley." Kristofer shrugs with nonchalance. None of us have told Kristofer yet about the long-lost twin brother.

Alex scoffs, then mumbles "Figures," Annoyance radiated from him.

Voices echo down the hall, increasing in volume as the people get closer to the living room.

"Riley, talk to me. Why are you being like this?" Riley stomps into the living room with Isabella closely behind.

"May I have my brother for a moment." Riley extends his hand to Alex.

I let go so Alex can decide if he wants to get up or not. Kristofer breaks his neck looking between Riley and then Alex, confused.

"They're twins," I smile at my Alpha, but that only adds to Kristofer's perplexed face.

"Alex!" Isabella gasps.

Alex accepts Riley's hand and they both leave a frowning Isabella.

She stands, baffled, as her sons walk away from her.

"Give them time," I tell Isabella.

She drops onto the sofa in shock. She probably expected her children to run into her arms, Instead, she got the silent treatment.

***

Most of the afternoon goes by and Alex is still with Riley in his room.

So much for ripping off the band aid and getting this over with.

Isabella went to the healer when he was done with Finn to have herself checked as well. She said she was fine, but being raped by multiple men while unconscious is not something you would be okay with so easily. She is bound to have some kind of internal damage. She tried to convince us that since she wasn't aware of it happening. She can simply put it off as it never having occurred, but her body will remember. If I've learned anything about mental and physical trauma while being with Alex is that if you don't deal with the past, it will continue to affect your future. I think reality just hasn't hit her yet. Then again, it can be the shock over her experience that has her mind trying to cope by ignoring the situation. Her mind may want to shut down and forget.

I sigh for the hundredth time while watching reruns on the television above the fireplace. I don't know what Riley and Alex are doing, but I am going a bit stir crazy not having my mate with me. I want to give him space with his brother as much as I want to monopolize his time. But this doesn't seem like the right time to be possessive. He and his brother probably have a lot to say to one another and are handling the emotions that come from the decisions of their mother. I am not familiar with this place or integrated with this family enough, so wandering around or finding something to do is out of the question.

I get up from the sofa and turn off the screen. My best bet is taking a nap since it is the only thing to keep my mind from running rampant. I turn down the hall and go up the stairs. Riley and Alex, walk by me and stop. Alex gives me a pensive look before grabbing my hand. I willingly follow my mate. We stop before a door and Riley knocks a bit angrily.

"Yes?" Isabella calls out.

"Mom, it's us," Riley answers and Alex squeezes my hand.

The door quickly springs open, and Isabella Neverdeen stands there with a tear-stained face. Her eyes are swollen. Her nose is red and irritated.

"Let's talk," Riley marches into the room with Alex and me attached. They sit on the bed, and I stand next to Alex holding on to his shoulders.

"Son I-"

"No, Mom. Listen to me first." Riley takes a deep breath and glances at Alex who is shaking beneath me. "I don't know what your reasons were for not telling anyone about Alex, and we will listen to what you have to say, but before you start, let me tell you this. I don't think the way you handled all of this was fair for either of us. My brother has been alive this whole time and you know how much I yearned for him. You told me I was crazy for feeling that way and convinced me he had died as a baby. You convinced all of us!" Riley raises his voice angry and hurt.

"Then you allowed my brother to be raised by a fucking psychopath. Do you not feel shame or guilt? Did you not love him enough to save him from the pain he had to endure?" Riley yells as Alex starts crying silently. Riley holds his hand tighter to comfort him or maybe to lend himself support, but they have each other and it's endearing. "We will hear you out before we decide how we will move on. I love you, Mom. I do. but right now... tell us what started all this?"

"What decision?" Isabella asks, biting her lip.

So that's where the twins get it from.

"Mom, answer the question?" Riley hits the bed with his fist making Isabella flinch.

"Okay." She pulls the chair from her vanity and sits. "When I met your father, Jon, and realized we were mates, we weren't sure what to do. I was nineteen and Jon was twenty-one, so we decided to take things slow and see where it went. Hugo then started to pop up around us all the time and even though Jon introduced him to me as his half-brother, I never liked him. Hugo just kept hanging around, but I didn't know why at the time. He then started using me to get information on the family. He would ask sly questions, catching me off guard, or bribing me with my favorite milkshake from the diner down the street. I didn't know he held the grudge that he did. I sort of knew his story when I asked Jon about it. But most of the time Jon would shrug it off because he didn't know much. All he knew was that his father refused to talk about Hugo." Isabella stood up and paced a bit before turning back to us and continuing the story.

"Jon never had the chance to grow up with his brother since Dad made sure to disown Hugo completely. One night I told Jon to come with me to meet with Hugo. Jon wanted to know his half-brother better and the only way to do so was to do it secretly. We would constantly all meet up in secret and spend time getting to know one another. I hated Hugo a little after spending so much time together, but he still annoyed me. The last time we went to meet up, I was already pregnant with the both of you. We were excited for the pregnancy only for me to have to return home without my husband. We were attacked by rogues and Jon was killed." Her face is distraught, recalling everything that happened, and Isabella reaches out to touch Riley's arm but he pulls away.

"Afterward, I ended up going into early labor due to the stress of losing Jon and had Alex. I was in the cabin that Jon and I shared during the summer in the woods alone when it happened. That cabin was where Jon and I would go to escape the pressures from both our families and where we wanted to start a life together. Alex was so weak and barely four pounds. I called a witch friend of mine who helped. Using her magic, she was able to help stop my labor. It was how I found out that I was pregnant with twins. She helped me so Riley could continue to grow and be born full term. I called Hugo so he could help me get home. Instead, he invited me over to his home so I could rest while he watched Alex. I was so tired and still half expected Riley to come out, so I agreed. We ended up arguing that night. He was trying to convince me to stay and marry him." Isabella sighs but continues as she wipes the streaks falling down her cheeks.

"I denied him of course. I'd just lost my mate and given birth. In his anger of being rejected, he snatched Alex from me. I tried rescuing you, but I had just given birth to you. I had no strength, and I couldn't shift. He beat me badly that night. When I returned home, I told everyone that you didn't survive after I had been attacked. Everyone believed the story I told and since my stomach was flatter than before, they didn't question it. I was terrified if I said something, and it got back to Hugo that he would harm you."

Alex trembles in my arms and I can only hold him tight in order to give him comfort while he confronts his mother. This story is a hard one to listen to and while I can understand Isabella being scared, I still would have made every effort to get back Alex. She starts to pace again around the room and fumbles with her fingers.

"I made several attempts to save you but in one of those attempts, Hugo beat me so badly that not even the witch's magic could stop me from going into labor. I laid on the ground beaten and broken from Hugo's abuse and cried from the labor pains. They were intense and worse than my initial labor with Alex. I thought I was going to die but an hour later, the labor progressed, and the contractions were just a few minutes apart. I dragged myself against a tree and braced myself while I gave birth shortly after and poor Riley was barely breathing.

"I came for you. I tried to rescue you a couple times. The last time I tried I was beaten to a pulp. He threatened to kill you if I attempted to come back or told anyone. And I believed him. Thankfully he didn't know about Riley. The only person who knew I was pregnant with twins was the witch. I tried contacting Hugo one more time, but he moved, and I had no idea where. I was scared of reaching out for help without giving away that Alex was alive or alerting Hugo of Riley. Yes, I knew what kind of man Hugo was and that his real goal I eventually learned was power. But I was more afraid of him killing Alex. I left you to protect you!" Isabella cries into her hands apologizing over and over as she drops to her knees in front of Alex.

Alex takes a deep breath and speaks. "You know Isabella, for the longest time I wanted a family. I wanted unconditional love and acceptance. I grew up thinking Hugo was my father and that you died because of me. I was abused every day until I moved out when I turned eighteen. From a young age I became a drug addict. I hurt myself. I even ended up with a health condition because I was so malnourished. I wanted to die. DO you not get that? I. Wanted. To. Die." I squeeze Alex tighter reassuring him to go on.

"I went through hell. Finding that necklace you sent, and the note gave me hope of finding you. Yet now that I have, I wish I hadn't. You gave up looking for me to protect me? No. I will not accept that. You had so many options that would have led to my salvation. Even the backing of the council and the founding family but you chose to stay in fear. Ignorant because it was easier for you. The only good thing out of this is finding my brother and grandparents. I thought there was some deeper reason for my abandonment. Instead, you were a better mother in my imagination than the one before me right now." Alex spits his words like venom, full of pain and sorrow.

Isabella began to bawl uncontrollably at his words.

"Mom, I'm going back with them," Riley announces.

Both Alex and I turn to Riley.

"You are?" I ask, finally speaking after being silent the whole time.

"Yes. I need to find myself and I want to get to know my brother better. That is if you and Kristofer are okay with it."

Riley smiles at me. The resemblance to one another down to their mannerisms was undeniable.

"Of course. You'll be my brother-in-law soon anyways," I smile back.

"You can't leave. You're next in line for the council seat," Isabella rushes her words while wiping her forgotten tears.

"I don't want that damned seat. I never did. It's what you want. Let Manny have it. He is older and better versed in our laws anyways."

"But-"

"But nothing Mom. I'm not changing my mind. Besides, I already spoke to Abuela. My decision is final." Riley stands up and so does Alex.

"Can I at least hug you before I never see you again?" Isabella opens her arms to Alex. He leaves her standing there but I nudge Alex. I know he will regret not doing so later. He stares at her for a bit and reluctantly accepts the hug. They cling tightly to each other.

"This isn't the last time but I'm too angry right now. I thought I could let it all go but I've gone through too much to simply forgive and forget. Give me time. I won't cut you off completely, but I can't smile that easily either. At least not at this moment," Alex pulls away from the hug.

"I understand. I'll give you all the time you need. Please take care of Riley." Isabella sniffles a bit.

"Don't worry. He is very capable, and my family will take him in as their own." Alex grabs my hand and walks towards the door. "By the way, this is my mate. He has shown me the person I am capable of being. I owe my strength to this man. I hope being gay isn't an issue." Alex never turns around but simply states the fact and walks out with me in tow.

A muffled cry leaves her room as we walk down the stairs and join the rest of our pack.

"It's time we go home."

25

Alex

I don't know why I have this anger welling up inside me. For as long as I can remember, I've wanted to meet my mother. I craved nothing more than to call her mother and hug her. Yet, the moment I looked at her, I felt nothing more than the urge to scream. An impetus feeling to show how much I hurt over the years. The closer the time approached to see her, the bigger my anxiety became. I kept ruminating over and over on why she might have abandoned me. Then looking into her green eyes…I just snapped. The hugs didn't matter. Calling her mother didn't matter. I want her to understand how alone I felt growing up. How I lived in fear every day. How there were times I wouldn't eat because Hugo denied me food. I want her to feel the pain I felt when all I could think of was why no one loved me and how I was better off dead.

Whether she deserves my anger or not, I don't know. All I do know is that I can't look at her with love right now. I can't love her like I want. Doing so would be as if I was okay with how it all turned out. But I'm not okay. Maybe it really was impossible to save me without risking my life like she said. Maybe she had no other choice but to remain silent but then I think of Demetrius. He went through hell and high water to get me back every time I was in need.

Why couldn't she do the same? Was I not worth it to her?

I lean against Demetrius as we wait for my grandparents to come out of their room. I don't want to have these feelings, nor do I want to think. All I need is the love of this man next to me, and then maybe, just maybe, I'll be able to open my heart to Isabella.

"Abuela, I'm gonna miss you. I will try to visit, okay?" I hug my grandmother, noticing Isabella watching from the entrance of the foyer. "Abuelo, thank you for everything." I hug my grandfather still stumbling over the words.

Getting used to calling them my 'grandparents' will take time. This is mi familia.

"De nada, mi hijo," My grandfather says. He turns to Demetrius. "I leave him in your hands. Welcome to the family mi otro hijo." He extends his hand to Demetrius and shakes it firmly.

"Gracias, Paul." Demetrius replies with a smile.

"Please, call me Abuelo."

They both smile at me, Demetrius, and Riley. It is heart wrenching to leave them so soon, but I am honestly ready to go home to my bed. I miss the comfort of my room and my other family. My first family. Riley waves goodbye to our mother and I simply look in her direction before turning to leave. The sad lines in her eyes are heavy, but so is my heart. It makes me wonder if this is how it would have gone had I left to find her sooner.

We all head out and pile into our vans. We sit with the same groups we rode in before. "Okay guys, into the sexmobile." Mark jokes with Dan laughing right behind him.

I smirk at the comment and look up at Demetrius who is walking beside me with his arm around my shoulders. Riley of course goes with Scott as they whisper to one another, which I don't find surprising. Scott has been eyeing my brother since last night and Riley has been relishing in it. Although I'm sure they are mates, I just wish Riley would tell me already. Maybe they need time to see if that's what they really want. It's not like being a mate suddenly means you have to spend your life with that person.

This time Demetrius and I are sitting in the middle seat. Mark and Dan make it in the van first and steal the back seats. I'm sure they want some alone time after what happened last night, but I was hoping to have those seats again for me and Demi.

Lenny takes the first shift to drive with his bag of chips ready to go in the center console. He and Spike strike up a conversation about sports and how baseball will be starting soon for spring training. The NFL Super Bowl has already passed, and they're excited for something new to gamble on.

I lay down and place my head on Demetrius' lap. He runs his fingers through my hair, and I fall in and out of sleep. I can't tell how much time has passed and I refuse to move. My Demi's thigh is really comfortable.

I'm going to kill you. Spike's voice pops into my mind. I blink my eyes open in surprise to find him still facing forward in his seat.

What the hell did I do? I reply.

I'm sure you're the reason why those two idiots have been making out the last 10 minutes.

Hahaha, leave them be. Are you jealous? I tease.

…. no. Maybe…um… actually, want to try your hand at Cupid for me?

Holy shit, yea! Who is it?

……

wait, no way… Lenny? You're crushing on Lenny?

…. yea.

Okay, I'll let you know.

Spike brings down his left arm between the seats extending it back towards me and wiggles his fingers. I reach over and wiggle mine over his. It's silly but that's how Spike is. He is a very mentally mature thirty-three-year-old but very much a child at heart with how he interacts with his friends. He met his mate last year, but she rejected him saying she was in love with someone else. It broke his heart, but he also isn't as upset as I thought he would be. Either that or he hides it very well. Luckily, she rejected him the second they realized the bond had formed so they never had a chance to strengthen it either. His heartbreak only lasted a few days at most.

Lenny on the other hand is very old-fashioned. Lenny could best be described as the sweetest and most respectful person but a clown around those he was very close to. Similar in that sense to Spike. It may be why they get along so well. He lost his mate four years ago during a complicated procedure to remove an aggressive brain tumor. Now at thirty-nine, he drowns himself in work or food, but the loneliness still makes an appearance when he stops for a second to breathe. If he doesn't think or surround himself with people, the way his walls crumble only serves to accentuate the hole in his heart.

At least that's what he told me on my birthday when I found him crying after many drinks. He admitted that seeing the Alphas find their mates recently reminded him of his late wife and he has been struggling with it. Yet recently things seem to have improved in his mood, and I am curious if it has anything to do with the man next to him.

I reach out to Lenny through the mind link. **Lenny don't react but I have a question. Are you looking to date anytime soon?**

Lenny keeps his cool as if nothing is happening. **Well, I'm not actively looking, but I wouldn't turn down a potential partner. Why?**

Oh, good. I have someone interested. Is there someone you like before I say anything?

Alex, what are you doing? Did someone ask you? Lenny changes his position, fidgeting in his seat.

No...

Well, I do like someone, but they are straight. Lenny sits up in his seat. This is making him nervous but now I am certain that I am right.

Lenny, are you bi?

Yes.

Wow didn't know that. So, who is it?

...Spike. But please don't tell him. I don't want to ruin our friendship. I'm fine as it is. I've grown used to hiding my feelings.

But didn't you guys jerk each other off when all of us were getting it on during our last drive? Lenny stiffens and looks up to the rearview mirror, but we can't see each other with me laying in Demi's lap.

Yes, but that was a fluke.

And what if I told you that he is the reason I'm asking?

What? Wait, what do you mean?

...I stay quiet smelling the slight panic coming off his body which makes me chuckle.

Alex, answer me. You can't just drop a bomb like that.

Haha, why don't you find out for yourself?

I switch my link to Spike. **He's all yours buddy.**

I close the link and watch them panic a bit, most likely from them trying to communicate with me, but failing. Lenny looks over to Spike and smiles. Spike gives him a cheesy grin. Then he looks over his shoulder to look at me. Goddess knows why. I signal for him to say or do something. If that isn't obvious then I don't know what is.

How did they keep it secret from one another this long?

I watch as Spike blushes and turns back in his seat to face forward again. Watching them all nervous is cute but Spike doesn't do anything. I thought for sure he would have at least said something.

I shrug it off and look up to my mate, who is looking down at me very amused. He must have put two and two together and understands what I just did. I sit up and lean in to give him a kiss when a wet, all too familiar sound catches my ears.

It is like a replay from last night, but in reverse when I get up and turn back to see Mark going down on Dan. The way I almost gasp out loud has me covering my mouth to stop myself. Dan is balls deep in Mark's mouth and moaning from the pleasure. They wasted no time in progressing. Dan opens his eyes and catches me gawking at them and smirks.

"If you don't mind the interruption. What are you guys going to do if you find your mates?"

Mark stops, but Dan holds his head down. "Keep going. I'm close," Mark resumes the blow job. "If he or she comes along, then they come along. Mark and I agreed to keep this open and if my mate doesn't accept an open relationship, then we agreed to stop." Dan throws his head back and moans, exploding in Mark's mouth. "Fuck!"

Mark swallows and comes up wiping his lip with a smile.

"How did I do?" Mark asks Dan like an excited little puppy.

"Fucking amazing. You sure I'm your first?" Dan kisses Mark on the lips with a chuckle.

"What do you mean your mate? What about Mark's?"

I look over at the blushing man sitting there practically wagging his tail at Dan. He is definitely smitten.

"I don't have a mate. When the years started rolling by, I started to wonder if anyone was really out there for me. I dated around and traveled trying to see if I'd come across them. But nothing. I then felt a weird pain in my wolf. He told me something was wrong, so I decided to talk to the Elders. We did a spiritual cleanse and reveal ceremony. My aura showed that my mate passed away not too long prior to my visit with them. That was the pain I felt. I know there's potential for someone else to be my mate, but the chances are low, and I don't feel like looking." Mark sighs, but Dan runs his hand over Mark's back bringing a smile to his face.

I wasn't expecting the conversation to go this deep, but they must have already had this conversation to be so calm about it. Either that or they are underplaying their feelings for one another so neither gets hurt.

I turn back around to Demetrius and chuckle at how they are sexually compatible. I have created sex monsters and possibly may have created two more up front. Maybe I'm the fairy gay mother to my pack. With that thought, I return my attention to mate so I can kiss him silly and then cuddle up for the rest of the ride home.

***

It's well past midnight and we are still driving. I am over being in the car. Spike is the one driving now and humming to a tune on the radio. The horny birds in the back are sleeping on each other and Demetrius is trying to sneak his hands in my pants, again. I smack his hand away with a smirk, getting Spike's attention.

"Is there ever a time you two aren't at it?" Spike looks at us through the rearview mirror.

"No," we reply in unison and laugh at how quickly we answered.

The van finally pulls up to our home, allowing us to stretch our bodies while we make ungodly sounds that could rival those of our sex-capades. It feels so good to be back home. I wait for Iris to drop off Riley and observe my little brother step out of the van with Scott. They hug each other and Riley whispers something in Scott's ear. He laughs and kisses my brother on the forehead. Riley lingers there for a bit and then walks towards me.

"Um, so you and Scott?" I whisper to Riley, unwilling to wait for him to tell me first.

He shrugs his shoulders with a giddy grin, "So, funny thing..." I laugh at how cheeky he is being.

I knew it. "You're mates, aren't you?"

"Shut up!" Riley tries to hush me and covers my mouth.

I really must be Cupid.

I shake my head and pull him inside the house. He has a lot of explaining to do. Plus, I want to show him everything in my room and introduce him to everyone.

We step inside the quiet home. Everyone is in bed due to how late it already is, so I send Demetrius to his room and bring Riley to mine. We are both too wired to sleep so we stay in my bed under the covers and talk about everything.

What are our favorite colors and foods? What a perfect day for us is like or our taste in music and movies?

We stay that way for two hours absorbing as much information about each other as we can. We discover we are a lot more similar than we thought. We both like black, our favorite cuisine is Japanese, we love rock music and Bachata, and we enjoy kung fu movies and fantasy alien books.

"Hey, so what's up with the four of you?" Riley adjusts his pillow and turns over to face me.

"Who?" I ask honestly, not following his train of thought.

"You, Demetrius, Mark, and Dan," Riley wiggles his brows.

"I have no idea what you're talking about," my face turns a deep red.

"Oh please, like if I didn't hear you all. Did you forget my room was next to yours? I saw when they entered your room when I was heading to bed. I didn't think anything of it until I heard you spouting commands and moaning like crazy."

I knew we ran the risk of being heard but damn it is embarrassing actually knowing we were.

"Okay, but you better not say a word." I stick out my pinky to Riley.

"Of course. Who am I gonna tell anyways?" He grabs my pinky and promises.

"Okay so Demi and I are into BDSM." Riley gasps. "I am the Dominant and he is the Sub. When we were driving to meet you all, I got a little aroused and initiated play in the van." I pause to laugh because Riley is scooting closer to me wide eyed.

"You had sex in the car?" Riley whispers really low.

"Yea and during sex I asked Mark and Dan to watch." I told Riley everything and watched his eyes grow wide with curiosity.

"Oh, my Goddess, my twin is a fucking freak. You need to teach me your ways." Riley makes hand gestures as if worshiping me and I laugh. Even our sarcasm and sense of humor is the same. It's incredible that despite having completely different upbringings, we are so much alike.

"Hardy har har. Anyways, are you still a virgin?" I ask and Riley stares at me.

"Well, with men I am." He finally answers.

"Do you think you're top or bottom?"

"I don't know. I guess I'm fine either way. Depends on Scott." Riley blushes at the thought of his mate. He didn't even make it out of his home, and he found his life partner. I am also sure that's the real reason for him coming with me. I was only part of that decision, I think. Makes sense. I can't be mad at that; I'd do the same if I were him. I'm just happy we could spend more time together.

"I guess you're right. Well, let's try and sleep. You have a long day tomorrow. I am introducing you to everyone." I pinch Riley in the waist, and he screams. I'm ticklish on my waist and it suddenly made me curious if he was as well. I laugh at the way he rubs his waist and dodge the pillow he throws my way from the bed.

"Keep it up and you sleep on the floor." I point a finger at him.

"You started it! No pinching." Riley huffs.

"Whatever." I wave him off and make a mental note that he isn't ticklish. We lay down and at the same time fake falling asleep and snoring. We both laugh at our silliness.

I cozy up with my pillow and close my eyes when Riley grabs my hand. "I'm happy you're not dead." Riley doesn't even give me a chance to respond to his weird word choice. His eyes close and he drifts into a deep slumber.

Me too.

Epilogue
Alex

It's been a few months since we returned from my family's home. Riley is adjusting well with us here, working with Dan at the butcher shop in town. Dan and Mark have been tied at the hip as well and I am really rooting for them to stay together. I also decided to start online classes for my associate's degree, but I haven't figured out what to major in yet. Riley is trying to help me figure that part out while Demetrius has been trying to get me pregnant despite that being impossible. Unless you're Cassius that is. He was shocked for his life when the Shaman spirit told him he made him a uterus. It was the only way to keep the Shamans' ability to reincarnate, by extending the bloodline. Kristofer and Iris are still crazy love birds making us laugh with their antics as we are all getting ready for Atlas and Cassius' wedding.

Now, everyone is running around with their heads cut off trying to pull the wedding together. We are up in the mountains in Ryan's village for the ceremony and the scenery couldn't be more perfect. I've never met the guy, but I've heard stories from everyone. Demetrius and I are getting ready, and Riley is somewhere with Scott doing Goddess knows what. Over these past few months, their bond strengthened. Since then, Scott has moved in with us. Lately they've had this uncomfortable tension. I can only assume it's because they haven't been intimate yet. Riley confessed to me that he got scared after seeing how big Scott's dick was. Scott isn't a bottom, and Riley doesn't want to pressure him to reverse the role. But this leaves them at a stalemate.

The vanity before me is a mess but with one good look at myself in the mirror, I'm happy at how good my hair and makeup turned out. This is my first time using makeup and I thought it would be fun to use to commemorate this occasion. Not sure if I will do it again though. It's too much work but I must admit, I love who I see in the mirror. I managed to gain some weight and have filled out very nicely. Now my brother and I are indistinguishable to most. I gained some muscle from all the training Demetrius puts me through as well, so my body is more aesthetically pleasing to the eye which does wonders to my confidence.

I adjust my tie a bit and walk over to stand beside Demetrius. We make a fine-looking couple. Suddenly my left ring finger feels very lonely. I know he still has Abuela's ring, and I don't want to pressure him especially since he technically already proposed to me however directly that was. Then he marked me and although faint, the mark of his teeth on my skin is still there. This mark seals our bond and it is now until death do us part. I can't help but wonder when he will propose.

"You look beautiful. I'm gonna have to kiss that gloss off your lips." Demetrius brings my hand to his lips and brushes a kiss gently onto my fingers.

"I expect no less," I reply.

We walk to our seats, greeting others as we pass. The ceremony setup is beautiful. Atlas chose a lodge by a lake surrounded by evergreen trees. The white gazebo that is placed in the middle is decorated with white and pink orchids with vines that wrap around the post. A long white runner leads from the last row of seats up the middle to the gazebo. The white chairs placed on both sides of the runner are wrapped in soft pink and burnt orange satin cloths that are tied in the back into a bow. Flower petals are scattered everywhere, and fairy lights decorate the roof of the gazebo and the treetops surrounding us.

The sun is almost ready to set, so we all take our seats. The music cues after Atlas and the officiator make their way into the gazebo. The music playing smoothly transitions to something upbeat but melodic. One of the little pups of the pack walks down the aisle. She spreads more petals and confetti by aggressively throwing it up in the air. We all laugh at how quickly she walks while doing it and sits down. Then the bridesmaids and groomsmen walk down to take their places up front by the groom. The music changes once again and the wedding march begins, signaling us all to rise.

Kristofer appears with Cassius hooked on his arm, and my breath is taken away. We fall silent with how beautifully Cassius strides in along with our Alpha. He is dressed in white fitted dress pants custom-made to fit his small growing belly. His shirt is also custom-made and perfectly tucked in. His cummerbund is a soft pale blush pink sitting comfortably low on his belly, accentuating the small bump. His jacket is short and white with a long tail in the back and a matching pink handkerchief that tops it all off in his left pocket. His long hair is loose in soft waves but pulled back into a half-up-do and tied with a long satin pink ribbon. Cassius holds his small bouquet of dragon lilies and locks eyes with his mate.

They walk down to the gazebo taking careful steps, so Cass doesn't trip. We all sit down and watch how love fills the air.

"We are gathered here today to take these two wolves in spiritual matrimony. They have found no greater love than the one within one another. Today we will bear witness under the Goddess five souls uniting as one. Atlas, Cassius, Leo, Wolfie, and their unborn child. Let us all howl our praise and bring forth goodwill and fortune to this couple."

We all howled as one into the now-set sun and the rising moon.

"If there is anyone who thinks these two should not wed... please leave!" We all laugh but look around making sure no one is dumb enough to protest. "Now, the grooms will exchange vows."

Atlas goes first and pulls out a note from his pocket.

"Cassius, remember when we first met? It wasn't with you naked in my basement but when you first saved Iris. I was lying in the grass when the most delightful scent caught my nose. It's what prompted me to sit up. When I saw you for that brief moment I was transfixed. I had never seen anything in this world as beautiful as you. Each day with you since, has been the best day of my life. I promise that I will do my best to give you those same feelings in return. To keep you excited, happy, warm, and satisfied. Most importantly I promise to always be there for you and our child. You are my greatest joy in life. So, thank you for healing this broken wolf."

Atlas folds the paper and tucks it away. I am already a blubbering mess because as my first wedding, I have never experienced so much happiness in one place. They are the epitome of a perfect couple. Cassius wipes his tears and pulls out his note.

"When I first realized what was happening, I was scared, and rightfully so. I mean you locked me in your basement for Goddess's sake." We all laugh at his exasperation. "But then getting to know you and the kind of man you are, how could I not fall in love? You stood by me through all of my trials and made me stronger. You even tolerate my pregnant mood swings which we all know is not pretty, but all jokes aside, I don't want to spend any more time without your last name because you are my home. You are my reason to breathe. You are everything I could ever dream of and more. Even without our bond, I know in my heart, I would have fallen for you regardless. I promise to always be by your side, to be a supportive and strong Luna, and the best father to our child."

Cassius puts away his note and grabs Atlas' hand.

"And now, do you, Atlas Ellwood, take Cassius Avelious to be your spiritually wedded husband? To love and hold. In sickness and in health. Till your wolves leave this realm?"

"I do."

"And do you Cassius Avelious, take Atlas Ellwood to be your spiritually wedded husband? To love and hold. In sickness and in health. Till your wolves leave this realm?"

"I do."

"I now pronounce you Mr. and Mr. Ellwood. You may kiss your husband." The officiator steps back and the grooms make out like teenagers behind bleachers.

We all shout and whistle while some howl at the new couple. They laugh with tears and hold hands walking down the aisle as happy as can be. My makeup is surely a mess, but I can't deny the bond we witnessed. Throughout the ceremony, my whole body warmed at the feel of their bond manifesting around us. As they said their vows, their auras lit up in swirls and spread among us. Our very own version of the Northern Lights. I have never witnessed anything like it.

The reception kicks off shortly after and we all break into dance and alcohol. Everyone is having the time of their lives smiling ear to ear, enjoying the love spreading through us all.

"Okay, everyone with a partner come on up. I will toss the bouquet." Cassius positions himself, but I stay rooted to my spot. I honestly don't want to get trampled by the ladies, so I stand next to my mate to watch. Cassius turns around and flings the bouquet hard. I follow it with my eyes and realize it is coming straight for me. Before I even have time to react, Demetrius catches the bouquet inches from my head. Everyone begins to whistle, and I blush into oblivion.

"I guess this means we're next," Demetrius kisses me and I chuckle.

"That's up to you now, isn't it," I wink and walk away leaving him speechless.

The rest of the night continues without a hitch. We dance the night away and then return to our rooms in the cabin we are renting. I trip my way into our room laughing for no apparent reason. I drank enough to kill a human two times over, but for me, I am at a comfortable drunk level. I strip my clothes off and throw myself in bed. Demetrius does the same and we fall asleep within seconds.

Epilogue 2

It's now the end of May and I make sure to plan a romantic birthday dinner for Demetrius. I set up my bedroom with a small table and dinner. If I did the dinner in the dining room, then we would have constant interruptions. I hang lights and put some champagne on ice. My phone is hooked up to small speakers giving the room a nice ambiance with soft classical music. All I need is to bring in the food.

I search for my brother since he promised to bring over a cake he is baking over to Atlas' place, but he is nowhere to be found. No one has seen him, and it is making me anxious. I go back to the kitchen and grab dinner to finish setting up in my room. Demetrius will be home soon from hanging out with the guys and everything needs to be perfect before he arrives. It's the first time I get to do a birthday for him. I open the fridge, grabbing a couple of waters, when a moan fills my ears. I pop up my head to find my brother getting the lights fucked out of him by Scott in our back porch.

I guess they finally went all the way.

Unfortunately, the cake is right next to them.

Well, I guess no cake.

I head to the room and wait for my mate with my nerves on fire. Even though it's just a dinner, for some reason, I am nervous as to whether he is going to like it or not. While I have cooked smaller meals for him before, I made sure to practice making him this dish. He's mentioned it on multiple occasions as a favorite from when he was growing up. He hasn't had it since he was a kid, and I wanted to bring some nostalgia to him. It honestly brings some to me as well since I only ever had it once. It's a Spanish dish that resembles a lasagna but made with yellow sweet plantains and meat and cheese. For some reason, though I couldn't get the flavor or texture right, this time I think I nailed it. It's a wonder to me how he came about eating this as a kid, but he mentioned having a Spanish nanny so I'm sure that's how he discovered it.

A car pulling up to the house steals my attention and laughter from the guy's filters through my open window. I hide my scent. Demetrius walks into the house and calls for me, but I stay quiet. He calls for me again and I giggle at how his steps quicken to find me, most likely worried. I stop hiding my scent and almost instantly his feet shift and come straight into my room.

"Happy birthday, mi amor!" I say sitting in a chair by the table naked with a loose red tie around my neck. His eyes drink in every inch of me and he growls in approval.

"Can I have dessert first?" He closes the door and kneels before me.

"No, I spent a lot of time making dinner. We are eating and then dessert."

I point to his chair so he can sit. His eyes bug out of his head when he realizes what is on his plate. He takes a small bite at first and the smile that spreads across his lips is all I need. He inhales his plate while singing me his praises. We finish the meal I prepared over the soft music playing while Demetrius keeps trying to fondle me with his foot. Half the champagne is gone, and I am ready for some amazing sex.

"Chiquito, thank you for dinner, it was delicious. You make a perfect wife." He licks his lips making me instantly jealous of them.

"Well, not like I see a ring on my finger," I tease with a smirk.

"I guess we need to fix that." Demetrius gets on one knee and pulls out the box from his pocket. "This is not a proposal, but a promise. I want to propose with my own ring and not on my birthday. Until then I want to make you a promise. With this ring, I promise to put no one else before you. I promise to make every day happier than the last. I promise to never make you feel lonely or hurt and I promise to always support you, in life, love, school, and your endeavors. Will you accept me?" My heart is pounding a million miles a minute.

Why is this man so perfect? How did he know exactly what to say?

"Yes, I accept." I give him my hand for him to slide the ring on my finger. He rises up a bit and kisses me. "Why was the ring already in your pocket?"

"Because I have had it with me since the day I got it. I love you, Chiquito."

I moan into his lips. "I love you, too." He picks me up and carries me to bed. "Demi, how about we don't role play. I want you to fuck me until you're satisfied." I lick his lips.

"No safe word?" I shake my head no.

"Nope, this little lobo wants you to have all of me. So, take it."

Forever grateful that I found such a great person and a great family. I finally have my brother, my pack, my grandparents, and even Isabella whom I kept in contact with. Everything is good and I owe it all to the man in my arms. The man that never gave up on me or us.

"Fuck me, Demi!"

The End

Trigger Warnings

Content includes:
Sexual Assault
Abuse
Drug Abuse
Mentions of r*pe
Age Gap (10 yrs)
Exhibitionism
Dom/Sub relationship

Author's Other Works

Paranormal Romance

Lunar River Series
1.   The Silver Lining
2.   Nothing Stays Buried
3.   Safe Word Lobo

Contemporary Romance

- Color Me, Sugar

Connect with the Author